# Of Serpents and Sorrow

## A Medusa Retelling

### Katherine Shaw

OF SERPENTS AND SORROW

Copyright © 2025 Katherine Shaw

All rights reserved.

www.katherineshawwrites.com

Published by Arteminion Books 2025

Hull, United Kingdom

No parts of this publication may be reproduced, stored in a retrieval system, or transmitted in any form or by any means, electronic, mechanical, photocopying, recording, or otherwise, without the prior written permission of the copyright owner.

This book is sold subject to the condition that it shall not, by way of trade or otherwise, be lent, resold, hired out, or otherwise circulated without the publisher's prior consent in any form of binding or cover other than that in which it is published and without a similar condition including this condition being imposed on the subsequent purchaser. Under no circumstances may any part of this book be photocopied for resale.

This is a work of fiction. Any similarity between the characters and situations within its pages and places or persons, living or dead, is unintentional and co-incidental.

Paperback edition ISBN: 978-1-8383786-6-0

E-book edition (Amazon) ISBN: 978-1-8383786-8-4

E-book edition ISBN: 978-1-8383786-7-7

Cover Design by Fay Lane.

Generative AI has not been used at any point in the creation of this book.

# Content Warning

It's important to protect yourself when reading. While some readers might be familiar with Medusa's story, each variation is different, and content warnings for this retelling can be found below. If you're the type of person who would rather not know in order to avoid spoilers, please skip ahead to the next page.

Below are warnings for topics that are typically considered triggering:

General warning for violence and death

Abusive parents (emotional, physical, and neglect)

Memories of receiving severe burns

Historically accurate misogyny

Attempted sexual assault, sexual assault (on page) and rape (fade to black)

Pregnancy, pregnancy-related illness and graphic on-page labour scenes

**monster**  /ˈmɒn.stə/

*noun*

**a strange or horrible and often frightening creature**

# Part One

The day she had been dreading had arrived, and it made Medusa sick to her stomach.

Butterflies ravaged her insides, a flurry of hot angry motes of anxiety desperate to get out. It was the day she had been preparing for her entire youth. Lessons in reading, writing, history, theology, elocution, poise... They all culminated in what would surely be the most significant day of her life.

It was terrifying.

'Medusa, pay attention!'

She blinked, her clouded vision sharpening into focus. Her gaze returned to the copper mirror, its surface so finely polished she could see the fear glinting in her dark eyes.

'I am paying attention, Mother,' she said with more confidence than she truly felt.

'All right, then,' the older woman snapped, tugging Medusa's scalp hard as she worked a piece of long walnut hair into a tightly coiled braid, 'what did I just say?'

'You were saying…' Medusa said slowly, fully aware she had been deaf to her mother's comments for several minutes, 'that I need to appreciate the gravity of what today means for me and this family?'

Her mother's reflection smiled, one of those small, tight smiles that suggested both irritation and amusement. She leaned in, pressing a cheek against her daughter's. 'That was a lucky guess.' Medusa's mother allowed herself a low chuckle before returning her attention to her daughter's hair.

Medusa grimaced, her scalp burning more with each twist. Her days of letting her hair hang loose around her shoulders were limited, she had known that, but now that the day of her ordination had arrived, each pin felt like the stone slab of a tomb being laid around her.

'How did you feel?' she blurted, surprising herself with her forward-ness. This was a question she had longed to voice, but the courage had never come.

Her mother's hands stilled. 'What?'

Medusa swallowed. There was no going back now. 'When you were ordained, and began your term of service. How did you feel?'

There was a moment of silence. Tension buzzed over Medusa's skin. She and her mother never discussed such things; it was improper. But, surely, today of all days, they could be candid with each other.

'I was proud,' her mother finally responded, her voice tight. 'As you should be.'

'But—'

'Daughter.' Firm fingers grasped Medusa's arm and turned her until she was face to face with her mother, the morning sunlight from the villa's high windows dappled across her skin. The older woman was handsome, there was no doubt about that, but years managing the household under the firm hand of her husband had given her a sharpness that hadn't yet touched Medusa's soft features. 'Priestesshood is an honour that has been bestowed on our family for generations, and I was grateful for the opportunity. Not many women have the chance to be elevated in such a way, and it's a joyous occasion. Next to my wedding day, it was the happiest day of my life.'

A broad smile swept over Medusa's mother's face, but it didn't touch her eyes.

She was lying.

There was a brisk wind blowing off the Mediterranean, filling Medusa's nostrils with the tang of salt. She knew she should be below deck with her parents, protecting her intricately styled hair and perfect makeup from the sea spray, but who knew when she would be able to cross these waters again? Once her term at the temple was complete, she would be married off to an eligible nobleman, and might never return to the island of Lade again.

Whether that would be a good or bad thing, she could not decide.

The butterflies threatened to return, anticipation swelling in Medusa's chest. She relished the opportunity to see a real city, and escape the tedium of the gynaeceum – the woman's area of the house where her greatest excitement was completing the day's weaving – but being thrust into the life of a public figure and all the pressure and expectation that came with it was overwhelming. The vow of chastity while she served the goddess Athena didn't worry her – the few men she had been permitted to meet hadn't interested her in the slightest – but the shift from relative solitude to being under constant scrutiny was daunting.

'Medusa!' Her mother's shrill voice erupted from behind her, almost swallowed by the howl of the wind and the crash of the waves against the bow of the ship. 'Come inside before the sun spoils your complexion!'

The words were immediately forgotten as something much more interesting came into view on the horizon – the skyline of Miletus.

Excitement gripped Medusa's insides. She had heard tales of the greatest city in Ionia – from housewives' gossip around the local well, and from eavesdropping on her father's discussions with other influential men as she loitered near the door to the male-only andron – but none of it compared to beholding it with her own eyes.

A tremendous harbour sprawled ahead of them, with a great number of ships moored in the glittering sapphire water, dock workers scurrying back and forth with goods from foreign and exotic lands. A breathtaking tapestry of urban life hugged the bay, a scattering of vibrant orange clay and striking white limestone dotted with accents of dark hardwood and glistening marble. Beyond the first ring of municipal buildings, temples and courtyards stood the grand amphitheatre, sweeping around the city in a huge crescent and standing taller than any structure Medusa had seen before. It was breathtaking.

She stepped forward to get a better look, wrapping an arm around the figurehead for balance and reaching up on to her toes, eyes scanning the city for the Temple of Athena – her new home.

Medusa's mother had told her scant information about where she would reside for the next four years, almost as if she couldn't bear to relive her time there, but Medusa imagined it as a tremendous, imposing place. As the ship drew closer to Miletus' shoreline, her sharp eyes picked out many impressive stone buildings, but as her gaze swept over the south-western edge of the city, her breath caught in her throat, and she knew she had found it. The Temple of Athena.

Even from her distance on the approaching ship, Medusa could pick out the towering granite columns and high vaulted roof that could only belong to the most significant place of worship in the city. It loomed over the surrounding area like some great guardian, watching over the people. Whether for protection or retribution, Medusa did not know.

A firm hand suddenly grasped Medusa's arm, forcefully pulling her back from the ship's prow.

'What do you think you are doing?' her mother hissed, dragging Medusa across the deck towards the inner quarters of the vessel. 'Do you want to arrive looking like some common, ungroomed servant?'

She pushed Medusa through an open doorway into a protected cabin. The wind immediately dropped and the fresh, sea breeze was replaced by stale, stuffy air.

'Sit down and tidy yourself up,' Medusa's mother whispered into her ear, shoving her forwards into the small space she had abandoned just minutes ago. 'I will *not* let you bring shame on your father and our family name on today of all days.'

Medusa moved deliberately slowly, crossing the dark room to a wooden bench where her father and brother sat straight-backed, dressed in the finery of aristocratic Grecian men, neither meeting her gaze. She lowered herself beside her brother, fighting the urge to sneer. Of course, the men of the family would put on a great show today, exuding pride and affection they had never felt for the daughter whose life had been planned out since before birth. To them, she was sub-human, just a pawn for them to use to their advantage to maintain their ranking as one of Ionia's most powerful families.

Medusa had always tried to accept her lot in life as a woman living in a world dominated by men. They decided her future, they told her where to go, what to do, and who she would marry, and she accepted it quietly and without argument. But right then, in that moment, she hated them for it.

Crowds surged towards the harbour, buffeting against Ismene as she tried to battle against the flow of bodies. She swore under her breath as a stranger barged past her, their rough shoulder dragging her headscarf back and revealing her face.

'Damn it!' she muttered, dashing to the side of the street to seek the refuge of the shadows between two narrow villas. Once out of sight, Ismene tugged the scarf back down, relief washing over her as she was hidden once more. Her gaze returned to the flow of people sweeping down towards the sea front, excited chatter buzzing all around them.

*Where are they going?,* she thought.

There were no festivals scheduled today, she was sure, but it wouldn't be surprising if there was something exciting happening in town and her parents had kept her ignorant of it. They wouldn't want to pique her curiosity and risk her slipping away into town. Again.

Ismene straightened her himation and wrapped it more firmly around her shoulders, the outer garment in disarray from the pushing and shoving of the crowd. She reached into the folds of the fabric, her heart fluttering as her fingers found the obols stitched into the lining. She rubbed her thumb against the linen, smiling as she felt the raised horsehead on the coins' surfaces. She had been saving for this opportunity for months; she should really hurry straight to the agora and back home before her absence was discovered. Ismene chewed her lip, watching the anxious crowd bustling past. Her father would be at the workshop until sundown – there was time to visit the market *and* see what was causing such excitement on the way.

Pulling her headscarf close, Ismene slipped into the crowd and let it carry her southwards, towards the sea.

She would find out what all this commotion was about.

People crushed in on every side, the forced proximity sending Ismene's pulse racing. So close to so many bodies, a heady aroma of scented oils, body odour and herbs flooded her senses. Men and women pressed against Ismene as they all gathered to see what was drawing so much attention, sending a small thrill up her spine. Hundreds of people surrounded her, and yet she was practically invisible. No staring, no frowns as she hid further beneath her headscarf, no shaking heads or whispers of 'such a waste'.

'What's going on?' a surly seaman shouted over the crowd, face screwed up in frustration. 'Some of us have a job to do here!'

'She's here!' a tall younger man ahead of Ismene yelled back, pointing to the row of small ships docked at the harbour. 'The new priestess of Athena arrives today!'

Ismene frowned.

*Is that it?*

Were these people really so excited about a woman on her way to live a chaste and tedious life in a temple for half a decade? Ismene was reverent of the gods, of course, but had never taken much notice of the people tending to their places of worship. Such roles were part of the political games in the city which her parents discussed at length, but which Ismene considered irrelevant and, frankly, boring. Her father's attempts to marry her off had been thus far unsuccessful, and so Ismene had become practically worthless in Miletus society. That suited her just fine; she had long ago had enough of the twisted faces of would-be suitors when they examined her features.

Ismene stood on her toes, head swivelling from side to side in search of an escape route through the mass of people. She had already spent too much of her precious time away from home on this anticlimactic investigation; her freedom was limited – she couldn't waste it.

'Excuse me,' she murmured, trying to squeeze between a large man and his wife. They didn't move, both too engrossed in the arrival of a woman who would be forgotten about within a few days, out of sight and out of mind. Ismene turned around, but the space behind her had already been filled by a throng of new people, all deaf to her pleas to step aside and let her through.

'I see her,' a well-dressed lady to Ismene's right called out, 'the new priestess! She's beautiful.'

Ismene rolled her eyes, but didn't continue trying to move away. She was stuck in the crowd now, and she might as well catch a glimpse of the person everyone else was so interested in.

It was a long time since Ismene visited a temple – her parents preferred her to worship at home – and she imagined the priestess to be a stern-faced, humourless woman, focused entirely on completing her service as easily as possible before moving on to bigger and better things.

Nevertheless, Ismene's curiosity had always gotten the better of her. She leaned forwards, rising on the balls of her feet to get a better look.

That's when she saw her.

A young woman, no older than Ismene herself, stepped off a gangplank onto the dock, waving shyly at the cheering crowd, a blush radiating across her plump, olive-skinned cheeks. She was tall – no doubt a trait inherited from the statuesque nobleman standing beside her, who Ismene presumed to be her father – and blessed with a voluptuous pear-shaped figure.

And, by the gods, she *was* beautiful.

The crowd fell away, the chatter and excitement silenced as Ismene's gaze focused on this entrancing woman. She stepped forward, moving with an effortless elegance Ismene could never hope to replicate, an uncertain smile playing on her full, crimson lips.

Ismene's skin tingled as the woman's large, dark eyes swept over the crowd, her heart skipping a beat as that unsure but piercing gaze seemed to settle on her face for just a moment. A blink and the connection was gone, but the burning in Ismene's cheeks lingered. Those eyes... They made Ismene feel light-headed, a deep and unfamiliar heat coiling in her stomach. It was exhilarating.

And petrifying.

'What in the names of the gods are you doing here?'

Ismene froze. The heat evaporated from her body as her blood curdled into ice.

*Oh, no. No no no no no.*

She knew she should turn and face him, but it was as if her feet were rooted to the ground.

'Answer me!'

Rough hands clamped onto Ismene's shoulders and spun her around so she was looking directly into the blazing eyes of her father. His face was contorted with barely controlled rage, his fingers digging into Ismene's flesh so hard she knew there would be bruises tomorrow.

'I... I just...' Ismene stammered, shame pooling in her gut at how pitifully meek she sounded. 'I thought—'

'You thought you could wander the city unescorted?' her father shouted, angry spittle spraying from his wide mouth. 'Have you not brought enough shame on our family?'

'I... I'm sorry.' Ismene's cheeks flushed. She could feel eyes on her from all around; people were starting to notice the scene they were causing. 'Father, please...'

'And where is your mother?' If her father realised they were drawing an audience, he didn't care. His anger had always blinded him. 'Did she permit this?'

'No!' Ismene finally found her voice. 'Mother is unwell – she thinks I'm home, I swear.'

Her father narrowed his eyes, searching for lies, whether real or imagined. 'We'll see about that.' His hand moved to Ismene's wrist, and he pulled her towards him. 'Come on.'

Ismene twisted in his grip, hoping to catch a final glance of that breathtaking priestess as her feet were put into motion against her will.

But it was too late. Ismene craned her neck to look past her shoulder just in time to see a head of perfectly braided dark hair disappear behind a closing carriage door. She tore her eyes away, stumbling as her father dragged her through the crowd, his thunderous expression clearing a path for them as he led his daughter like a disobedient bullock.

Ismene's adventure was over before it had truly begun, and all she had gained for her efforts was an already fading memory of the most beautiful woman she had ever seen.

By the gods above, she swore she would see her again.

Once all the pomp and ceremony was over, Medusa's new elevated status seemed to evaporate.

After several days of meeting politicians and ambassadors, being paraded in front of foreign dignitaries, and receiving offerings from the wealthy and powerful so that their families might receive preferential prayers (always implied, of course, never said explicitly), her world was plunged into silence.

The Temple of Athena transformed from a bustling centre of music, speeches and processions to an empty cavern, each footstep echoing a thousand times off the cold marble surroundings as Medusa drifted through the great space like a ghost.

In a way, she enjoyed the peace. There was a paradoxical freedom to being bound to the temple, out of the sight of her critical mother and cold, distant father. No more reminders of her duties to come, that her pivotal role was to ensure the ambitions of the family were achieved no matter the personal cost. Medusa had been lonely her entire life, alone even when surrounded by the people who claimed to love her, and this new form of solitude settled around her shoulders easily.

The assistants and acolytes who shared Medusa's new home treated her with polite indifference. They offered the appropriate respect and reverence as warranted by her status as priestess, but there was no warmth between them, no companionship through their shared bonds to the goddess Athena, no whispered secrets or girlish chatter. The nights were near silent, each woman wrapped in a cocoon of their own thoughts and dreams, never shared or spoken aloud. Medusa would often lie awake, wondering about the girls she saw each and every day but knew so little about. Were they happy with the roles they had been allotted? Would it matter if they weren't? One day, as they tended to the great altar outside in the morning sunlight together, Medusa had caught Kephissa, a senior acolyte within the temple, smiling the kind of private smile revealed in a moment of remembrance or thoughts of the future, and Medusa wondered if she was thinking of a loved one. A friend or lover, perhaps. She would likely never know.

Medusa tried to convince herself she didn't need the company of others, that she was content with her quiet detachment and would never long for human touch, but with each day that slipped by, cracks in her resolve reached deeper. She knew she was to be married someday, wed to an important and wealthy man of her father's choosing, for whom she would bear children and fulfil her expected purpose, but when she imagined this future, no desire or joy stirred within her. There would be no love between her and this faceless husband – just as she had never witnessed love between her own parents – only a shared sense of duty and a cold marital bed. She hoped, at least, that he would be kind.

Medusa's favourite activity was visiting the naos – the small, windowless inner chamber of the temple – and worshipping the statue of Athena that dwelled within its walls. Lit only by a single shaft of sunlight through the doorway and overlooked by the goddess of wisdom herself, the shadowy, narrow room felt like a private sanctuary, a secluded space away from prying eyes and judgemental looks.

It was within the small haven of the naos that Medusa's mood was its lightest. As priestess, she had a small office to tend to her administrative duties, but it was by no means private; acolytes would come regularly to receive their work orders, and often appear beside Medusa if there was anything they needed help with, especially if a wealthy or prestigious visitor demanded the priestess' attention. But in the naos, Medusa could light the oil lamps and sit beside the goddess, reading theological texts in their soft amber glow and basking in the peace that came with Athena's company. She would not dedicate her entire life to religious worship – that was not the destiny decided for her – but she enjoyed immersing herself in the lore of the gods, their fantastical creation, their wondrous powers, and their impact on the world and its people. Alone in the naos, she could pretend she was truly part of their world. While Medusa was still unused to her high authority within the temple, and would not dream of wielding it unfairly, she knew no one would disturb the private worship of the priestess, and she revelled in every moment of gentle tranquility before she stepped back through the threshold and into the harsh light of reality.

As spring transitioned into summer, Medusa found herself waking early with the rising sun, padding through the empty temple grounds on bare feet to seek the company of the goddess. One morning, she was roused from her sleep as the sun was barely on the horizon, Helios and his chariot just beginning their flight across the pre-dawn sky. Medusa blinked, eyes quickly adjusting to the gloom. She surveyed the sleeping quarters around her, searching for what could have woken her before the sunlight crept between the pillars and illuminated the room, but there was nothing there aside from her acolytes, lost in slumber in their own cots.

Wide awake despite the early hour, Medusa slipped a shawl around her shoulders and crept past her sleeping sisters towards the inner sanctum of the naos. Being in the presence of the goddess always soothed her. Perhaps after some quiet meditation she would be able to sleep until the morning sun graced the temple.

With well-practiced movements, Medusa was near-silent as she manoeuvred through the temple grounds. This early, the silence was almost complete, the birds not yet woken by the rising sun. As she drifted through the courtyard towards her destination, the only sound was that of her own beating heart. That... and something else.

Medusa halted and strained her ears. The sound was quiet, but unmistakeable. Footsteps.

Goosebumps erupted over her skin. While the temple was never strictly closed to the public, there was an understood etiquette, and no one entered outside of daylight hours. There were treasures in the naos, votive offerings to the goddess Athena, but what thief would dare desecrate such a holy place and incite the wrath of the gods?

Medusa crept to the end of the courtyard, staying close to the columns that lined its edges in case the intruder appeared and she required additional cover. Thick shadows pooled around their bases and gathered in every corner, but amidst the gloom she could see an orb of light swaying back and forth towards the inner sanctuary. A lamp. Someone was there, and they were almost at the naos.

Heart pounding, Medusa hurried after the intruder, thankful she had kept her feet bare. She padded across the cold marble in near-silence, long strides soon bringing her close enough to see the stranger's hooded cloak disappear through the doorway of the naos. They were smaller than she expected, shorter than Medusa, narrow-shouldered and surprisingly slight for a late-night burglar.

As the figure swept out of view, Medusa crept up close behind, clinging to the stone wall as she leaned out and peered into the naos. A frown creased her brow as she watched them, standing in the centre of the small space with their oil lamp held aloft, head swivelling side to side as if unsure of their surroundings. On the stone table ahead of them sat fine jewellery, exquisite statuettes and bronze vases – all recent offerings to the goddess, and worth more than an average Ionian would earn in a year – but these were seemingly unnoticed by the intruder.

Emboldened by their uncertainty, Medusa stepped into the doorway. 'Are you lost?' She spoke softly, but in the dense silence she might as well have been shouting.

The figure spun around, startled. Their hood shrouded their face in mystery, but amidst the shadows two amber almond-shaped eyes widened with alarm. Before Medusa could say another word, they sprang at her, barrelling through the doorway.

'Wait!' Medusa snatched at them as they passed, fingers grasping a handful of their himation. The linen was thin, and tore as the stranger pulled away. Something small clattered to the ground, hidden in the shadows. The stranger turned and hesitated, gaze shifting between the dropped item and Medusa. They made to snatch at what they had lost, and as the lamp in their hands tilted, hot oil spilled over and onto their fingers, no doubt burning them.

'Damn!' they shouted, and Medusa blinked, shocked by their piercing female voice. It shattered the silence, reverberating off the surrounding walls and out into the temple grounds, the echo ricocheting off each column until the air was filled with her cries.

Eyes bulging as if surprised by her own curse, the strange woman spun around and darted away from Medusa. The sound of her footsteps rattled through the darkness until she was out of the temple, leaving Medusa frozen in uneasy silence, cheeks flushed and heart hammering in her chest.

Who was this strange, striking woman, and why had their interaction flustered Medusa so?

Taking a deep breath to settle her frayed nerves, Medusa set off back to her sleeping quarters, halting as something on the ground glinted at her in the gloom. She squatted and picked up what appeared to be a small coin. Holding it up to the dawn light beginning to filter into the temple, she could just make out the shape of a horse's head.

Ismene sprinted up the alleyway, her legs burning as she forced herself to keep running. The sun was almost fully risen; she had to get home before her father left for the workshop.

Her lungs screamed at her to stop as she weaved through the Miletus streets, and the pulsing tips of her scalded fingers cried out for cold water, but there was no time. Her sandals slipped on the packed dirt when she careened too sharply around a corner, almost sending her colliding into an already-cracked limestone wall. She recovered just in time and stumbled onwards, relief flooding her body as the high class city townhouses gave way to more modest dwellings and places of work.

*Almost home.*

Spurred on by the more familiar surroundings, Ismene surged forwards, breathing hard. She had been foolish to think she could go to the temple and return before sunrise, and now she was going to pay for it.

Finally, the small, square building that was her family home came into view. Ismene slowed, eyes scanning for any sign of her father. It would do her no good if she made it home just to crash into him in the doorway. Thoughts of his ire brought a twinge of pain to Ismene's sides as she approached the house, sticking close to the walls of the neighbouring buildings. With the adrenaline of her flight from the temple beginning to ebb, her bruised ribs, a gift from her father the last time he'd caught her out unescorted, throbbed.

*Damn that man to Hades.*

As if summoned by her curse, the door to the house burst open, revealing the frowning face of Ismene's father. The breath froze in Ismene's lungs and her pulse raced as she pressed her body into the wall, praying to every god and goddess that his gaze didn't drift in her direction.

'Anthea! Anthea!' Ismene's father shouted over his shoulder, each word dripping with contempt. 'Where are you, woman? I need my tools!'

Anger burned through Ismene's fear, but she pushed it down. She despised the way her father spoke to her mother, but now was not the time to challenge him. While he was distracted, she sidestepped slowly towards the house, hoping the early morning sun would hold off just a little longer and maintain the shadows clinging to the wall behind her. Her breath quickened as she inched closer, drawing level with the doorway, tantalisingly close to escaping his line of sight.

Ismene stepped to the side. Her foot caught on a rock and she stumbled, her hurried steps to right herself clattering like thunderclaps in the quiet street. Her father began to turn towards her, but halted as a high, strained voice called from inside the house.

'Here, Thaddeus!'

Ismene cringed at her mother's placating voice, but wasted no further time, sprinting to the back of the house while her father berated her mother for her less than satisfactory cleaning of his potter's tools.

Ismene burst through the rear doorway, her surroundings a blur as she dashed upstairs and bolted into the gynaeceum – the only place within the house her father would never tread. Once inside, Ismene threw herself onto the hard couch, where she lay panting, every muscle in her body aching. She trembled all over, from the fear, panic, exertion and... something else.

Her eyes fluttered closed, and Ismene saw her again. The priestess.

She wasn't supposed to have met her, not yet. Ismene had just wanted to see the temple, to understand the place where this enchanting woman now held residence. Since the accident, her prayers had been limited to the small altar in her living quarters, where she wouldn't have to cover her face to avoid the cruel stares of strangers, and such grand – and public – places of worship intimidated her.

And yet... The Temple of Athena was tended to by exclusively women, and Ismene had always felt more comfortable in the company of her own gender. Perhaps she could convince her father to escort her there...

*No.*

Ismene sat upright and shook her head. She knew better than to ask her father for unexpected and unexplained journeys – how had her once-sharp mind become so addled? She rose and strode to the basin in the corner of the room, straining to lift the terracotta water jar beside it.

*Mother must have already been out to fill it*, Ismene thought bitterly. Frail and barely recovered from her recent illness, and yet still up with the first glimmers of dawn light to begin the housework. Ismene wanted to be impressed by the fine example of a model housewife her mother provided, but where she should have felt pride she only found resentment. Her mother worked so hard, catered to her husband's every whim, and what did she get in return? No love, no warmth, no income or agency of her own, just barked orders and cutting remarks.

'Men,' she muttered as she eased the jar forward to let some water into the basin. Even the fine terracotta was a reminder of her father. Ismene's eyes swept over the pattern painted on the its smooth surface. To her, it looked immaculate, a skilled series of classic Ionian images – leaves of laurel, charging horses, great ships – but her father had deemed it unsatisfactory and unsuitable for sale, and brought it home from the workshop in a great temper.

Ismene's gaze lingered on one of the painted horses, and her stomach dropped.

*The obols!*

She hastily placed the water jar back on the ground and rifled through the folds of her himation, desperate fingers searching for the secret pocket she had stitched into it. Her breath hitched when she felt the familiar weight of the hidden coins; she had only dropped one. And now the priestess had it.

At the thought of her, Ismene's face flushed, fresh heat scorching her cheeks. She dipped her hands into the cool water in the basin and scooped great handfuls over her face. After several minutes, she stood back, the front of her tunic soaked through. Pulling back her hood and letting her bronze curls burst free, Ismene placed the back of one hand against her forehead.

Her skin might have cooled, but her heart still fluttered like the furious wings of a bird in flight.

What was this sickness that had infected her? When she closed her eyes, the priestess' face appeared unbidden, and Ismene's body thrummed with an energy that was both exhilarating and terrifying.

She returned to the couch and threw herself down onto the pillows. No matter how much she tried to blink them away, images of the priestess' wide, surprised eyes and her dark lips, parted ever so slightly, drifted across Ismene's field of vision. She truly had an affliction, and visiting the temple had exacerbated it ten-fold.

It was too much.

Ismene should never have gone there, and she would never return. Whatever fantasy had driven her to the temple had to be forgotten.

It was over before it had truly begun.

Second only to the Temple of Athena, the North Agora was the grandest area in all of Miletus.

Medusa attempted to maintain an indifferent expression – the calm serenity befitting of a priestess – but her eyes widened as she took in the bustling marketplace. Her father had described it once to Medusa as a child, when he had returned to the island of Lade following a successful political meeting and she had assaulted him with questions until he relented, but his brief words did not do the place justice.

All around Medusa merchants and artisans called for her attention, display tables draped in the finest wares in all Ionia. Stores held shelves of gold, bronze and silver, delightful aromas of baking bread and roasting meats drifted through the air, and the sound of hammers pounding and wheels spinning echoed from the workshops. Compared to the sedate quiet of the temple, it was a cacophony of activity that sent Medusa's pulse racing.

Heads turned as she swept through the agora, the nods of acknowledgement, knowing smiles, and raised eyebrows sending a blush across

Medusa's cheeks. Being recognised would never feel entirely comfortable to her, and every significant family in the city vying for her favour made her stomach churn. During their meetings, the faces of her petitioners had become a blur, each ambitious husband and obedient wife blending into the next. Medusa worshipped the goddess of wisdom and reason, and had no doubt the great Athena would frown upon such vain and shallow attempts to gain social and political superiority.

Bribery would not grant these people access to Medusa's prayers.

As her gaze drifted over the stallholders and the bustling crowd, she was frozen in place by two piercing blue eyes, locked on her from across the marketplace. People weaved in and out around her, but that stare remained focused on Medusa, sending a dreadful chill radiating through her body. The rest of the face was indistinct, the eyes drawing her attention completely. The shouts of merchants and bartering customers faded into nothingness, leaving only Medusa and those pale, penetrating eyes.

She blinked, and the figure was gone. The cold uneasiness that had settled on her skin dissipated as if it had never existed, and the sounds of the busy agora refilled Medusa's ears. She shook her head, bewildered. Had that really happened, or were her early mornings and periods of prolonged solitude affecting her more than she had realised? A nearby spice merchant called to her, pulling Medusa out of her thoughts, and she ducked back into the crowd, letting the stream of bodies carry her onward.

Finally, the potter's studio came into view. She clutched the amphora in her arms closer to her chest and hurried through the crowd, weaving between bodies until she could slip into the sanctuary of the small store.

A short, stocky man turned as Medusa stepped through the doorway, his attention shifting from the array of fine vases and sculptures around him to his visitor, a frown creasing his prominent brow. He sported a dense beard which was more grey than black, and the smears of wet clay streaking his linen apron suggested Medusa had interrupted the finishing of one of his pieces. He looked Medusa up and down, his eyes slowly tracking over her body, coming to rest on her uncovered head and the finely braided hair which marked her as a priestess of high status.

'Can I help you... Your Grace?' he said warily, his gruff voice contrasting the polite words.

Medusa lifted the large vase in her arms and the potter raised an eyebrow, silently demanding further explanation of the task expected of him.

'This is from the Temple of Athena,' Medusa began, this finally piquing his interest. 'It is very old, and a sacred vessel for several of our rituals. However...' She twisted the amphora so the potter could see the deep crack marring one of its sides. 'One of the new acolytes was... not as gentle as she could have been. Is it salvageable?'

Evadne – the new and extremely nervous acolyte who had dropped the vase during her first ritual – had been distraught by the damage she caused, and it had taken a great deal of reassurance from Medusa that she would not be severely punished to finally calm her. Many of the girls under her instruction had not been provided the level of education and practice that Medusa had gained before serving the goddess, and she would not see them punished for that.

The potter lifted the vessel away from Medusa, tugging it roughly from her fingers. She frowned at his impoliteness, but held her tongue. Her status as priestess granted her greater privileges than most – it was only this status that allowed her to be out in public unescorted at all

– but she was still a woman, and the wrong words from an influential man could have devastating consequences.

'Hmm,' the man murmured, holding the amphora up and running a calloused thumb over the fissure in its surface. 'Yes. Yes, I believe I can fix this.'

Medusa opened her mouth to respond, delighted at this news, but she was cut short by the potter's bellowing.

'Girl!' He yelled over his shoulder at an open doorway, presumably leading to some sort of storeroom or workshop. 'Girl!'

'Yes, Father?' A high voice called back. It was oddly familiar to Medusa. She had never been to this studio – had never been to the agora at all – and yet she was sure she knew that voice.

'Amphora for repair,' the potter continued his command. 'Make room on the rack and come get it. Quickly, now!'

'Yes, Father.'

Medusa's eyes widened as realisation struck her. It could not be... and yet only one voice had struck Medusa in such a profound way. That woman. The intruder.

She swallowed, her throat suddenly tight, her mouth dry. The potter was speaking, but his words didn't reach her through the throb of her pulse in her ears.

'Girl!' His shout shook Medusa out of her trance. 'What is the hold up? Get out here!'

'Allow me,' Medusa mumbled, snatching the amphora out of his hands. He opened his mouth to protest, but Medusa swept past him with as much authority as she could muster and glided through the doorway into the back room.

There she was.

Medusa watched, entranced, as the young woman shifted between pots of all sizes, moving them from place to place with purpose. In the privacy of her father's studio, she had let her headscarf fall around her shoulders, releasing a magnificent array of honey-coloured curls. She was slim, with an athletic frame, and carried herself with a self-assured determination that was bewitching to watch.

After several long, captivating moments, Medusa felt she must make her presence known. As beguiling as this young woman was, it seemed intrusive to watch her for any longer in what she thought was a private activity.

'Excuse me.' Medusa spoke softly, but the other woman started, spinning to face the priestess with wide eyes. She frantically tugged her headscarf up, taking great pains to draw it forward so it shadowed almost all of her narrow face, with only her striking amber eyes truly visible. Medusa caught a glimpse of what she believed was the reason for the other woman's shyness, but kept quiet, patiently waiting for her to finish rearranging her clothing.

'Um... Can I help you?' the young woman asked, once she had somewhat composed herself. Her eyes fell on the amphora still clutched in Medusa's arms, and she reached forward to relieve her of it. The ends of her fingers were red, the tell-tale shine of a recent burn streaked across each one. Medusa's pulse quickened a little; it was definitely her.

'Thank you.' Medusa smiled as the woman gently pulled the vase from her hands and carried it to the rack by the wall. 'Perhaps, now we're meeting in more pleasant circumstances, you can grant me the pleasure of your name?'

The other woman froze, the amphora hovering above the rack in paralysed fingers. 'Oh, no... Oh, gods, no.'

Sympathy stirred in Medusa's chest at the panic in the other woman's voice. She hurried forward and placed a gentle hand on her shoulder, which was met with another wide-eyed stare.

'It's all right,' Medusa soothed, using her free hand to guide the amphora to its proper place in the rack before it slipped from the other woman's trembling hands. 'You are not in any trouble. It's purely by chance that our paths have crossed again – I swear I did not seek you out.'

The young woman nodded, releasing the amphora safely into the rack and clasping her hands together, but she continued to thrum with nervous energy.

'And your name?' Medusa prompted again, maintaining a gentle tone to her voice so as  not to fluster the other woman any further.

'Ismene.'

'That's beautiful.' The simple compliment elicited a small, shy smile from Ismene, partially obscured by the headscarf she continued to tug over her face. 'If you would forgive my boldness,' Medusa continued, not wanting to fray the woman's nerves further, but unable to quell her curiosity, 'why did you come to the temple that night?'

Though Ismene's ochre face was still shadowed by the scarf, Medusa thought she spied a hot blush sweep across the small area she could see. She felt her own cheeks heat to match, whether in sympathy or some other undefined emotion, she could not quite tell.

'I...' Ismene began, her voice little more than a squeak. She cleared her throat and continued with greater conviction. 'I just wanted to see.'

A smile twitched at the corner of Medusa's mouth. There was something about this woman – shy and unsure of herself one moment, and bold and reckless in another – that piqued her interest.

'Well,' Medusa said slowly, watching carefully for the reaction to her next words, 'if you want to see the temple and our work there, I would be happy to escort you around and teach you about our worship.' She swallowed, hoping she was not being too forward. 'You would be very welcome.'

For a moment, Ismene's eyes lit up with something akin to delight, but it was quickly replaced by something else, something dark. 'While I'm sure that would be... lovely,' she said wistfully, 'I don't think it would be possible.'

A subtle flit of Ismene's eyes to the doorway and back – so fast Medusa almost missed it – told her everything she needed to know. 'You're afraid.' She held out an arm to gesture through the doorway to the storefront. 'Afraid of *him*.'

Ismene nodded, chewing her bottom lip in a way that made Medusa's stomach flutter strangely.

'Well, then,' Medusa said brightly, squaring her shoulders and summoning all of the priestessly authority she had learned in recent weeks. 'I shall have to convince him.'

Before Ismene could protest, Medusa hooked an arm through hers and led her swiftly through to the front of the store, where the potter was waiting. A perplexed expression coloured his face, and as his gaze landed on Ismene, it shifted to one of barely concealed outrage.

'What are you—'

'Good sir, I am astounded!' Medusa beamed at the potter, using every modicum of charm she had been taught growing up to lace her voice with honey and her body language with grace. 'Your wife has shown tremendous aptitude for the wisdom of our lady Athena. You have married a woman with great promise.'

The potter blinked, his bewildered gaze slowly shifting between the two women stood before him. 'She,' he began, pausing to clear his throat, 'is my *daughter*.'

Medusa forced a dainty, surprised laugh. It was as she'd suspected – and hoped, judging by the odd sense of relief that fluttered in her chest – but the information would serve her purposes perfectly.

'Forgive me,' she said, placing a gentle hand on the man's upper arm. Friendly, perhaps a little flirtatious even, but not inappropriate. 'But I struggle to believe that! You are far too young a man to have sired a woman of her age, surely?'

A flush of heat reddened the man's cheeks, and his confusion transformed to a beaming grin. Medusa's mother had been right – flattery was by far the quickest way to a man's affections.

'Well, I don't know about that...' he muttered, eyes on his feet and a hand running through his thinning hair.

This was her chance.

'In that case, I am sure a man of superior breeding and good graces such as yourself is thrilled his daughter will be extending her education to the divine arts. The Temple of Athena is the most prestigious and sacred holy site in the city, and I can personally guarantee her training will be of the highest quality.'

'Wait.' Ismene's father raised his head, joviality replaced by concern, bordering on suspicion. 'What is this?'

'Not full time, of course,' Medusa continued brightly, determined to ignore his shift in mood and successfully charm him. 'Her valuable assistance here takes priority – I will see to that.' She gestured to the array of admittedly expertly crafted vases and sculptures around them. 'After all, an artisan of such high calibre must be extremely busy.'

That elicited the beginnings of a grin. 'Well, of course, but—'

'And,' Medusa interrupted, lowering her voice to a faux-conspiratorial whisper, 'I am sure I don't need to tell a canny man – and *father* – like you what such a distinguished education can mean for a young woman's... *prospects*.'

The implication landed as intended, and the potter's expression shifted, his eyebrows furrowing and his lips puckered as if he was calculating the worth of a prize bull. Medusa hated pandering to his desire to marry off his poor daughter to some wealthy or powerful man, but Ismene clearly wasn't happy here. Throughout the conversation, Medusa had felt her grow increasingly tense by her side, ready to bolt back into the back room at her father's direction as soon as Medusa's persuasive words failed and his mood soured beyond even her talents to remedy.

The older man deliberated in silence, the few moments they waited stretching on until the silence was almost painful. Ismene was practically vibrating with nerves next to Medusa. The priestess laid a soft hand on her arm, the energy passing between the two women sending an odd thrill down her spine. Ismene glanced at Medusa, eyes wide and her teeth once again working at her lip in that strangely endearing manner. Medusa nodded and flashed her a small, confident smile.

'Yes.'

Medusa blinked at the potter's sudden and abrupt exclamation. 'Yes? Is that to say, you consent to Ismene's training at the temple?'

He nodded stiffly, his face concerningly neutral. 'I do, but I have conditions.'

Medusa's stomach clenched, but she kept her features smooth and her expression positive. 'Of course. Please, go on.'

'Ismene is permitted to attend the temple three days out of seven, no more.' Medusa nodded, and opened her mouth to speak, but the potter continued. 'She is to remain in the temple grounds *at all times*, and must never travel to or from the temple unescorted. With no offence intended, my *lady*,' he said without a trace of reverence of Medusa's station, 'she must be escorted by a male member of her family. In most cases, me.'

The unspoken message was very clear: Medusa might have some status granted by her position, but she was no man. In his mind – and in the laws that bound all citizens of Miletus – Ismene belonged to him, and only he was allowed to be seen with her in public.

'I see,' Medusa responded mildly. As much as it pained her, this man had shifted the power in the room to himself, and she could not wrest it from him. 'Those conditions are acceptable. Are you satisfied with that proposal, Ismene?'

'Of course she is. Now,' he gestured to the doorway. 'If you do not mind, Priestess, we have considerable work to do today, and now an additional amphora requiring repair.'

'Of course.' Medusa's smile was sickeningly sweet. She removed her arm from its link with Ismene with reluctance, and turned the other woman to face her. 'I do look forward to you joining us at the temple.' She leaned forward, her lips finding Ismene's cheek and settling there for a brief moment. Heat erupted in Medusa's chest, and she pulled away, startled by the fire burning through her skin. 'I will take my leave,' she muttered, strolling to the doorway, willing the blush to leave her cheeks. As she turned to face the store's interior again, she noticed Ismene's head was down, her face hidden by her headscarf, her expression unreadable.

Drawing herself up to her full height, Medusa addressed the potter a final time. She would not leave this man's presence cowed into submission. 'You will bring the amphora with you when you bring Ismene to the temple, yes?'

He blinked. 'Yes, that won't be a problem.'

'And when will that be?'

He frowned, taken aback by her questioning. 'Two days to make the repair, a further two to fire and finish. Five days maximum in total, I imagine.'

Medusa nodded. 'See that it is done. Good day to you both.'

With that, she swept through the doorway and out into the bustling agora, her stomach swirling and her pulse racing.

With excitement or anxiety, she couldn't be sure.

The Temple of Athena rose high above the Miletus streets, both re-splendent and intimidating, like the statue of a ferocious warrior.

It sent a shiver down Ismene's spine.

Her excitement had been growing by the day ever since the priestess persuaded her father to allow regular visits to the temple, but now her destination loomed before her, its shadow filled her with dread.

The women who tended to holy places were educated, with some being high-born from families of power and status, and it wouldn't take long for them to realise she was not one of them. Nervous fingers tugged at her headscarf, the urge to hide her face – and the shame that came with it – rising with each step.

'Here we are,' her father announced gruffly as they reached the pala-tial entrance to the temple grounds.

Wide marble steps ascended ahead of them, leading to an elevat-ed terrace paved with what appeared to be granite, but banded with minerals in different shades which sparkled in the early morning sun. Beyond, the temple buildings towered over them, a great colonnade guarding the entrance as if protecting the sacred grounds from those bearing ill will towards the goddess.

Ismene chewed her lower lip as she took it all in, suddenly feeling very small.

'Here.'

Her father's voice snapped Ismene back to reality. She turned to see him holding out the priestess' amphora, skilfully returned to its former splendour. Ismene cradled it in her arms, shifting her feet to manage its weight.

'Do you not want to present it to her yourself?' she asked, peering at her father over the finely sculpted handles. He had gone beyond merely filling and repairing the crack in the vessel's surface, reworking many aspects of its decoration and fine finish until it looked freshly made. It was a thing of beauty, certainly, and Ismene felt a sliver of resentment writhe through her gut as she ran her fingers over the perfectly glazed surface. If only Thaddeus took this much pride in all his creations.

'Not this time,' her father grunted, dark eyes sweeping past Ismene and up the steps. 'Never been comfortable in these places.'

Ismene nodded, not understanding his unease, but grateful for it nonetheless. The sooner she could part ways from her father and be free from his constant supervision, the better.

'Go,' Thaddeus ordered gruffly, waving an arm towards the temple. 'I will collect you at sundown.'

Ismene frowned. He didn't even trust her to go into the temple without him watching over her. Eager to be free of his gaze, Ismene hurried up the steps, holding the repaired amphora tightly against her chest as she walked.

As the temple entrance loomed closer, butterflies erupted in Ismene's stomach. She stood before the columns, peering into the sanctuary beyond, afraid to cross the threshold. It had been easy when she arrived in the depths of night, when there was no one to stare at her or question her presence. But now, in the light of day, there were acolytes hurrying through the rooms, arranging altars, preparing rituals, and tending to offerings. There was a quiet hum of activity Ismene had never experienced before, and she didn't know how to become part of it.

'Ismene, I am so glad you made it.'

Ismene turned to see the priestess from the studio – Medusa, had she said her name was? - gliding across the paved temple floor towards the entrance. The butterflies in Ismene's stomach grew faster as she approached, their wings beating into a whirlwind when she placed a hand on Ismene's shoulder.

'It looks wonderful, does it not?' Medusa smiled, and Ismene blinked in confusion. 'The amphora,' Medusa continued, pointing to the vessel Ismene had forgotten she was holding. 'Your father has done an excellent job.'

'Oh,' she murmured, heat flaring across her cheeks. 'Yes. He does fine work.'

'Here, allow me.' Medusa lifted the amphora from Ismene's arms and carried it to the nearest acolyte, who was arranging some flowers – a beautiful bouquet of roses, anemones and hyacinths. Medusa murmured some instructions to the young woman, who nodded, taking the amphora and scurrying off into a side chamber at the far end of the entrance hall.

That done, the priestess returned to Ismene's side, those wide hips swaying with each step. Ismene could not pull her eyes away.

'I'm still not entirely comfortable with giving people orders,' Medusa whispered, her breath tickling Ismene's cheek and sending goosebumps erupting over her skin. 'Come on.' She wrapped an arm around Ismene's, heat pooling under her soft touch. 'I'll give you a tour of the temple grounds.'

Eyes closed, with the sound of birds singing in her ears and the late afternoon sun bathing her face in warmth, Ismene felt more at peace than she had in a very long time.

'It's so peaceful here,' she murmured slowly, leaning back as she sat and enjoying the cool stone against her palms. The priestess had shown Ismene most of the temple during the morning hours, carefully and patiently explaining each area's purpose and religious significance. It had been interesting – and certainly a refreshing change to assisting her father with his work while he berated her constantly – but Ismene welcomed the break. She took a deep breath, revelling in the quiet. 'How do you get anything else done when you could sit out here all day?'

A soft, melodic laugh rang out, and Ismene's eyelids fluttered open. Medusa stood a short distance ahead of her, between the large marble bench Ismene had chosen as a resting place and a great pool in the centre of the courtyard. She was looking at the tall olive tree which stood in the pool's middle – standing sentinel on its own small island within the man-made water feature – but turned on hearing Ismene speak, the sunlight shimmering in her deep brown eyes.

*Gods, she is beautiful.*

Fresh heat flooded Ismene's cheeks and she dropped her gaze, hoping the priestess hadn't noticed her staring.

'I actually like to keep busy.' Medusa answered Ismene's question as if nothing had happened.

'Oh,' Ismene replied, embarrassment worming through her gut. 'If you would rather me not be here, interrupting your duties…'

'No!' Ismene looked up to see Medusa approaching her, a frown creasing her perfect face. She lowered herself onto the bench next to Ismene, and took one of her hands in her own. 'I hope I didn't make you feel unwelcome with that remark! I welcome your company, truly.' A sigh fell from her plump lips, and her eyes fell. 'It's just… It gets lonely here, you understand. Focusing on my duties and keeping myself occupied helps me forget.'

Ismene blinked, bewildered. 'But… the temple is full of people, all the time. Worshippers, acolytes…'

Another laugh, but this time hollow and tinged with sadness. 'Being alone is not a requirement for loneliness.' Medusa looked up, her eyes shining with the threat of tears. At Ismene's puzzled expression, she continued, 'I value the company of the others here – they are all pleasant and well-meaning – but it is all on the surface. We smile and nod and pray together, but there is no connection. I don't know their hearts, or their souls, and they don't know mine. I feel… somewhat cold inside. Empty.'

Ismene frowned, taking in the priestess' solemn words. That someone who radiated such warmth and light could be hiding a profound sadness inside them was jarring. It was a high honour to be selected to be priestess of the Temple of Athena, and although Ismene generally avoided the city's social and political manoeuvring, she had always assumed those selected were overjoyed with their coveted position. They were on their way to a life of high society and privilege, offered the opportunities and social status Ismene had always been – and always would be – denied. Perhaps things were not so black and white, however.

'I apologise,' Medusa continued, drawing her hand away and dabbing at the moisture forming around her eyes. 'You came here to learn and see the temple, not to listen to my woes.'

'No, not at all.' Ismene chewed her lip, struggling to find the words to express her true intentions. How could she tell this enchanting woman – who was laying her soul bare without expecting anything in return – that the real reason she had first crept into this religious sanctuary was because of her, because she'd felt drawn to her, and needed to get closer?

She couldn't. It would sound absurd.

Medusa had been nothing but honest and earnest since they met, and Ismene was taking advantage of that. It was wrong, part of her knew that, but the thrill of being in the priestess' company was intoxicating. It was like Ismene was under a magnificent spell that she would do anything not to break.

The two women locked eyes, and Ismene knew Medusa was waiting for her to say more, to reassure her that her vulnerability was not misplaced.

'If it helps,' she said softly, the words finally coming to her, 'I know your soul now, or at least a part of it, and it's beautiful.'

A real smile flashed across Medusa's lips, lighting up her face and forming small dimples in her plump cheeks. Ismene's heart soared. What she wouldn't give to make her smile like this every single day.

Perhaps she could.

It was a foolish notion, and Ismene shook it away before any hope could latch onto it. That line of thinking would lead only to heartbreak.

'You warm my heart, Ismene.' Medusa squeezed the other woman's hand, sending fresh waves of heat spreading over Ismene's skin. 'Come,' she said brightly, rising to her feet, 'let me show you the naos. I don't think you got a proper look last time.'

The giggle that burst from the priestess' lips sent Ismene's stomach tumbling. She stood, and followed Medusa across the courtyard.

She would follow her to the end of the world.

Time spent with Ismene was nothing short of joyful. As the hours slipped into days, the potter's daughter opened up to Medusa little by little, delighting her with the bright personality she was slowly letting shine through. Conversation drifted from theological teachings to more personal matters, with Medusa speaking of her childhood on Lade, being groomed for her future duties as a dutiful housewife, while Ismene shared the resentment she held for her overbearing father. For the first time in her life, Medusa had a true companion, someone she could confide in without fear of reprisal or judgement.

'Do you miss them?' Ismene asked her one morning as they strolled through the courtyard. It seemed to be becoming their favourite spot, and they often found themselves unconsciously drawn there several times each day. 'Your family, I mean.'

Medusa couldn't help but smile. Where she had been taught to be subtle and guarded when trying to extract information from someone – even in private – Ismene spoke plainly, speaking her mind without hesitation.

'Sometimes I think I do,' Medusa answered almost wistfully, 'but then I realise it's more the place that I miss. The island was peaceful and quiet, the air fragrant with fig, orchid and wild herbs. But...'

'But...?' Ismene prompted, sitting on the edge of the pool in the centre of the courtyard and gesturing for Medusa to do the same. Her almond-shaped amber eyes swept over Medusa's face, full of kindness and understanding.

Medusa took a deep breath. She had started to open up to Ismene, but after years crafting the mask required to navigate Miletus society as the daughter of a nobleman, it was still difficult to let it slip. 'My life was so... *empty* there. I was trapped in the gynaeceum learning how to weave, and sew, and hold myself in the right way while with company, and flutter my eyelashes just so at an eligible gentleman... And all the while, Father and Adrastus – that's my brother,' she added, seeing Ismene's forehead crease slightly with confusion. 'All the while, they were downstairs hosting influential Ionian leaders, discussing politics, trade and philosophy. I would hear them talking and laughing as they filled their cups and celebrated new alliances while I languished in solitude. I was a forgotten shadow, a ghost haunting the upper floor until they could finally be rid of me.'

Her breath caught, and she swallowed down the sob rising in her throat. It wouldn't do for one of the acolytes to see their priestess breaking down in tears. 'I was told I was lucky. What a great honour to be raised to the position of priestess, to be a woman of what little status and independence we are able to be granted. I *am* grateful – I understand there are women who would relish this opportunity – but none of it is my choosing. I'm an object, with no agency of my own. First I belong to my father, then to the goddess, then to my husband.'

Medusa squeezed her eyes shut. She didn't realise she was crying until a gentle finger brushed her cheek, sweeping away a stray tear. When her eyelids fluttered open, Medusa found herself once again staring into those beautiful golden eyes of Ismene's. For a moment, the two women simply stared at one another, lost in each other's gaze. Heat pooled in Medusa's abdomen; Ismene was so close. Her knee grazed Medusa's ever so slightly, only the thin linen of their chiton tunics preventing their bare flesh from touching. Medusa's pulse quickened as she noticed Ismene's dark lips part a little, tantalisingly close yet impossibly far.

Ismene broke the spell first, glancing away and tugging her headscarf to further cover her cheeks.

Medusa leaned back a little, blinking away her stupor. Her eyes remained on Ismene, however, suddenly timid and hurrying to hide her face even more than usual. It was curious.

'Ismene?' Medusa spoke softly, her stomach twisting as she prepared to ask the question which had been lingering in the back of her mind ever since the potter's daughter had joined her at the temple. She waited for Ismene to turn to face her again, trying to gauge if she would be open to this discussion. It would be heartbreaking if Medusa lost the only real friend she had because she could not contain her curiosity.

'Yes?' Ismene was still half-hidden to Medusa, but her honey-coloured eyes were warm and open, and a shy smile pulled at her lips.

Medusa would ask. She wanted to know Ismene, truly know her, and this was the only way.

'Please forgive me if this is an inappropriate question,' she began slowly, wary of provoking a panicked reaction. When none came, she continued. 'But can I ask, why do you hide behind your headscarf so? The temple is a sanctuary, a safe space where women do not need to be veiled or cover their hair. There is no obligation, of course, but... I worry you are not entirely comfortable here, with me.'

Medusa fought to maintain a mask of neutrality as she awaited Ismene's response. Were Ismene to reveal she despised her company, it would devastate her entirely.

'Oh, Medusa, you wonderful woman.' Ismene threw her arms around the priestess, drawing her in for a warm embrace. 'If only everyone in this world was as kind and considerate as you.'

A slight shiver ran through Medusa as Ismene's body pressed against her own. She breathed in her scent: earthy and clean, with an undertone of fruit, reminiscent of a fine olive oil. Butterflies fluttered in Medusa's stomach as she tentatively placed her hands on Ismene's slender back, energy thrumming through her fingers. Ismene seemed to respond to her touch, inching closer to the priestess and holding her tighter against her breast. Medusa's breath caught as she realised their legs had interlinked, Ismene's thigh now pressed between hers. A fresh burst of heat blossomed between Medusa's legs, startling her with its intensity.

An unfamiliar and almost overwhelming urge gripped Medusa. Her touch grew firmer as she slowly slid her hands down Ismene's back, a thrill running up her spine as she took in the gentle curves of her body.

A soft exhale tickled Medusa's neck. She wanted to linger in this moment forever, to drink in the feel of Ismene's body, the warmth of her embrace, but it wasn't proper. The temple was quiet today, but she was the priestess, and such displays of affection would not be appropriate in front of the acolytes.

With great reluctance, Medusa drew back. Her hands traced the backs of Ismene's arms as she pulled away, and Medusa briefly imagined Ismene's fingers hook onto hers, retaining their physical connection for just a little longer.

'All right,' Ismene said firmly, her amber eyes sparkling.

'All right?' Medusa's chest tightened with anticipation.

'I trust you,' Ismene continued. She took a breath, her fingers moving to the fringe of her headscarf. 'I'll show you why I hide my face.'

Medusa gasped. 'Ismene, you do not have to do that. I'm sorry if I—'

'No, no it's all right,' Ismene interrupted, waving a hand to quieten Medusa's worrying. 'I feel safe here, with you. Out there, in the street, or even in Father's studio... people stare. And although I trust you, and know you wouldn't be cruel...' Ismene's eyes dropped, and Medusa thought she saw a slight quiver in her lips.

'Yes?' Medusa gently prompted, her heart racing.

Ismene raised her face, and her eyes shone with tears. 'I thought you might find me hideous,' she said, her voice breaking. 'And I couldn't bear that.'

'I could never—'

Ismene raised a hand. 'Don't, please. Just... be kind, I beg of you.'

Medusa held her breath as Ismene drew back her headscarf and let it fall around her narrow shoulders.

'Oh,' Medusa breathed as Ismene's full face was finally revealed.

A shining pink scar stretched over the left side of her face, starting from underneath her eye and widening over her cheek before it disappeared under the tight auburn curls covering her ears. It had clearly healed, but against her smooth dark skin, the scarred flesh appeared raw.

Medusa licked her lips, considering her next words carefully. 'Is it a—'

'Burn?'

Medusa nodded, thankful the other woman did not seem offended by the question.

'Yes.' Ismene's eyes dropped, and she raised a hand halfway to her face before noticing her self-conscious movement and dropping it again. 'I was a child, full of curiosity and following my parents everywhere, trying to figure out how all manner of things were done.'

A smile pulled at Medusa's lips as she imagined a younger Ismene, that bold spirit of hers sending her charging around the household asking a never-ending string of questions.

'While Mother was happy to indulge me,' Ismene continued, eyes still downcast, 'Father was not.'

She took a shuddering breath. Medusa ached to reach out to her, to reassure her with her touch, but she resisted. This was Ismene's story, and she would respect that and allow her some space.

'I sneaked into his studio. You've seen it.' Ismene looked up, eyes shining with tears. 'It's full of interesting bits and pieces, equipment and materials and tools.'

Medusa nodded. Of course Ismene had been drawn to the potter's workshop – what child wouldn't be fascinated by such a place?

'I'd always wanted to know how it worked, and thought if I learned enough he'd let me help him, maybe even allow me to make my own pieces eventually.' A sad smile ghosted across her face as she remembered. 'It was a naive notion, stupid really, but, full to the brim with the overconfidence of youth, I decided to take a look at the kiln. I didn't know...' Her breath hitched, but she forced herself to continue. 'I didn't know how hot it could get. Father wouldn't tell me anything – he refused to teach me! So, I opened it up myself and... Well.' She waved a hand over her face, the bitterness plain on her features. '*This* happened.'

'Did it hurt?' Medusa asked, immediately cringing at the banality of her question. 'I'm sorry, that was a foolish question.'

'No, no, it's all right.' Ismene closed her eyes and took a deep breath, as if even the memory of the incident caused her pain. 'Yes, yes it did. It was this white hot, searing pain, as if my flesh was being ripped from my skull. I remember screaming until my lungs gave out, and Mother soothing me with soft words and cloths soaked in cold water while Father berated me for my idiocy, for my foolishness and disrespect, for my... my *selfishness*.'

'Selfishness?' Medusa asked, confused. 'What did he mean by that?'

A bitter laugh burst from Ismene's lips, though a touch of fondness glittered in her damp eyes. 'My dear Medusa, haven't you ever wondered why I am unmarried at my age? Why I have never mentioned suitors or a betrothal?'

Medusa blinked. Not once had she considered Ismene's marital status, or lack thereof. Protected by her temporary position within the temple, it was a reality Medusa had managed to postpone longer than most young women were able. Realisation dawned on her, and it must have shown on her features, as Ismene slowly nodded in affirmation.

'You don't mean...?'

'Yes,' Ismene confirmed. 'Father says I am damaged, ruined even. What man will want to marry me, now that I look like this? No dowry will convince a high-standing family to ally with mine and raise us into nobility. I am worthless, nothing but a burden.'

Tears streamed down Ismene's face now, and Medusa's heart swelled for the poor, broken woman before her. Her gaze did not linger on the scar that had caused Ismene such pain and torment, instead taking in the rest of the young woman's appearance, finally presented to Medusa in what she now understood to be a moment of supreme trust.

A heart-shaped face, a narrow brow, and arched eyebrows framing the loveliest almond-shaped eyes. Where Medusa's cheeks were plump and round, Ismene's were angled with high, prominent cheekbones, giving her a look of elegance and strength.

She was striking.

'May I?' Medusa asked softly, raising a tentative hand. Ismene nodded. turning her head for the priestess to examine her scar more closely. Instead, Medusa cupped Ismene's cheeks with both hands, turning her face so their eyes met again. 'Ismene,' she whispered, gentle thumbs brushing away the lingering tears, 'you are *beautiful*.'

A gentle shake of Ismene's head loosened Medusa's fingers. 'You cannot mean that.'

Medusa smoothed Ismene's loose curls behind her ears, revealing the other woman's face in its entirety for the first time, and let her hands fall gently to rest on her shoulders. 'I have never meant anything more sincerely in my life.' Ismene's gaze drew her closer, so vulnerable and open, willing Medusa to be speaking true. 'You are beautiful, Ismene. You are bright, you are warm, you are bold, and...' She leaned closer, placing a delicate kiss on Ismene's brow. 'You are worth so much more than you know.'

Something between a sob and a laugh burst from Ismene's lips. The two women melted into an embrace, their foreheads touching, tears flowing down both of their cheeks.

It was with great reluctance that Medusa waved to Ismene as she departed the temple to be escorted home by her father. The sun was low in the sky, its light glittering off the finely polished stonework of the temple grounds. As per Thaddeus' wishes, Medusa remained standing in the entrance, her escort not acceptable for his daughter in public. The man was a fool, but if gratifying him provided Ismene with an easier home life, Medusa would do it.

A twinge of sadness pulled at Medusa's heart as she saw Ismene tug her headscarf further over her face when they reached the public roadway. Despite Medusa's protestations that she did not need to hide herself away, Ismene was insistent, and had covered herself before they even reached her father at their usual meeting place. Thaddeus did not – and most likely never would – realise what a treasure he had in his daughter, and the effect his presence had on Ismene's confidence was profound, and infuriating.

It was in this moment, as Medusa watched her friend depart, already shrinking into the shadow of her tyrannical father, she realised how privileged she had been. Her status as a nobleman's daughter had never been in doubt, and she knew that this provided advantages other women would never possess, but she had been blind to the blessing that was her appearance. All her life, she had been reminded that her beauty was her greatest asset. She had been trained to accentuate her good looks, to use them to charm those around her, to elevate herself in society and to eventually – once her tenure at the temple was complete – secure her that grand prize of a good marriage.

And she had hated it.

Since blossoming into adulthood, Medusa had despised being nothing but a pretty face, an image to be desired, a prize to be offered to lure a man of quality and status to her bed. But now there was Ismene, who believed she did not even have that, who had grown up understanding she lacked this one thing that made a woman hold any value. The thought filled Medusa not only with great sadness, but a heavy shame. She would not allow her friend to feel this way any longer. If it was the last thing she did, she would prove to Ismene that she was valued, and that she was loved.

As father and daughter disappeared around a corner in the distance, Medusa stepped forward into the sun. Soon, darkness would settle over the Temple of Athena, and she wished to allow herself a few moments to enjoy what remained of the day's warmth.

Then she saw him.

The figure – a man, she now realised – with the piercing blue eyes. He stood, motionless in the middle of the public road, his gaze locked onto Medusa, his expression unreadable. Unlike the other people milling to and fro down the Miletus streets, his features were not dark and his clothes were not plain. Instead, he was fair, his long, loose hair and curled beard shining golden in the sun, his skin impossibly pale for one who dwelt on the Ionian shore. Where others mostly wore undyed himations or chitons, he was dressed in great robes of blue and green, edged with glittering gold. On his chest he sported a bronze breastplate that gleamed in the sunlight, as if freshly polished.

Ordinarily such a striking figure would create a stir amongst the locals, but the men in the street passed him by without a second glance. Where he stood directly in their path, they did not complain or even seem to notice, seamlessly stepping aside and rejoining their original trajectory, not once breaking their stride.

In a similar fashion, the man paid them no mind, his attention entirely fixed on Medusa, his eyes boring into hers and sending her blood running cold. It was unnerving. A vulpine grin twisted his face, and his eyes flashed dangerously, suddenly dark and threatening.

Medusa stepped back into the shelter of the temple's shadows, but it wasn't enough. She felt the man's gaze still locked onto her, finding her in the gloom, watching her every move.

She turned, a chill running down her spine as the feeling of being watched lingered. She scanned the temple, searching for someone, anyone, she could call over. Medusa craved the comfort of an ally, another person to not only draw this man's uncomfortable gaze away from her, but perhaps provide some explanation of who he was, and why he was fixated on the temple.

Finding no one, her stomach dropped, but when she turned back to peer outside again, the strange man was gone.

Thaddeus' ramblings about his insolent and miserly customers – and the inconvenience of yet another day without assistance – drifted over Ismene's head without permeating her thoughts.

All she could think of was Medusa.

Even now, hours after their embrace, Ismene could still feel the priestess' soft lips on her brow, her thighs pressed against her own, her gentle fingers sliding down her back...

Ismene stumbled forward as her foot caught on something sticking out of the surface of the road. Her arms flailed, and she clutched onto her father's himation to prevent herself from falling face-first into the dirt.

'Get your head out of the clouds, girl!' her father scolded, roughly pushing Ismene away. He shook the material out, a scowl on his face, as if his daughter's touch repulsed him. 'This training is supposed to be making you more intelligent, and yet you seem more stupid each day.'

Usually, her father's barbed words hurt, but right then Ismene didn't care. Medusa had seen her face. More than that, she had seen her face *and* called her beautiful. Ismene could hardly believe it. All her life she had received sneers and stares from anyone who caught so much as a glimpse of her deformed face, shakes of the head and whispers of "such a shame" and "used to be so pretty", each one chipping away at Ismene's self-esteem until she folded in on herself.

But Medusa saw past it. She saw Ismene as a person, not a mistake, or a lost opportunity. Medusa saw her as... Well, Ismene didn't know. "Friend" didn't seem quite enough to capture the closeness she felt in the priestess' presence, or the energy that seemed to thrum between them when they were alone. It was something beyond friendship, something deep and warm and terrifying.

She only hoped Medusa felt the same way.

'Come along!' Thaddeus grasped Ismene's arm, his strong fingers jolting her out of her thoughts. 'You've wasted enough time today already. Your mother needs help collecting the water before it's fully dark.'

He tugged at her so aggressively she almost fell, but even her father's rough treatment couldn't shake the smile from her face.

Medusa had called her beautiful, and that meant everything.

Holding the copper disc in her palm and raising it to the window, Ismene angled her arm to catch what she could of the sun's rays. They reflected poorly off the old copper mirror she had dug out of her mother's things, each scratch and dent warping the image of herself she was confronted with.

She stretched her arm out further, turning her face to try and get a view of the scar she had hidden from for so many years. Ismene had never possessed a mirror of her own; as she grew into her teen and adult years and it became obvious her face would never return to normal, her parents didn't deem it necessary, and so Ismene grew used to being estranged from her reflection, only occasionally catching glimpses of it in the wash basin or her father's metal tools.

Resisting the urge to toss the mirror aside and continue to hide, Ismene raised her chin to finally bring the patch of angry pink skin into view.

She blinked. It seemed impossible, after a lifetime of scorn and self-loathing, but when Ismene cast her eyes over her damaged face, she felt… relieved. Was it possible that her disfigurement was less severe than she had thought? Perhaps Medusa's kind words were blinding Ismene to reality, but as she stared at the tight scar tissue which crawled across her cheek, it seemed almost fine. It was true she would never be a great beauty, but neither was she monstrous.

Ismene glanced over her shoulder, where her headscarf lay spread out on her bed, waiting. They would be leaving soon – Ismene could already hear her father clattering around in the next room, muttering and ranting to himself as he prepared for another working day. It was time to decide how brave she really was.

Taking one last look at the face staring back at her in the dappled copper surface, Ismene squared her shoulders and marched through the door.

Her father had his back to her, hunching over a satchel of small tools and muttering to himself as he rummaged. On hearing her footsteps, Thaddeus waved an arm behind him, gesturing his daughter over.

'Finally! Make yourself useful, girl, and find my good callipers. Your fool mother cleaned them and now can't find them.'

Ismene resisted the urge to defend her mother. Thaddeus was already in a foul mood; she would have to choose her battles wisely today.

'Yes, Father,' she muttered, moving warily to the other end of the room to search the shelving by the door. Her mother was noticeably absent, and Ismene sent a silent prayer to the gods that Thaddeus hadn't punished her too severely for misplacing a piece of his equipment. 'Is this it?' She pulled what looked like a measuring device from beside a squat vase on the shelf. It was in plain sight, at eye level, but of course her father hadn't noticed it in his petulant state.

'Yes,' he answered gruffly, snatching the callipers from Ismene's hands without so much as glancing at his daughter. 'Come, we're late.' He placed the tool into his satchel, slung it over his shoulder and strode out of the house. 'Now, Ismene!'

Ismene scurried out after him into the bright morning sun. It was strange to feel the light bathe her entire face, the gentle warmth caressing her cheeks. There was nowhere to hide, no scarf to pull at whenever a stranger drew near, but Ismene wasn't afraid. She was somehow… *excited*. A thrill shivered through her as she followed her father down the dirt road. People would see her – see *that* – but it would be fine. Medusa had called her beautiful, and she had meant it.

'Hurry along, girl! Why are you—'

Thaddeus froze as his eyes fell on his daughter. His face twisted into a thunderous sneer, sending Ismene's stomach plummeting.

'What are you doing?'

Ismene blinked, words failing her under the heat of her father's glare.

'Go home.' His words were stone cold. 'Cover yourself.'

His blazing eyes slid to Ismene's cheek. A look of disgust flickered across his features, igniting a small spark of anger in Ismene's chest.

'Why should I?' She stood up straight, willing confidence into her spirit as she faced off against the man who had diminished her for so long. 'What is so wrong with me?'

Her father's eyes bulged. 'What is... Have you taken leave of your senses? Look at you!' He waved a hand at Ismene's face, revulsion plain on his face.

'I see it!' Ismene shouted back, heat flushing her cheeks. 'Everyone sees it! Hiding it won't make it go away, Father!' Tears filled her eyes, but she continued, bolstered by the years of fear and self-hatred. 'I'm not some vile monster to be locked away from view, and I won't be ashamed of my face anymore. I won't!'

Thaddeus stepped closer to his daughter, his face red. Viper-quick, he snatched Ismene's arm with a painfully tight grip, and yanked her towards him. When he spoke, his slow words were cold, and full of venom.

'Girl, you have forgotten your place.' Thaddeus squeezed tighter, his fingers digging deep into Ismene's flesh. Pain radiated up Ismene's arm, sending fresh tears bursting from her eyes. He pulled her so their faces were barely a hair's breadth apart. 'I am your *father*, and everything you do, everything you say, everything you *are* is a reflection of me. You would do well to remember that.'

'Stop,' Ismene moaned, twisting in her father's vice-like grip. 'You're hurting me!'

Thaddeus squeezed tighter, a fresh wave of agony almost sending Ismene to her knees. 'You have no idea.'

He strode back towards the house, dragging Ismene behind him. She stumbled as she was forced backwards, her sandals unable to gain purchase on the ground, so she slipped, the skin of her legs grazing against the hard dirt as her father continued to pull her along.

'You say you're not ashamed?' Thaddeus growled through gritted teeth, dragging Ismene to the door of the house. He kicked the door open and threw her inside so she landed hard on the ground, sending pain shooting up her back and elbows. Thaddeus loomed in the doorway, staring down at his daughter with blazing fury in his dark eyes. 'I'll give you something to be ashamed about.'

Nervous energy fluttered in Medusa's chest as she looked out through the temple entrance for what must have been the tenth time that morning.

Ismene was late.

The priestess paced back and forth, not caring that she was attracting inquisitive looks from the acolytes and worshippers going about their business behind her. It was likely unbecoming for someone of her position to be so visibly rattled, but she did not care. Ismene was never late – in fact, she was typically early, dropped off by her father promptly so he could get started with his own work.

No, something was not right. Medusa could feel it in her gut, like a hot ball of lead burning her insides. She needed to see Ismene, to know she was all right.

Medusa stood still, clasped her hands together, and took a deep breath. Her new friend and trainee was having a profound effect on her. Medusa missed Ismene the moment she left her sight, and could think of little else until she returned, and now the other woman was running late to her lessons and Medusa was frantic with worry. Was this how friendships were supposed to feel, intense and all-consuming?

In truth, Medusa had never had friends growing up, not really. Cousins had visited the family home, but it was always a formal affair, the boys whisked away to learn politics or hunt with the men while the girls were locked away in the gynaeceum under the watchful eyes of their mothers. Medusa had tried to gossip with them, to learn more about the world beyond their island home, but she was quickly reminded it was unbecoming of a lady of her status, and her relationships with her cousins had remained as cold and unfeeling as those with her brother and parents.

Perhaps the emotions stirred by Ismene's presence were the formation of a real friendship at last.

Movement in the corner of her eye drew Medusa's attention, and her heart soared as she turned to see Thaddeus and Ismene making their way up the road towards the temple. Her unease did not fully lift, however. There was something wrong with Ismene. She walked a step behind her father, head bowed and shoulders hunched, headscarf smothering her features – the very image of submission.

Medusa stood frozen in place as she watched father and daughter approach, the anxiety never lifting from her chest. Thaddeus marched with purpose, arms swinging by his side, and gaze fixed straight ahead. When he walked up to Medusa, any thought of questioning his late arrival evaporated from her mind. Thaddeus glared at the priestess, his eyes full of a fury so cold it turned her blood to ice.

'Go,' he said forcefully, not turning to address his daughter directly. 'Now.'

Ismene scurried around her father and into the sanctuary of the temple, not looking up at Medusa as she passed.

'And you,' Thaddeus continued, looking to Medusa, his words dripping with venom. 'I do not know what form your *education* is taking, but I raised my daughter to have a sense of propriety, and to know her place. I expect your training *not* to undermine that.' He closed his eyes and took a breath, calming himself fractionally. When his gaze fell on Medusa again, it was hard as stone. 'Have I made myself clear?'

Anger bubbled up inside the priestess, but she swallowed it down. Such brazen disrespect against a Priestess of Athena in front of her acolytes was painful to ignore, but Ismene could only attend the temple with her father's blessing, and it would break Medusa's heart to have their friendship severed by this vile man.

'Perfectly clear,' Medusa forced through gritted teeth. 'Of course.'

Thaddeus nodded curtly and turned to leave.

'Thaddeus?' Medusa called before she could stop herself.

He turned, an irritated eyebrow raised. 'Yes?'

'I am confident that, should you choose to attend a service and worship the goddess yourself, you will witness your daughter's tremendous capability, and attest to the quality of her training.'

A scowl twisted his face, but Thaddeus did not offer a response. He turned and strode from the temple without another word.

Medusa did not waste time revelling in her barb, instead pivoting on her heel to observe her friend. Ismene was not grinning at Medusa's jibe at her father, nor was she rushing to speak to Medusa and discuss their plans for the day, as was their typical greeting. Ismene stood by the temple wall, half-hidden in shadow, head bowed and clutching her elbows as if cowering from those who served the goddess.

'Ismene?' Medusa tentatively asked, stepping closer. 'Are you all right? You... don't seem yourself.'

The other woman nodded, but it was a weak gesture, with no feeling to it. Medusa's stomach churned; Thaddeus had done something terrible, she just knew it.

'Ismene,' Medusa repeated, fighting to maintain a calm voice, anger and worry warring in her chest. 'What has he done to you?'

Ismene shook her head, gaze downcast. Though she could not see her face, Medusa knew she was hiding tears. The priestess placed a soft hand on Ismene's shoulder, turning her gently so they faced one another.

'Show me,' Medusa whispered. 'Please.'

Ismene raised her head, pulling back her headscarf as she did. Shockwaves crashed through Medusa's body as Ismene's face was revealed. Those beautiful honey-coloured eyes were swollen horribly, and ringed with deep blue and purple bruises. Her lips were split and bloody, and further bruising peppered Ismene's jawline and disappeared under her clothes.

'May I?' Medusa asked, reaching for the collar of Ismene's himation. The other woman nodded, and Medusa gently pulled at the fabric, revealing angry crimson bruises around Ismene's slender throat. Several distinct shapes stood out, five small patches that were darker than the rest.

Fingerprints.

'Gods,' Medusa gasped, letting the fabric drop from her fingers. 'Oh, my dear, sweet girl.'

She swept Ismene into her arms, clutching her tight to her breast. It didn't matter that every acolyte and worshipper in the temple could see their embrace. It didn't matter that tears flowed freely down the priestess' cheeks in full view of her subordinates. All that mattered was Ismene. All Medusa wanted was to ensure Ismene's safety and happiness. She wanted to take her away from that oppressive, violent household and protect her, to pluck her from her father's clutches permanently.

Perhaps, one day, she could.

A whimper sounded from Medusa's shoulder, and Medusa blinked back her tears. Such fanciful ideas would have to wait. She needed to take care of Ismene.

'Come,' she murmured, reluctantly releasing Ismene from her arms and taking her by the hand. 'I know where we can soothe your injuries.'

Cool air washed over the two women as they descended the steep stone steps, Medusa leading Ismene carefully by the hand.

'What is this place?' Ismene asked, her voice quiet and still carrying a slight tremble.

'Mainly a storeroom,' Medusa replied, halting at the bottom of the steps to light a wall-mounted torch. It partially illuminated a cavernous room, an array of crates, jars and large amphorae coming into view. 'I don't usually come down here myself, but it seemed the best place, given the situation. Plus,' she continued, draping a cloth over a row of crates and gesturing for Ismene to sit. 'It's one of the only truly private areas in the temple.'

'It'll be nice to be alone for a while,' Ismene murmured, a shy smile twitching at her broken lips.

'I told one of the acolytes we were coming down here, so we won't be disturbed, don't worry.'

Medusa's heart fluttered a little as she turned away and opened the nearest water jar. Though she and Ismene had snatched peaceful moments in each other's company throughout their studies, they had never been truly alone. A temple was a busy place, even on the quietest days, and there was always a chance of disturbance. Here, however, underneath the temple proper, privacy wasn't only promised, it was guaranteed. Nothing that transpired between them would be seen or heard by anyone else.

Goosebumps which had nothing to do with the cold room blossomed over Medusa's skin.

'Here.' Medusa dipped a small cloth into the jar, waiting a moment for it to become saturated with cool water before wringing it out and returning to Ismene. 'This should help.'

Medusa sat beside Ismene and dabbed the cloth against the other woman's lower lip, taking care to be as gentle as possible. Ismene closed her eyes, allowing her mouth to open slightly for Medusa to wipe away the dried blood.

'Curse that man to Hades,' Medusa muttered as she smoothed the last of the blood away and held the balled cloth against the worst of the swelling.

A small laugh escaped Ismene's throat, and her almond-shaped eyes flickered open.

'What?' Medusa asked, raising her eyebrows.

'I never thought I'd hear a priestess of Athena cursing in such a way.'

Medusa smiled. Despite everything, Ismene had managed to retain some of her sense of humour. The woman was a wonder.

'Sometimes,' she replied with an exaggerated air of authority, 'it is necessary.' The lopsided smile her words conjured on Ismene's lips made her heart leap. 'Here.' She took Ismene's hand and raised it to where she was holding the damp cloth to her lips. 'Take hold of this while I get another for your eye. It seems to be swelling more than the other.'

Ismene did as instructed as Medusa soaked another scrap of material and brought it back. 'Come here,' she said softly as she sat close to Ismene, their legs interlocked.

Brushing a handful of curls back from Ismene's face, Medusa laid the freshly damp cloth against her right eye. A soft moan fell from Ismene's lips as the cool water soothed her skin. Heat blossomed in Medusa's cheeks at the sound, and she tried to ignore the way her heartbeat quickened.

'That feels nice.' Ismene's soft breath whispered over Medusa's cheek to her neck, sending a shiver down her spine.

'Good.' Medusa moved closer to study Ismene's eye, tracing a tentative finger across the bruising on her upper cheek. 'Does that hurt?'

'No.' Ismene's voice was quiet, almost a whisper. 'You're the one person I trust *not* to hurt me.'

Medusa's hand stilled, and her gaze met Ismene's. Something shone behind those golden eyes. Trust, yes, but something else, something more.

Medusa withdrew the cloth from Ismene's eye and cupped the other woman's face with both hands. 'Ismene, I swear, I would never, ever hurt you.'

Fresh tears spilled down Ismene's cheeks, glistening rivulets meandering over smooth skin until they reached her tender lips. 'I know,' she whispered, closing her eyes and giving the slightest of nods, her face still cradled in Medusa's fingers. 'I know.'

Medusa's gaze settled on Ismene's mouth – broken but perfect, and inviting in a way that struck her with excitement and terror in equal measure. A strange urge pulled at her, willing her to move closer, to draw Ismene's lips up to her own and drink her in completely.

Medusa's heart pounded in her chest and her fingertips trembled where they rested on Ismene's skin. Her own lips parted as her breath quickened. Ismene was so close. Medusa shivered as she leaned in, heat thrumming through her body.

Ismene's soft breath caressed Medusa's lips, and she stopped.

What was she doing? Ismene was injured; Medusa should be taking care of her, not taking advantage of her vulnerability.

With great reluctance, Medusa pulled back, and let her hands fall softly to her lap. Ismene's eyes fluttered open, confusion shining in them. Confusion... and perhaps disappointment? Medusa dismissed the thought as soon as it arose. Ismene was Medusa's friend and apprentice, and she was sure that was where her fondness for the priestess ended. It was wrong to presume she shared Medusa's urges, that she held any of the desires Medusa now felt throbbing within herself.

No – Ismene was her friend, and nothing more.

'Here,' Medusa said hurriedly, rising from her seat before she found herself drawn to Ismene again. 'Let me get you some milk and honey. It will soothe you, and give you some much-needed energy after your ordeal.'

Before Ismene could respond, Medusa strode to the far side of the storeroom and began rummaging amongst the smaller amphorae until she found a jar of milk and an even smaller pot of honey. She returned to their makeshift bench to find Ismene sat with her eyes downcast, slender fingers crossed on her lap. Medusa longed to embrace her, to wrap Ismene in her arms and take all her pain away, but she resisted. Instead, she balanced the two amphorae in the crook of one elbow and held out her other hand.

'Come,' Medusa said softly. Ismene lifted her head, and the fresh sight of the swollen bruises that marred her otherwise beautiful features ignited a spark of rage in Medusa's chest.

Thaddeus would pay for what he had done today, she would make sure of that. But that would have to wait for another day. For now, all that mattered was Ismene.

'I have cups and spoons in my office,' she continued, gesturing for Ismene to take her hand. 'Let's have a quiet drink together before we get to work for the day, shall we?'

A small smile tugged at Ismene's broken lip, and Medusa's heart fluttered. The other woman slipped her hand into hers, slender fingers entwining her own, and a shiver ran down her spine. One day, Medusa would have to learn to be around her friend without such potent bodily reactions, but it seemed today would not be that day.

Ismene could not focus, and it had nothing to do with the lingering injuries following her father's latest attempt at getting her under his control.

She drifted through his workshop as if in a trance, her movements automatic and, more often than not, clumsy. She knew she should pay more attention, that if she broke something or damaged a piece of equipment he might lose his temper so badly her prior beating would seem like nothing, but she couldn't bring herself to care.

Ismene's thoughts kept drifting to Medusa, to that strange moment in the storeroom where the energy had changed between them. They had been so close Ismene could feel Medusa's breath on her cheek, could feel her pulse thrumming in her fingertips as the priestess held her face in her hands, and for just a moment, the impossible had seemed possible.

That is, until Medusa pulled away, and Ismene had been overwhelmed by a crushing regret that she still did not fully understand.

*What did I expect,* she thought bitterly to herself as she lugged repaired amphorae to the storage rack, ready for collection, *that she would kiss me, and declare her undying love?*

Ismene shook her head. Medusa was the Priestess of Athena – yes, they had developed a close friendship, and Ismene didn't doubt that Medusa was fond of her, but it was madness to hope for anything more.

'Hurry up, girl!'

Thaddeus' gruff voice brought Ismene back to the present, but she could not escape her thoughts of Medusa. She worked in silence all day, her father's insults washing over her as she cleaned and carried and organised. She tried to concentrate, to notice the fine designs of each piece, to scrub old clay off used instruments with intention, but her mind continued to wander back to the storeroom, to the touch of Medusa's fingers on her skin, the warmth of her breath on her lips.

Was it so wrong to dream of more from their relationship? Ismene was reminded every day that no man would want her, but was it so inconceivable that Medusa might?

*She called me beautiful. She saw my face, and called me beautiful.*

That had to mean something.

The day wore on, Ismene's thoughts continuing to spiral. She convinced herself that Medusa hated her as often as she was convinced she could love her, words and emotions tumbling around in her head until she could no longer think straight. By the time her father announced it was time to go home, she was utterly drained. Thaddeus practically dragged her back to the house in a daze, throwing her through the doorway in frustration so hard she tumbled forwards onto the ground.

'What in Hades is wrong with you, girl?' he shouted as he stood over her, hands on his hips. 'You have been useless all day, and now you can barely manage walking home.'

'Apologies, Father,' Ismene mumbled, no heart in her words. 'I must be tired.'

'Tired?' Thaddeus asked, incredulous. 'You have barely lifted a finger all day. Come on.' He wrenched Ismene to her feet by the arm and dragged her through the hallway to the gynaeceum. Shoving the door inwards with his shoulder, he pushed Ismene into the women-only space with rough hands. 'Given you are so in need of rest, you will go to bed immediately. I will instruct your mother to bring no food. Ensure you are more lively tomorrow, girl, or you *will* be sorry. Now,' he continued, pointing to the bed at the opposite end of the room, 'go to sleep. I am sick of looking at you.'

The door slammed and Ismene was left standing in the middle of the room, dazed and alone. Perhaps the cure for her stupor truly was sleep. She kicked off her sandals and padded to the bed, ripping her headscarf from around her head and lying back on the lumpy hay-stuffed mattress.

Even there, in the dim light of the claustrophobic gynaeceum, Ismene longed for Medusa, craved her company like a man dying of thirst craves even a single drop of water.

What if Ismene would never get to quench her thirst? Medusa had pulled away from her, severed that momentary tie that held them so close and sent Ismene's pulse racing just remembering it. Had the priestess felt it too, or was it all in Ismene's mind? Was it wishful thinking, or had the pulsing energy building up between them truly existed?

Ismene threw her arms over her eyes, blocking out what little light illuminated the empty room. The questions roiling in her mind were maddening, especially as no one could help her answer them. No one but Medusa.

Ismene had no siblings she could ask for advice. No one older and more experienced who could guide her through the maelstrom of emotions plaguing her body and mind. No doubt her mother and father had tried to conceive a son, or even a second daughter to replace their defective first child, but no brother or sister had ever materialised. Their only progeny would be Ismene, and Thaddeus hated her for it.

She rolled onto her side and hugged her knees up to her chest. Thoughts of Medusa continued to swirl through her mind, but eventually fatigue overwhelmed her, and she slipped into an uneasy doze.

A creak sounded behind her, and Ismene started. She sat up and stared at the doorway, pulse racing. Surely Thaddeus' anger had abated by now – even in his worst fits of rage he had not demeaned himself by entering the gynaeceum. The door swung inwards, and a sigh of relief tumbled from Ismene's lips as she saw the silhouette of her mother creep into the room.

There had been a time when Anthea and Ismene were close, back when Ismene was very young and her mother's spirit had not yet been broken by her father's constant berating and punishment. In recent years, though, the two women merely existed together in the same space, barely acknowledging each other beyond assisting in tasks doled out to the pair by Thaddeus. He ruled the house like a king ruled his palace, and even the most strong-spirited woman would bend to his will eventually. Even so, Ismene hated what her mother had become. She yearned for the days when her mother stood up to Thaddeus when he was wrong, when Anthea protected and advocated for her daughter, even sometimes shielding her from his blows, but the woman standing before her now was a ghost of the person she used to be. She was married to a man who had drained her of everything she once was, and left her a shell.

'Mother?' Ismene called through the gloom, reaching out to Anthea in a way she had not for a long time. 'Can I ask you something?'

'Of course,' Anthea responded weakly. She sounded bone-tired, but strode slowly to Ismene's bed and sat beside her. 'Are you unwell?'

'How old were you when you and Father were wed?' It was difficult to see her mother's expression in the dimness, but Ismene thought she saw the older woman flinch.

'I had fifteen years, I believe...' Anthea spoke slowly, the discomfort clear in her thin voice.

*Fifteen.*

The thought turned Ismene's stomach sour. Anthea had been married off to Thaddeus when she was several years younger than Ismene was now. A mere child, who would not have known the severity of the life she was destined for.

'And when you met him...' Ismene continued, uncomfortable herself with this line of questioning, but needing to know the answers. 'What was he like? Did you... Did you feel anything for him?'

Silence settled over the two women, and for a moment Ismene wondered if her mother had heard the question, or in her exhaustion had slipped into a daze herself. Finally, Anthea responded.

'He was older,' she said quietly, as if lost in the memory, 'had almost thirty years at the time. And was tall, his hair fuller and darker than it is now. He was already a respected artisan in the city. My parents were quite thrilled with the match, especially my father.'

Thirty years, almost double her mother's age. Ismene had always known there was a difference in age – it was the norm, a man typically having established himself in his position or trade before seeking a suitable wife – but the years had been cruel to Anthea. Decades of toiling for her husband had ravaged her features and stolen her youth.

'But how did *you* feel?' Ismene probed. Of course her grandfather had approved of his daughter marrying a man of influence and modest wealth, but that wasn't what she was asking. 'Did you love him?'

A laugh burst from Anthea, so cold and sharp it took Ismene by surprise. 'Ismene, my girl, I know you are no fool. Why would you ask me that when surely you know the answer?'

Ismene's mouth dried up, and she struggled to find the words to respond. What had she expected her mother to say, really? That she was overwhelmed with desire upon their meeting, like Ismene was with Medusa? That somewhere, despite the cruelty bestowed on them both by her tyrannical husband, Anthea bore an all-consuming, undying love for the man?

'I thought he was handsome,' Anthea continued, rescuing her daughter from the burden of providing an answer. 'He looked strong, like he could carry me to safety if the need arose.' She laughed again, but this time there was a tinge of sadness in the sound. 'But when I looked into his dark eyes, I saw cruelty there. I knew... I knew there would never be love between us.'

Ismene's head drooped. Her mother's words were not unexpected, but hearing them spoken aloud made everything so much more real.

'Don't despair, my child.' Anthea's arm slipped around Ismene and pulled her closer. Ismene let her head fall onto her mother's shoulder, the two women closer in that moment than they had been in years. 'Love is a great luxury in this world, and it is no great injustice that it wasn't bestowed on me. We women have our place in society, and we must do what we can with that.' She turned her head and laid a soft kiss on Ismene's forehead. 'Don't worry yourself further with this. Get some sleep, and things will be better in the morning.'

With that, Anthea rose and moved to her own bed, leaving Ismene sat in silence, staring into the gloom. Her mother's words rang loudly in her mind.

*Love is a great luxury in this world.*

She was right. What Ismene felt for Medusa was not what many women had the opportunity to experience. It may be terrifying, it might be painful, but it was also exceptional, and incredibly special.

In that moment Ismene knew what she had to do.

She had to tell Medusa she loved her.

The early morning sunlight beamed down on the grounds of the Temple of Athena, bathing everyone who stood within them in a pleasant, invigorating warmth.

Medusa stood behind the great altar in front of the temple building and looked out over the small crowd who stood waiting to hear her speak. Today she would be doing one of her favourite duties as priestess – teaching the acolytes a new ritual. While she performed her other tasks proficiently enough, she got little enjoyment from assigning duties or running the administration of the temple itself. She had spent her youth learning all there was to know about the rites of Athena, and passing on that knowledge to enthusiastic pupils was a joy.

'As you all know,' she began, raising her arms so all eyes were on her, 'summer is almost over, and with that comes the harvest.' Medusa gestured to an array of items laid out on the altar in front of her: sickles, a sheaf of wheat, a cup of grains, a bowl of olives, and a small amphora of the highest quality olive oil with an empty shallow bowl sat beside it. 'Our lady Athena granted us the gift of the olive tree; she bestowed the knowledge of agriculture upon us and invented the plough so we might sustain ourselves, and so at this time of year we thank the goddess for her generosity and wisdom with the following ritual.'

Medusa lost herself in her teaching, explaining the relevance of each item as she raised it before her pupils, and showing them how to expertly pour the oil from amphora to bowl while reciting a solemn prayer to the goddess. The eyes of the acolytes followed her every movement, and while under any other circumstance the undivided attention of so many people might fluster her, there was no such shyness while she shared her wisdom. Medusa knew the education she had received in preparation for this role was a great privilege not offered to many, and she would gladly impart her knowledge to anyone who was willing to receive it.

As she concluded her lesson, Medusa cast her eyes over the crowd once more, her heart swelling at the sea of enthralled and delighted faces, until her gaze settled on Ismene, and her stomach fluttered.

There, standing at the back of the crowd and flanked by her sour-faced father, Ismene stared up at Medusa, her golden eyes gleaming in the morning sun that bathed her face, revealing her beautiful features often hidden under her headscarf.

Medusa's throat tightened as Ismene locked eyes with her, a broad smile forming on her lips which sent Medusa's heart pounding. Ismene was early – Medusa had not expected her to be in the audience at all – and while her presence was a pleasant surprise, it knocked Medusa off balance. She tore her gaze away and stumbled through the rest of her speech, a heat that had nothing to do with the rising sun burning into her cheeks. If the acolytes noticed her change in demeanour, they showed no sign of it, applauding the priestess' final words, some even approaching the altar to ask further questions. Medusa answered willingly, all the while feeling Ismene's golden eyes watching her.

As the final acolyte turned to leave, a gruff voice came from behind Medusa.

'Is that how you spend your days? Pouring oil and uttering nonsense?'

Medusa turned to see Thaddeus, arms crossed and eyebrows raised, Ismene by his side. She wanted to ignore him, to tell him how little she cared for his opinions on how she conducted her worship, but instead she held her head high. 'Good to see you, Thaddeus. I would be glad to talk you through the finer points of the ritual, if you would like to know more. I know such things can seem strange to the untrained.'

Ismene smirked silently at that, but Medusa kept her expression passive; perfectly neutral, just as she had been taught growing up.

'That won't be necessary,' Thaddeus grumbled, his eyes darkening. 'Here.' He pushed Ismene towards Medusa, who stumbled and almost fell.

Anger pulsed through Medusa's veins, but she did not show it. This man would not provoke her with such petty acts of aggression. 'Careful, Ismene,' she said with all the politeness she could muster, looping her arm through Ismene's and holding her steady before she faced Thaddeus again. 'Your dear father does not know his own strength.'

'Just teach her something useful, rather than this drivel.' With that, Thaddeus turned and stomped away, out of the temple grounds and to the road beyond. Medusa shook her head and she and Ismene turned to head into the temple building proper.

'You were amazing.' Ismene said, using her free hand to tug back her headscarf and let her mass of curls tumble to her shoulders.

'I cannot stand the man, or the way he treats you.'

'No, not that.'

The two women stepped through the colonnade into the temple building, goosebumps erupting over Medusa's flesh in reaction to the sudden drop in temperature.

'Then what?' she asked, reluctantly letting go of Ismene's arms so they could speak face to face.

'Out there – your lesson!' Ismene beamed. 'You come to life when you teach. It was wonderful.'

'Oh.' A sudden shyness washed over Medusa, and her cheeks flamed once more. 'Thank you. It was nothing special, just a celebration ritual I thought would be good for the temple to adopt.'

'The ritual might not be special, but *you* are. You made it special.'

The now-familiar sensation of fluttering butterflies erupted in Medusa's stomach. 'You're too kind,' she murmured, pulse racing under Ismene's gaze. 'Really, you are. But thank you.'

'Have I embarrassed you, Priestess?' Ismene's smile widened and Medusa's throat tightened. The chill from the cool morning air had disappeared entirely, replaced with a swirling heat in Medusa's chest. 'I just wish...' Ismene continued, chewing her bottom lip in a way that sent Medusa's heart fluttering. 'I wish I had seen the whole lesson. I was enthralled by what I did see, but do you think you could show the ritual to me? All of it?'

'Oh, of course! I hope you are not offended – we needed to conduct the lesson before the temple opened for the day's prayers, but I didn't intentionally exclude you. I thought it would be over before you even arrived... You must think me so rude.'

She was rambling, Medusa knew that, but she did not seem to be able to stop. While Ismene's eyes were on her, the composed, professional demeanour of the priestess seemed to slowly melt away.

'I'm not offended, Medusa, truly.' Ismene moved as if to take the priestess' hand, but thought better of it, instead clasping her own hands together in front of her chest. 'I know your work here can't revolve around me and my schedule. It's just...' Her teeth scraped across her lower lip again, and Medusa's stomach tumbled. 'Since the ritual looked so interesting, and you delivered it so well... Perhaps you could give me a lesson... privately.'

It could have been a trick of the sunlight streaming in from between the columns, but Ismene's golden eyes seemed to flash with intent, and a thrill ran up Medusa's spine. Ismene wanted to be alone with her again. And this time, she wasn't injured or upset, she was wholly herself, and was the one initiating the move to a private space.

Medusa's heart pounded. She might be wrong. Ismene might want to learn the ritual in earnest, might simply want to benefit from the focus of one-on-one teaching.

Medusa licked her lips, and could not help but notice the way Ismene's gaze flitted to her mouth for the briefest of moments. 'Will the storage room do for the lesson?' Medusa asked tentatively, nerves thrumming as she waited to see if Ismene understood her invitation.

Ismene's eyes flashed once more. 'Yes.'

'It *is* peaceful down here,' Ismene observed as Medusa led her into the coolness of the storeroom. 'If a little dusty.'

Medusa chuckled and laid a lamp on top of a crate near to where they had sat in such close proximity mere days before. 'It's a small price to pay for absolute privacy, I suppose.'

The air between the two women became charged, the unsaid implication within Medusa's words clear to them both.

She cleared her throat, and tried to continue in a level tone. 'If you could place the items on one of these crates, that would be perfect.'

Ismene moved to stand beside her, setting the tray holding the items needed for the ritual on a crate beside the lamp. The yellow light from the flame danced over them and, not for the first time, Medusa wondered if they would even be needed.

The thought sent her stomach fluttering, and for a moment the two women simply stood side by side, a taut energy strung between them, begging Medusa to act. What was Ismene thinking in that moment? Would she welcome Medusa's touch, or would she push her away?

The brush of a fingertip against the back of her hand sent a shiver through Medusa. 'I meant it when I said you were special,' Ismene murmured, her slender fingers feather-like as they made small circles on the back of Medusa's hand. 'Especially to me.'

Medusa turned to face Ismene, lacing their fingers together, the simple gesture accelerating her heart rate. She yearned to hold Ismene, to pull her close and feel more of her skin under her fingers.

'And you are special to me, also,' she managed to whisper, her mouth dry and her throat tight. 'More special than I think you realise.'

'You'll think me mad,' Ismene murmured, lips parted slightly, her breathing rapid and her golden eyes sparkling in the undulating lamplight, 'but I think I love you, Medusa.'

The words had barely reached Medusa's ears when she leaned in, barely conscious of her movements. Blissful heat radiated through her as their lips met, energy thrumming deep down inside with the gentle caress of their kiss.

For a brief, terrifying moment, Medusa worried she had made a mistake, but then Ismene's hands were clasped tightly around her waist, drawing her closer still.

'Don't stop,' Ismene whispered, her lips parting just enough for Medusa's tongue to tentatively explore, which she eagerly reciprocated.

Medusa's fingers reached into Ismene's hair, and she revelled in the softness of her curls, the heat of her mouth, and the firmness of her hands. A feeling stirred between Medusa's thighs that she had never experienced before: an intense longing, a throbbing urge that only Ismene's touch could quench.

Reluctantly – almost painfully – Medusa withdrew, letting her hands fall to rest on her thighs. Her lips burned with desire.

Ismene's eyes flickered open, a lust blazing in them that almost drove Medusa to move forward and take her in her arms once again. A smile spread across Ismene's tender lips, and she took Medusa's hands in hers. Gentle thumbs stroked the back of each hand, sending fresh shivers rippling through Medusa's body.

A rush of joy swept over Medusa, and she pulled Ismene close, where she rested her head against the priestess' chest.

'You know,' Medusa said quietly, stroking a soft hand over Ismene's hair. 'I think I love you too.'

Medusa felt as if she was walking amongst the clouds as she made her way to her bed that night.

She and Ismene had spent a long while in the storeroom together, wrapped in each other's arms and revelling in their newfound intimacy. It had been difficult to untangle themselves and return to the temple proper, veiling themselves in the guise of friendly acquaintances, pretending that nothing had changed despite their entire worlds being turned upside down.

Ismene said she loved her, and Medusa had said it back.

It was almost unbelievable, but it was real. It was real, and terrifying, and thrilling, and wonderful, all at once.

She had never loved before – not in the true sense of the word. Her mother and father she respected and honoured as was required, and her brother she felt like she barely knew, so often were they kept separated growing up. None of that was real love. It was nothing like the euphoric energy swirling in Medusa's gut whenever she thought of Ismene.

Medusa could not suppress the smile creeping across her face as she climbed into bed and under the thin woollen blanket. As her head rested on the straw-filled pillow, Medusa was quickly swept into sweet dreams of Ismene.

They were alone, and not in a cold, dusty storeroom, but on a beach, strolling hand in hand in the glow of a beautiful sunset as they stepped through the flawless white sand.

A soft breeze blew Medusa's hair back, and she closed her eyes. The gentle lapping of the waves, the tang of salt in the air, the feeling of Ismene's fingers entwined with hers... It was perfect.

Then it went dark.

The world fell away around her. The sand dropped from beneath Medusa's feet, and Ismene's fingers were torn from her grasp. There was no beach, no sunset, no breeze, just Medusa in the abyss, blind in the impenetrable darkness.

Her senses overwhelmed by the total nothingness, Medusa brought her hands to her body to ground herself, and found – to her horror –

that her clothes were no longer there. Even in the void of blackness, she felt exposed, as if she was stood alone on a pedestal on public display.

All of a sudden the seemingly unending darkness was broken as pinpricks of light blossomed all around Medusa. Small oval sapphires, strangely arrayed in pairs at an indeterminable distance, seemed focused entirely on her. A stone cold dread crawled over her as Medusa realised they were not lights at all – they were eyes.

Hundreds of them.

She turned away, frantically attempting to cover herself with her arms, but there were more eyes behind her. Unblinking. Staring. Watching.

Medusa started at what felt like a warm breath on the back of her neck. She spun around again, but there was nothing there but those menacing blue eyes, still gazing down at her from the void. She flinched as something touched her arm, creeping down her flesh like the caress of invisible fingers. Medusa swatted at her skin, heart pounding as she desperately tried to free herself of the unwelcome sensation.

But it did not stop. More unseen hands fell upon her, roaming her body as Medusa swiped at each touch, panic rising through her, heart hammering in her chest.

'Who are you?' she screamed into the emptiness, but no answer came. Just more hands running over her legs, her torso, her back, swarming her like locusts ravaging a field of wheat. 'Stop this!'

Hot tears burned down Medusa's cheeks as invisible fingers curled around the back of her neck, digging into her flesh. The eyes grew larger, blazing down as if hungry and ready to devour her. Medusa's chest grew tight. An otherworldly whisper breathed into her ear, and terror truly set in.

'Mine.'

She woke gasping, thrashing against the sweat-soaked blanket which had wrapped itself around her limbs. Sitting upright, Medusa stared into the gloom, her breathing rapid and her pulse throbbing in her ears. The sleeping quarters were empty, save for the other servants of Athena sleeping soundly in the other beds, their gentle snores the only sound.

Unease remained, weighing heavily on Medusa's shoulders. Each time she blinked she saw the many eyes staring at her naked form, and her skin crawled. She threw off the sodden blanket and took a deep breath, willing the cool night air to bring her calm. After several long moments, some semblance of normalcy settled over her, and she dared risk sleep again.

As she lay down her head, an uncomfortable itch blossomed between her shoulder blades. For hours she remained awake, eyes wide open, as she could not shake a horrible feeling that she was being watched.

Nothing that Thaddeus threw at her could dislodge Ismene's smile from her face.

He would never admit it, but Medusa's dismissal of his condescension had stung, and rather than direct his ire towards the respected priestess in a public place, it came at Ismene. Thankfully, there was no further physical violence, but his sour mood once he collected her from the temple that afternoon meant a barrage of insults and gruelling work cleaning his studio late into the evening. The fact that Ismene took it all without complaint outraged him further, and when they returned home he stormed off to bed without another word.

It was almost impossible to sleep that night. Every time she began to doze, Ismene's mind wandered back to the kiss she and Medusa had shared just hours prior, and her heart raced all over again. It was nothing like anything she had ever experienced before. Thrilling yet tender, passionate yet delicate, and it sent heat flaring through Ismene's body. The memory of Medusa's lips against hers, the gentle caress of her hair, the hot, overwhelming urge blooming between her thighs... It was almost too much. Ismene rose from her bed and padded barefoot to the water jar, taking care not to make a sound. Her father's temper was a fragile and unpredictable thing at the best of times, and tonight he would no doubt be on the verge of another explosion.

Ismene reached into the cool water and splashed it over her face and neck. She took a deep breath, trying to calm herself. She would see Medusa tomorrow, and perhaps they could even get some time alone together again.

No. She couldn't think of that.

She needed to calm down, to get some sleep. Deep under her excitement and longing, Ismene was still battered and bruised from her father's beating, and she would be no use to anyone if she didn't rest. Sprinkling water over herself one more time, Ismene returned to her bed and closed her eyes. She recited sacrificial prayers to Athena over and over in her head until sleep finally came.

As she and Thaddeus made their way to the temple the following morning, Ismene made sure to play the obedient daughter. She covered her face as per his wishes, head bowed and silent, though the joy of Medusa's kiss never fully dissipated. Anticipation fluttered in Ismene's chest with each step closer to being reunited with the priestess, though she kept her expression carefully neutral, in case her father chose to look at her.

Thaddeus walked in silence, an aura of cold anger surrounding him, his face twisted into a scowl. It was unusual for his rage to linger for this long, but Ismene had to ignore it. She couldn't afford to lose his blessing, not when her relationship with Medusa was blossoming into something amazing.

Finally, the temple came into view, and Ismene had to fight the urge to race past her father and into her love's waiting arms.

Except, this morning, Medusa wasn't waiting for her.

As Ismene left her father seething outside and passed into the shelter of the temple walls, she couldn't avoid the disappointment that washed over her. Medusa was always there, every morning, to greet Ismene with that bright smile and those sparkling chestnut eyes. Acolytes milled back and forth as usual, preparing for the day's rituals, but there was no sign of the priestess.

Ismene stepped tentatively through the temple. She wasn't used to walking these floors alone, without Medusa close by her side, and she felt strangely vulnerable, like the priestess had shielded her from the whispers and stares of the other worshippers of the goddess. She tugged her headscarf further over her face and kept her eyes down, scurrying out into the quiet sanctuary of the courtyard.

Then she saw her.

Medusa – usually tall, proud and striking – sat on the edge of the pool, curled in on herself and staring down into the still surface of the water. Ismene approached slowly, but the priestess didn't look up. It was as if she was in a trance, deaf and blind to the world around her, the only movement the stroking of her thumb against something she held hidden in one hand.

'Medusa?' Ismene asked softly, but the other woman didn't stir, too absorbed in her own thoughts to hear a thing. Ismene laid a tentative hand on her shoulder, startling the priestess.

Medusa gasped and jumped up, eyes widening in horror as the item she had been holding slipped from her grasp and plunged into the pool in front of her.

'Oh…' She stared into the water, arm partly outstretched as if she couldn't make up her mind whether to go in after the object or not.

'Here,' Ismene said, pulling off her sandals and handing them to the priestess. She hiked her chiton over her knees and stepped over the low wall, chuckling at the shocked intake of breath behind her as her feet plunged into the water.

'Ismene!' Medusa cried, 'what are you doing?'

'There are worse things in life, dear priestess,' Ismene responded, bending to retrieve the lost token from the crystal clear pool, 'than getting a little wet.'

Ismene's fingers closed around a small, metallic object, and she turned to step out of the pool, a triumphant grin across her face.

'See?' She smiled as Medusa reached for her hand to help her over. 'Not a problem at— Ah!'

Her foot slipped on the wet tile, and she tumbled forward, landing haphazardly in Medusa's arms. Not so long ago, such a public display of clumsiness would have mortified the potter's daughter, but here, in the safety of the temple courtyard, being held by the one person she trusted most, Ismene did nothing but laugh.

'You were saying?'

Ismene's heart fluttered at the amusement in Medusa's voice. When she righted herself and faced the priestess again, she was delighted to see a small smile replacing her previously sullen expression.

'I believe thanks are in order.' Ismene smiled back, unfurling her fingers from around her hard-won prize. 'I went to great pains to retrieve your... Oh.'

Recognition stirred within her as Ismene looked at the small coin in her hand.

*It couldn't be.*

Gentle fingers traced the image of a horse's head moulded into the small round obol. 'Is this...?'

'You'll think me foolish,' Medusa murmured, a rare blush creeping across her olive cheeks, 'but I couldn't bear to part with it. When I first picked it up, I kept it because you intrigued me, and I hoped I might see you again and return it to you. And then...' Medusa's gaze dropped, and an uncharacteristic shyness fell over her. 'Well... It soothes me. Whenever I look at it, or hold it, I think of you, and my heart feels lighter. You probably think me strange.'

Fondness stirred in Ismene's chest, and she placed the obol in Medusa's palm. 'I wouldn't have thought it was possible,' Ismene said softly, cupping her hands over Medusa's. 'But I think you're even more wonderful than I imagined.'

'You flatterer.' Medusa smiled, her large brown eyes glittering in the shimmering light reflecting off the pool's surface.

*Gods, she is beautiful.*

'Here.' Medusa lifted Ismene's hand away and offered her own to the other woman. 'You should have it. I have already kept it much longer than I had any right to.'

Ismene smiled, but did not take the coin. Instead, she curled Medusa's fingers over it, gently pressing it into her palm. 'You keep it. Consider it a gift.'

The priestess placed her other hand on the small of Ismene's back and pulled her close, lowering her head so that their foreheads just kissed. When she spoke, her words were barely more than a whisper. 'You have already given me the greatest gift I could ever have wished for, my love.'

Joy as sweet as honey flooded Ismene. Her heart raced and her skin burned with desire for the woman before her. A great need overwhelmed her senses, the urge to touch her, to feel Medusa's body against her own, to taste every inch of her perfect body.

'Come,' she murmured, taking Medusa by the wrist and leading her back towards the temple building. 'I think we need to get something from the storeroom.'

Medusa took a deep breath, and Ismene couldn't help but smile as her head was lifted with the rise of her chest.

They should get up and get back to their duties – they both knew that – but lying there together, arms and legs entwined, half-undressed and coated in a fine sheen of sweat, neither could bring themselves to move.

It was all a blur now, but the ecstasy that had washed over Ismene as the two women came together and became one lingered still. Medusa had been incredible. She was tender and gentle, and beheld Ismene as if she was something precious and wondrous, not some defective specimen to be pitied or hidden away.

Neither of them had experience in amorous acts – women were expected to remain untouched by any man until they were married, and Ismene's accident had rendered any search for a potential suitor futile in the eyes of her parents – but that hadn't mattered. Their hands had explored each other's bodies as if they knew them as well as their own, lips brushing against skin as natural as breathing.

'Mmm,' Medusa hummed, running a hand over Ismene's curls. 'They will be wondering where we are.'

'Probably,' Ismene murmured, burying her head deeper into the soft folds of Medusa's chiton. Iris, rose and mint filled her nostrils as she breathed in her scent: light yet rich, refreshing and comforting in equal measure. 'I wish we could stay here forever.'

'I would lie with you for eternity if I could.' Medusa sighed and gently eased Ismene off her chest, planting a tender kiss on her forehead. The priestess rose to her feet, leaving Ismene sitting on the storeroom floor, chiton pooled around her legs, breasts and shoulders bare, the cool air sending goosebumps rippling over her naked flesh. 'Only...'

Medusa shook her head and turned away. Ismene watched in silence as the priestess redid her own chiton, covering her legs and torso and tying a ribbon around her waist. Unease tickled the back of Ismene's mind as Medusa's movements became slow and pensive, as if the morning's despondency was falling over her again.

'Only what?' Ismene asked, pulling her chiton up over her chest and shoulders, suddenly feeling cold and vulnerable. 'Please don't tell me you've tired of me already!'

'What?' Medusa spun around, eyes wide. 'Never!'

A breath she hadn't realised she had been holding tumbled out of Ismene, and she rose to join her lover, grasping her hands. 'Then what? What could possibly worry the strongest and bravest woman I know so much? The woman who can stare down my raging father without so much as flinching?'

A smile pulled at Medusa's lips and she pulled Ismene closer, wrapping her arms around her waist. 'Flattery again? Remember whose house we're in, young apprentice.'

A flutter of butterflies passed through Ismene's stomach. Would she ever not be affected by being in such close proximity to this beautiful woman?

'I'm sorry, I'm out of sorts,' Medusa continued, gentle fingers tracing up and down Ismene's back, sending a shiver down her spine. 'This temple has always felt safe, a place I could never be harmed, not amongst my fellow sisters of the goddess and under Her watchful eyes, but last night...'

'What? What happened?'

'You will think me mad.' Medusa dropped her arms and stepped back, hugging her elbows. 'It was... It was a dream.'

'A dream?' Ismene frowned. She was no stranger to nightmares – and had been especially plagued by them in the years following her accident – but she would never have expected someone like Medusa to be so rattled by one.

'Not just a regular dream, it was... different.' Medusa began to pace back and forth, wringing her hands. 'And it isn't only that, it's the climax of a few instances. I shrugged them off at first, but after last night, after what I felt... I just can't.'

'Medusa, please.'

The priestess stopped her pacing and looked at Ismene, eyes shining in the torchlight. 'Ismene, I think I'm being watched.'

Dread pooled in the pit of Ismene's stomach. 'What do you mean?'

'It happened two or three times. A man, like none I've ever seen, watching me. In the agora, outside the temple, and... last night.'

Ismene's pulse quickened. 'He was here?'

'No! Yes... maybe.' Medusa sat on a crate and buried her head in her hands. 'I don't expect you to believe me – I'm not sure I believe it myself – but in the dream, he was watching me again, and when I awoke I could still feel that horrible stare, making my skin crawl. I couldn't shake it until morning. I couldn't see anyone, but it was dark. He could have easily been hiding amongst the shadows.' She raised her head, tears slowly creeping down her round cheeks. 'I know it sounds ludicrous, being terrified of a phantom man no one else has seen, but he is real, Ismene. I swear he's real, and he's dangerous.'

Ismene sat beside Medusa and placed a gentle arm around her shoulder. 'I believe you. Of course I believe you.'

Medusa dropped her head onto Ismene's shoulder, throwing her arms around her. Ismene couldn't be sure, but she thought she heard a quiet sob.

'No, no – not that one! Here, try this.'

'I have done this before, you know!'

Medusa ducked as an orchid flew in her direction, and stifled a laugh. It had been Ismene's idea for them to spend the day working on the flower arrangements around the temple – one of Medusa's favourite duties besides teaching – and it was proving to be an excellent distraction.

'I think these are my favourite.' Ismene beamed as she fanned out a vase of orange lilies, their strong, sweet scent heavy in the air.

'I think I prefer the pink ones,' Medusa mused, reaching over Ismene's shoulder and dropping small bunches of vivid asters and delicate oleander flowers in between the stems of Ismene's lilies. The result was a vibrant floral display evocative of the early autumnal season blossoming outside. 'See how well they go together?'

Ismene studied the arrangement. 'You're right. How did you know to put them together?'

'I had lessons growing up.'

Ismene turned, confusion creasing her brow. 'Really?'

'Yes.' Medusa cleared her throat and glanced away. 'As part of my preparations for marriage.'

'Oh.'

Silence settled between them, and Medusa's heart sank. The pair never discussed the future, and the expectations of them within Ionian society. They had been enjoying each other in the moment, but perhaps that had been naive. Time kept moving forwards, towards a future they could not share with each other.

'I never had any lessons like that.'

Medusa looked up at Ismene, surprised to hear a tinge of sadness in the other woman's voice. 'Do you wish you had?' she asked, incredulous.

Ismene shrugged. 'No... Yes...' She sank onto a marble bench beside the plinth the vase stood upon. 'I don't envy you for what your family has planned for you. I hate that you're expected to marry a man of your father's choosing, whether you like him or not. But...' She lowered her head. 'As ridiculous as it sounds – as ridiculous as it *is* – I never even got that. You're this perfect prize men are going to be falling over themselves to win, and I've already been thrown aside as useless.'

Medusa sat down beside Ismene and took her hand. 'I'm sorry. I sometimes get so wrapped up in my own frustration I forget the privileges I've had. But...' Medusa placed a gentle hand on Ismene's cheek and turned her head to meet her gaze. 'Your worth goes far beyond whether you are a good marriage prospect. You're an amazing, beautiful woman, and I consider myself lucky to know you.'

Ismene's eyes dropped, but Medusa noticed her lips twitching into a smile and, despite her dark skin, a notable blush heated her cheeks. 'You always know what to say.'

'I just tell you the truth.'

Evadne walked past the pair carrying the latest votive offerings brought to the temple – with great care, as if she was afraid she would break them like the amphora she'd damaged – and Medusa withdrew from Ismene, folding her hands on her lap. It was no secret that the priestess was close with her trainee, but rumours of a romance between the two women could cause a scandal. While relationships between unmarried women were not entirely unheard of, they were rare, and certainly never witnessed in public. The Priestess of Athena having any sort of pre-marital affair would be considered sordid at best, but to be found cavorting with another woman would cause a sensation Medusa was very keen to avoid.

Medusa and Ismene watched in silence as Evadne disappeared into the naos, suddenly very aware that they were not in a private place.

'I wish *we* could marry.'

Ismene's whispered words hung in the air, and the resulting silence said everything. They both knew their time together at the temple was finite. Medusa's tenure as priestess would end, and she would be married off to some wealthy, influential man, and Ismene could have her training privileges revoked by her father at any time. Their time together was precious, but precarious, and limited.

But did it have to be that way?

Medusa looked at Ismene, still gazing off into the distance. Faint bruises lurked underneath her dark complexion, yet they did not diminish her beauty. When the two women were together, the horrors inflicted on Ismene by her brutish father were forgotten, but that blissful ignorance could not last forever. What would happen to her when Medusa went home to Lade and Ismene returned to her old life, at the mercy of Thaddeus' brutality each and every day, and with no one to protect her? The thought made Medusa's blood run cold.

And what of her own fate? Medusa had never relished her future as a nobleman's wife, but she had accepted that it was what was most likely to come to pass eventually. That was before Ismene, though, before Medusa felt such love in her heart and fire in her veins that she had never dreamed was possible. No husband could elicit such desire in her belly, or such profound longing every moment they were apart. If she was lucky, he would be kind and patient, and if she was unlucky... Images of Thaddeus flashed in her mind, and a cold shiver ran down Medusa's spine.

Could she really let Ismene go, try to live her life as planned and spend eternity yearning for something – and someone – utterly irre-placeable?

'No.'

'No, what?' Ismene turned to face Medusa, confusion creasing her brow.

'We can't keep doing this,' Medusa replied, her words firm, and her resolve even firmer, as the beginning of a plan formed in her mind. This was the right decision, she was sure of it. 'We can't keep pretending the future doesn't matter.'

Ismene's eyes widened, and her face dropped. 'You want to... end things?'

'Of course not!' Medusa smiled warmly at Ismene; she seemed to expect rejection at every turn, but Medusa would never send her away. She would die first. Taking Ismene's hands in hers once more, Medusa continued, 'I don't want to have the greatest love affair of my life, only for us to go our separate ways and live apart, desolate and despairing, and dreaming about years past.' She squeezed Ismene's hands tight, tears pricking the back of her eyes. 'I want to be with you, Ismene. Forever.'

Ismene stared at Medusa, mouth agape.

'But... how? Your parents would never allow it, and my father... Well, you know how he is. I can't imagine the rage it would provoke.'

'I don't plan to ask for anyone's permission.'

Ismene blinked, utterly dumbfounded. 'If you have a plan, Medusa, you have to explain it to me, because you're not making any sense.'

Medusa leaned forward, excitement shining in her deep brown eyes. Ismene had never seen her like this before.

'We're going to leave,' she whispered, 'permanently.'

'Leave?' Ismene realised she had shouted, and quickly glanced around to ensure no one had overheard. When she was certain they were alone, she continued, lowering her voice. 'Are you serious?'

'I am deadly serious.' Medusa closed her eyes and took a deep breath. When she opened them again, there was more than simple excitement in her gaze. There was a great need, a fire burning under the calm exterior. 'I love the time we spend together, Ismene. It brings me a joy I never could have never imagined. But...'

'But?'

'Our love exists in a bubble. The moment you leave at the end of the day, reality floods back in, and it's like all the colour drains from the world. Each night I pray I'll see you the next day, and every morning I thank the goddess when I see you come through the gates. But what if, one day, your father decides to rescind his permission for you to be here? My position grants me more power than other women in the city, but it's a fraction of the power held by any man. If Thaddeus decided we could no longer see each other, I could do nothing to change that, and it would kill me.'

Ismene nodded. She understood Medusa's fear, and she realised now that she had only escaped it herself through sheer denial. She had spent so long under her father's stern hand that every moment away from him had been a blessing, and Ismene had chosen to revel in those moments rather considering they might one day be snatched away from her. And they would – of course they would. Thaddeus was a selfish tyrant, and if he found another way to bring some modicum of status to the family he would divert his efforts there, and Ismene's training would be forgotten in an instant.

'I understand,' she finally said, her stomach already fluttering with nervous excitement. 'And I'd truly love nothing more than to spend my life with you, Medusa, please believe that. But how could we possibly leave? It took months for me to be able to scrape together a few obols for the market. I don't have the means to secure even a short passage to the nearest island.'

'I think I have a solution.' Uncertainty flickered across Medusa's features, and Ismene's stomach clenched. The priestess was usually so sure of her actions; it was unsettling to see her doubting herself.

'As priestess,' she continued, 'I am granted very occasional visitations during my tenure, including one to my former home to see my family.'

*Family? How will a visit to Medusa's parents help us?*

As if sensing Ismene's confusion, Medusa hurried on with her explanation. 'I can take you with me. I will tell my family you're my apprentice.' Her self-assurance was returning as her plan seemed to solidify. 'We make for Lade, and under the guise of a visit to my parents, I collect clothes, jewellery, coins – as many items of value as we can reasonably carry – and then we slip away into the night and head for somewhere new. Perhaps Rhodes, Krete, or even Kythira! I'm certain, given our training, we could find refuge in one of Aphrodite's sanctuaries there. Who better to shelter two runaway lovers than the embodiment of love herself?' The priestess was grinning ear to ear now, evidently very pleased with the conclusion she had brought herself to. 'What do you think?'

Ismene opened her mouth, but no words came. Medusa was a highly intelligent woman, educated to a level far beyond most Ionian women, but it was a lot of information for Ismene to process. She wasn't worldly – she had never even left the city – and the thought of travelling to one of these far-off places was terrifying and exhilarating in equal measure.

Could they really do it? Leave their lives and families behind and start afresh, together? It sounded almost too good to be true.

It wasn't like Ismene hadn't taken chances before. The day she'd first laid eyes on the beautiful priestess she would fall in love with, she had been sneaking out of the house to visit the agora, and had later even broken into the temple just to be close to her again. But this... this was so *big*.

'Ismene?'

She blinked, coming to her senses with a slight shake of her head. Medusa was waiting for an answer.

'Yes,' Ismene finally responded, adrenaline rushing through her body as the next words tumbled out of her mouth, 'let's do it. Let's leave, together.'

A smile flickered across Medusa's face as the hot wax pooled on the surface of the papyrus. This was it. Her final missive before she shed her duties and moved on to a thrilling and completely unexpected new period of her life.

As excited as she was to start her adventure with Ismene – especially after spending the previous week planning and preparing for their trip – Medusa wanted to do right by the temple she had devoted her life to these past months, and both her fellow temple servants and the great goddess they had served together. They had grown used to her quiet leadership, and she didn't want them to be bereft when she didn't return from their visit to Lade.

Medusa picked up a small clay seal and pushed it into the cooling wax, and her smile widened with satisfaction as she pulled it away to reveal the perfect indentation of an owl grasping a snake in its talons; the symbol of the priestess of Athena. She brushed the image with gentle fingers, and an odd sadness struck her. The role of priestess wasn't something she had ever asked for, but she had felt more welcome at the temple than she ever had back in the family home. With her parents, she wasn't a person, not really. She was a pawn, one they must use strategically for the sake of furthering the family's status, and when she was not fulfilling that role, she was swept aside and forgotten about until she could be useful again.

Medusa took a deep breath, blinking away the tears threatening to spill from her eyes. This would not be an unhappy day. Tomorrow, she would set her plan into motion, and leave this place with the love of her life. That was something to be celebrated. She drove any lingering negative thoughts out of her mind and dipped a sharpened reed into a jar of ink, using it to scrawl a short note on the front of the folded letter.

'What does it say?'

Ismene's soft breath on the back of Medusa's neck sent a small thrill down her spine. How she wished she could take her into her arms and kiss her, and finally unleash the passion that had been building up inside since they first met...

Just one more day and they could be together properly. Just the thought of being completely alone with Ismene – where they could freely express their love for each other and not hold back – sent Medusa's pulse racing.

'Well?' Ismene gently poked Medusa in the ribs, jolting the priestess out of her thoughts. 'Can you tell me what it says?'

'Oh, of course.' Medusa stepped aside so Ismene could see the papyrus, neatly folded and sealed, with her final note written on the front. She traced a finger under the words as she voiced them aloud, so Ismene could follow along. 'To be opened should the priestess be lost for any reason.'

A small laugh fell from Ismene's lips as she leaned in closer to observe the angular characters. 'Incredible.'

Fondness warmed Medusa's chest. Literacy was an expectation back at home – for all members of the family – and so Medusa had always taken knowing her letters for granted. Moving to the city and meeting Ismene and others within the temple had shown her differently. Literacy was expected for most *men* in Greece, but was rare for women. Another privilege she had been blind to growing up.

'Would you like me to teach you properly?'

Ismene turned to Medusa, her eyes wide. 'Do you think you could?'

Medusa smiled. 'Of course! How about this – I'll pick up my writing materials while we're at Lade, and once we get settled in our final destination, I'll teach you how to read *and* write.'

'Really?' Ismene's amber eyes glittered with excitement. 'Do you promise?'

The priestess took Ismene's hand and raised it to her lips, planting a soft kiss on the back. 'I promise.'

Medusa almost fell out of her chair as Ismene threw her arms around her and squeezed her tight.

'You really are a dream come true, Medusa.'

Breathing in Ismene's light and earthy scent, Medusa wished she could spend all day in her arms, but it wasn't time for that, not yet.

'And you,' she said, gently pushing Ismene away, 'forget we are not alone quite yet.'

Ismene opened her arms wide, gesturing around the small administration office, an impish grin on her face. 'No one else is here, *Priestess*.'

Heat flooded Medusa's cheeks at Ismene's teasing tone, but she tried to ignore it. 'No,' she replied, unable to stop the small smile forming on her own lips, 'but you know as well as I do that acolytes pass in and out of this room freely, and we don't want to sabotage our escape when we're so close.'

As if summoned by Medusa's words, a small voice called out from just beyond the open doorway, startling both women. 'Priestess?'

Medusa's heart settled as she recognised the gentle tone of Kephissa, her senior acolyte, and if she was honest, one of Medusa's favourite attendants.

'Come!' she called, giving a warning glance to Ismene to behave herself. Medusa trusted Kephissa – they had worked side by side since Medusa first arrived at the temple – but she and Ismene were too close to pulling off their escape to do anything that might put their journey at risk.

Kephissa – always polite to a fault – peered around the doorway, and on seeing Medusa's welcoming smile, walked into the small office. Like Ismene, she was a smaller woman than Medusa, with a petite frame, a narrow but delicate face, and a warm, almost copper-coloured complexion. Quiet and unassuming, but dedicated to her duties and eager to help anyone who struggled to master the rites and rituals required of them, she had become the closest thing Medusa had to a friend within the walls of the temple.

'Good morning, Priestess,' Kephissa remarked cheerfully. Her gaze found Ismene, but where others might have wondered why a junior apprentice was standing besides the priestess while she carried out her administrative duties, Kephissa beamed a genuine smile. 'And Ismene, good to see you, as always.'

'And you, Kephissa.' Ismene returned the smile, a twinkle of mischief glittering in her amber eyes. 'I hope you haven't forgotten that you promised to help me with my honey libation this afternoon.'

'How could I?' Kephissa scoffed, with an exaggerated roll of her eyes. 'The last time you handled honey without assistance the altar was sticky for a week! Evadne helped me clean it after you went home, and she cursed your name for days.'

The two women giggled, and a pang of sorrow struck her heart. While Medusa was beyond delighted to be beginning a new life with Ismene, she was fond of Kephissa, and seeing Ismene form a kinship with her when she had spent so much of her life hidden away and alone had been a joy. They would both miss the senior acolyte dearly.

As if remembering she was in the priestess' company, Kephissa cleared her throat and her tone grew more formal. 'Here, Priestess.' She handed Medusa a bundle of papers, neatly tied with a thin leather cord. 'Given your journey tomorrow, I thought you might want to read them now and prepare some responses to be delivered while you are away. I'd be happy to see that it's done in your place.'

'Of course – thank you.' Medusa retrieved the papers from Kephissa's hand and laid them on the desk. She would see to them this evening, once Ismene had departed for home for the final time. It would keep her mind busy while waiting for the morning to come. 'I will ensure they are left on my desk before I depart for Lade, and I trust you will keep everything in order. I know I am leaving the temple in good hands with you.'

Kephissa offered a shy smile – despite being the most proficient acolyte in the temple, she still struggled to take compliments. 'Thank you, Priestess. That means a lot coming from you. I'll leave you to your duties. Ismene,' she continued, raising one playful eyebrow, 'come and find me when you're ready to try the honey again.'

Ismene chuckled at that and waved Kephissa off as she turned and left the office, leaving the two women alone once more.

'See,' Medusa faced Ismene with a knowing look. 'I told you we are never truly alone here.'

'Kephissa doesn't count.' Ismene shrugged. 'She always calls before coming in, and in any case, we can trust her, I'm sure of that.'

'Even so,' Medusa glanced behind her, towards the still open doorway, an uncomfortable itch forming between her shoulder blades. 'I still get that feeling I'm being watched here.'

Concern flitted across Ismene's features, and Medusa immediately regretted mentioning the comment. She didn't want to worry Ismene unnecessarily with a paranoia that would soon no longer be an issue.

'Let's focus on getting through this next day.' she said hurriedly, with what she hoped was a reassuring smile. 'Is everything in place for getting past your father?'

Ismene nodded, but there was uncertainty in her eyes. 'I've been gathering what few supplies I need, and I should be able to conceal them in my chiton.' She hesitated, and Medusa's chest tightened.

'What's wrong? Has Thaddeus done something?'

'No,' Ismene said slowly, and Medusa felt the breath she was holding escaping her lungs. 'Quite the opposite.'

'What do you mean?'

Ismene took a deep breath and ran a hand through her loose curls. 'He's been... distant. Cold, even. He has never been kind or loving to me, but I'm usually being shouted at for something, or told I'm being too slow, or too careless, or... *something.*' She let out an exasperated sigh. 'I don't miss his rage, but being ignored completely somehow feels worse. It's... unsettling.'

Medusa frowned. Granted, she didn't know Thaddeus anywhere near as well as Ismene, but even she was unnerved by this shift in mood. Sudden and unexpected tranquillity often foretold something terrible, like the calm before a storm.

'That is strange.' Medusa spoke carefully. She wanted to acknowledge Ismene's unease, but everything had been arranged, and their escape plan hinged on Ismene successfully leaving without drawing Thaddeus' suspicion. Sending her into a panic could ruin it all. 'Are you sure his behaviour is related to you? Could it be due to your mother?'

Ismene's teeth worried her bottom lip. 'I suppose it could.'

Medusa stood face to face with Ismene and placed a firm but gentle hand on the other woman's shoulders. 'Ismene, we don't have to do anything you're uncomfortable with. If you have doubts, we can postpone our journey until you're ready.' She leaned in, looking deep into Ismene's eyes. 'I love you, with all my heart, and I will wait as long as I need to so that I can be with you. I swear it.'

Mischief glittered in Ismene's eyes. 'You're making lots of promises today, Priestess.'

Medusa brushed the backs of her fingers down Ismene's cheek, her stomach flipping as the other woman leaned into her touch. 'And I plan to keep each one.'

'I believe you.' Ismene took Medusa's hand in her own and squeezed it tight. 'And I trust you. I trust *us*.'

Medusa's pulse quickened. 'So, you'll come?'

'Yes.' Ismene smiled, and Medusa's heart swelled. 'This time tomorrow, we will be on a ship and free from this city forever.'

Nervous excitement threatened to burst out of Ismene as she bade goodbye to Medusa. Their eyes locked as she turned to leave, a knowing intensity shared between them for just a moment.

One more night. That's all they had to get through before they could be together.

'Come,' her father commanded, as if she was a dog.

*One night, old man. One night and you will never speak down to me again.*

Ismene shot Medusa one more longing gaze before scurrying after Thaddeus. She would be the perfect daughter until the morning.

They strode through the city in silence, an uneasy tension growing with each step. Thaddeus walked straight-backed, hands balled into fists by his side and his jaw clenched so tight Ismene could see the surrounding muscles twitching. Unease curdled in her stomach. Her father was angry more often than not, but this was different. A cold rage radiated from the man, lurking just beneath the surface, and Ismene just hoped it wouldn't be unleashed in her direction.

As their home came into view, relief flooded Ismene's body. Once inside, she would head straight to the gynaeceum, and hide from her father until morning.

When they reached the door, Ismene resisted the urge to run. She kept her head down and walked inside, but a rough hand grasped her shoulder and wrenched her to one side. She spun around and came face to face with Thaddeus, his eyes burning with unbridled rage.

'Did you think I wouldn't find out?' He spat, every word laced with venom.

Ismene's blood ran cold. Dread crept up her spine as her mouth worked but no words would come.

Thaddeus tightened his grip on Ismene, his strong fingers digging painfully into her skin. 'Answer me, damn you!'

Ismene felt sick. She swallowed, her throat so tight it was almost painful. 'Find out w-what?' she murmured, finally finding the words.

Bringing his face even closer to hers, Thaddeus spoke through gritted teeth. 'About the two of you. You and that *whore* priestess.'

'I-I don't—'

A burst of pain shot through Ismene's face as the back of her father's hand landed hard, knocking her back several paces. 'Don't lie to me!' he bellowed, his face red. He approached Ismene again, and she shrivelled under his red hot gaze, her jaw throbbing. 'You think you're safe in that temple of yours, don't you? That no one is watching?' The laugh that fell from his lips was pure hatred. 'I'm always watching, girl, whether through my own eyes or others'. I know you've been cavorting with that viper, letting her lure you away from respectable society so she can have her way with you. You are too repulsive for any decent man to want you, so you let yourself be sullied by a *woman*.'

'She didn't—'

'SHUT UP!'

Thaddeus stared down at Ismene, his eyes bulging and his breathing heavy. He had always been a frightening man, but Ismene had never been as terrified of her father as she was in that moment. His arm shot out again, but instead of striking Ismene, his hand found her throat. He pulled her closer, his fingers clamped around Ismene's neck.

She could breathe, but only just. If he squeezed any tighter, he would kill her.

'It ends now,' he snarled. 'You will shame me no further. You are no longer permitted to leave this house.'

Thaddeus pushed his fingers harder into Ismene's throat. For a horrific moment her airway closed completely before he threw her away from him and she tumbled to the ground, gulping for air. Thaddeus loomed over her, his face twisted with disgust.

'If you defy me,' he said, his voice low and hard as iron, 'I will slit her throat, and then yours.'

He turned and walked away, leaving Ismene crumpled and trembling.

any moment, and once the coast was clear, the pair of them would be away.

The priestess paced the temple in an attempt to burn off her excess nervous energy. Everything was ready: the acolytes had been briefed that their priestess was attending her family home for a brief visit, a leather satchel was packed and by the temple entrance containing the essential items required for their journey across the Ionian Sea to Lade, their voyage was arranged and paid for, and – most important of all – her gift for Ismene was safely stored in the folds of Medusa's himation.

It was something Medusa had been preparing in secret since they started planning their escape. She halted her pacing by the temple entrance and reached into her himation, smiling as her fingers found cold metal. It had been difficult to keep the surprise from Ismene, but it would be worth it when Medusa finally gave it to her. She pulled out the small coin from their first meeting – buffed so the horse-head imprint gleamed and threaded with a fine gold chain. A lasting reminder of the encounter that changed both their lives forever.

Medusa smiled and hid the necklace back in her himation – close to her heart, where Ismene always would be. Her smile faded a little when she looked out at the sun creeping higher into the sky.

Ismene was late.

She took a deep breath and willed her nerves away. Thaddeus was as capricious as he was obnoxious, and his mood often dictated his daughter's arrival time. No doubt he was being difficult and stalling their departure. Even so, unease threaded its way through Medusa's insides. She eyed the satchel resting against a marble column, and a cold knot of anxiety formed in her chest.

She wanted to believe everything was as it should be. That Thaddeus was being his stubborn self and unnecessarily delaying Ismene just to reassert his dominance, to remind the priestess that he was the one in charge. She wanted to believe it, but what were the chances he would choose the day of their departure to pull such a stunt? It seemed too great a coincidence to Medusa. Ismene could be in danger, and no amount of rationalising would steady her nerves.

She needed to pray.

Medusa swept through the temple, hands clasped and jaw clenched tight. As if sensing her fraught disposition, each acolyte in her path scurried away without a word, avoiding the priestess' gaze. Finally, she reached the naos. She sighed in relief as she stepped inside the small space, the presence of the goddess already soothing her frayed nerves.

A small oil lamp cast an orange glow about the room, illuminating the statue of Athena and giving her an ethereal quality. Shadows danced across the goddess' face, softening her stone features so she appeared to be with Medusa in the flesh. Medusa dipped a rush candle into the flame, lighting it. The fragrant oils in which it was soaked wafted about the naos, the scents of iris and rose filling Medusa's nostrils. The finest fragrances to honour and appeal to the lady of the temple.

Medusa knelt, head bowed. She took a deep breath, letting the goddess' presence fill her lungs.

'Lady Athena,' she said with as strong a voice as she could muster, her heart racing as she willed the goddess to hear. 'Please watch over and protect Ismene. Lend her your wisdom and strength, so that she may safely reach the sanctuary of your temple, and bless her with your continued protection as we embark on our voyage.'

'I hope you are not leaving quite yet, Priestess.'

Medusa stiffened. That voice – deep, masculine, and so powerful it sent a shiver down her spine – was not one she recognised.

'Turn, fair one, let me once again look upon your beautiful face.'

Medusa rose to her feet on unsteady legs. She turned, and her heart jumped into her throat as her eyes fell on... *him*.

Tall and broad-shouldered, with fair skin, long golden hair and beard, and those piercing eyes that Medusa could never forget. The man she had seen everywhere – in the agora, outside the temple, even in her dreams – stood in the naos entrance. He was staring at her, a terrible hunger in his eyes.

His gaze burned into Medusa, sweeping slowly over every inch of her body. 'There you are.' His voice, even when quiet, seemed to shake the very air around them. 'I have had my eye on you for some time, Priestess. Quite the chatter arose when a beautiful new priestess arrived in the city, and naturally I had to see her for myself.' His sapphire eyes blazed with hunger as he stared down at Medusa. 'I have always found it such a waste,' he continued, stroking his bearded chin, 'that my niece – as chaste as she is dull – attracts such stimulating servants.'

'Niece?' Medusa stared at the formidable man before her, taking in his features anew. Her eyes grew wide as realisation struck like a hammer.

Long, golden curls, sea-green robes, a powerful presence unlike no other...

This was no mortal man. This was Poseidon, the god of the sea himself.

'Ah, you recognise me, then?' Poseidon chuckled as Medusa could only gape in shock, and he moved towards her with a grace only the divine could possess. He was tall, looming over her. 'So, what say you, Priestess? How does it feel to lay your eyes on a true Olympian – Son of Kronos, Master of Horses and Lord of the Sea?'

Medusa's heart pounded in her chest. When she spoke, she could conjure little more than a whisper. 'I... I am astounded.'

That brought a wide grin to the sea god's lips, and he moved closer. 'Of course you are. It is quite an honour to lie with a god. I only select the finest specimens, and you are very fine, indeed.'

'Lie with—?' Medusa's blood turned to ice as she understood Poseidon's meaning. 'Oh... no, no.'

'Do not be modest, Priestess.' Poseidon drew so close Medusa caught the scent of seawater on his breath. He leaned into her, and placed a hand on Medusa's upper arm. She stepped aside, shrugging it off, and backed away towards the naos wall.

Poseidon's expression darkened, his eyes flashing. 'What are you doing?'

His powerful voice was cold and hard. Medusa swallowed, her throat suddenly very tight.

'N-nothing,' she managed, cringing at the squeak in her voice.

'Then come to me.' He reached out his hand, a dangerous smile twisting his lips.

'I... I cannot.' Medusa forced herself to stand up straight and meet the sea god's hard gaze. 'I am flattered and honoured by your interest, my lord, but my heart belongs to another.'

A dark chuckle rumbled in Poseidon's throat. 'Your heart is of no interest to me, Priestess.' He grabbed Medusa's shoulders and pushed her back against the wall. 'I am much more interested in your *flesh*.'

Poseidon leaned in close and Medusa tried to pull away, but there was nowhere to go. She pressed back against the wall, shrinking away from the forceful deity before her.

'Please,' she whimpered, struggling in his vice-like grip. 'Let me go.'

Poseidon wasn't listening. His hard body pressed against Medusa's, pinning her in place. Strong fingers dug into her skin almost to the point of pain as Poseidon leaned in and planted his lips on her neck, sending a shiver down her spine. His kisses were hot and hungry, as if he would devour the priestess then and there.

Medusa pushed back against the sea god, but the more she struggled, the tighter he held onto her. Each touch of his lips against her bare skin sent ripples of revulsion through her body, but she couldn't fight off someone with godly strength — it was impossible. She had to try something else.

Though it went against her every instinct, Medusa softened her body against Poseidon's. She leaned into him, and he responded immediately, bucking his hips against her as his lust heightened. Her stomach churned, but hope flickered in her chest as the sea god's grip loosened a little. His mouth traced along her collarbone and up her neck, and she clamped her eyes shut, praying for a chance – any chance – to get away.

Poseidon's lips found Medusa's own, crashing into her with a startling urgency. There was none of the tenderness of Ismene's touch. The sea god was taking what he wanted from Medusa with no thoughts of love or affection, fuelled by a primal passion she couldn't dampen. His hands shifted, and Medusa's chest tightened.

As his fingers moved from holding her by the shoulders to fondling her breasts, Medusa seized her opportunity. She twisted to the right, extracting herself from beneath Poseidon's hulking body, and made for the doorway. She moved as fast as she could, desperate to get away, but she wasn't fast enough.

Medusa lunged forward, but had barely taken one step before she was wrenched back by a powerful hand clamped around her wrist. The sea god pulled the priestess back and tossed her to the floor. He stood over her, his eyes incandescent with rage.

'This could have been easy, Priestess,' he growled, fixing Medusa in place with his burning gaze. 'But you have elected to be difficult. I will have you, whether you are willing or not.'

Before Medusa could protest, Poseidon was on her, tearing open her himation so everything she had stashed within its folds went scattering across the naos floor. His eyes shone with hunger as he took in her naked form, his vicious grin almost feral with lust.

Medusa pushed at his chest with all her strength, but a mortal woman such as her could not make much of an impact on an Olympian god. Poseidon grabbed her wrists and pinned her arms down with ease. She thrashed and screamed, but he simply laughed.

'No one will hear you, Priestess. I have made sure of that.'

The floor beneath Medusa was hard and cold. She clamped her eyes shut and tried to focus her mind on that as Poseidon stole everything from her.

Sob after sob wracked Ismene's body. Her throat was raw, her eyes aching and dry. So close. She had been so close to escaping with the love of her life and finally being happy.

Then her father ruined her life.

She hated him. She hated him for what he had done to her, hated him for what he had done to her mother, and hated him for what he threatened to do to Medusa. Ismene buried her face in her blanket as another sob shook her.

Ismene's stomach tightened as she thought of Medusa, waiting for her. What would she do when Ismene never arrived as they had planned? She would be confused, worried.

Heartbroken.

It made Ismene sick to her stomach to think about. Medusa had opened her world to a life filled with love and happiness that she had never thought possible, and Ismene was abandoning her with no warning and no explanation. It wasn't fair.

Ismene turned onto her back and stared up at the ceiling of the gynaeceum. She was safe here, in the one part of the house Thaddeus would never tread –not because of his reverence to the feminine sex or out of respect for his wife and daughter, but because of the damage it would do to his reputation if word got out that he had stooped so low.

Anger coiled in Ismene's gut. Her father didn't love the women in his life; they had value until they were no longer of use to him, and were then hidden from view. Ismene knew she was merely an inconvenience, a defective progeny destined to inherit her mother's chores and nothing else. When she was with Medusa, Ismene could forget about life at home. She could ignore the coldness, the loneliness, the resentment.

Now, it was all she had.

Ismene sat up, the heat of her anger spreading into a fury. She couldn't live like this, punished for merely existing, never knowing love or affection again. Thaddeus might be the ruler of this house, but how far was his reach in reality? If Ismene could get out of this house and get to Medusa, and they could reach the sea and leave Miletus behind, her father's threats would be meaningless.

It was high risk, but worth it for their freedom. Ismene would not let her father control her anymore, and she would not let him hurt Medusa.

She would die protecting her if she had to.

Heart pounding, Ismene crept forward. Her trembling fingers clutched the loom weight cradled in her palm. It wasn't much, but the gynaeceum had little to offer in terms of weaponry, and the heavy lump of clay provided some reassurance. She strained her ears for any sound, but the house was quiet. Her mother was out collecting water – Ismene had heard her lugging the water jar outside some time ago – and Thaddeus should be at the studio this late in the morning, but if he had gone already, he had done so more quietly than usual. Ismene could only pray to the gods that that was the case.

Treading as lightly as she could, Ismene padded across the hallway on bare feet. It was dim – this room also being used for storage, so containing no windows – but the sunlight outlining the door shone like a beacon, drawing Ismene closer.

*Not much farther.*

Adrenaline pulsed in Ismene's veins, willing her to move faster, to run and get out while she could. But she couldn't panic. She couldn't risk rushing and alerting someone to her escape. Holding her breath, Ismene took the last few steps to the door.

'How disappointing.'

Ismene's heart leapt into her throat. She turned to see Thaddeus standing in the corner of the room, his face half-obscured by shadow. His dark eyes glittered in the darkness, radiating hate towards his daughter.

'I'm leaving,' Ismene murmured. Her grip tightened on the loom weight in her hand. 'Don't try to stop me.'

A dark chuckle rumbled from her father. 'Try? Girl, I am going to ensure you can never defy me again.'

Panic flooded Ismene's body, and she bolted for the door. Her fingers had barely brushed the handle when she was violently jerked backwards. Pain seared across her scalp as Thaddeus wrenched her back by her hair. Ismene twisted in his grasp, terror and anger warring in her gut. Their eyes met, and as Ismene took in her father's venom-twisted features, her rage won out.

She didn't hesitate. Summoning every iota of strength she possessed, Ismene swung her fist at Thaddeus. There was barely time for his eyes to widen in surprise before the loom weight collided with his temple. The heavy clay did its job, and Thaddeus buckled. The hand grasping Ismene's curls fell away and there was a dull thud as her father's body hit the ground.

Ismene didn't check if he still breathed. She ran through the door, leaving her father and her old life behind.

She was going to be with Medusa, and she was going to be happy – finally.

After what felt like a lifetime, the nightmare was finally over.

Poseidon pulled away, leaving Medusa ragged and raw. She trembled as he rose to his feet. She couldn't look at him, couldn't meet the eyes of the monster who had violated her in the most holy of places.

'You were exquisite,' he murmured; Medusa cringed at the unfeeling satisfaction rumbling in his deep voice. 'As I expected of such a fine specimen, of course.'

Medusa said nothing. She let the silence stretch between them as she lay there, hollow and numb. Eventually she heard Poseidon kneel beside her, and she curled in on herself, clinging to the torn remnants of her clothing, dreading his touch.

'Now, is that really the way to treat one's paramour?'

A strong hand grasped Medusa's chin. Poseidon tilted her face up, but she avoided his gaze.

'Look at me.'

Medusa complied, if only to pacify the sea god so he would finally leave her. She looked into Poseidon's face, blinking back fresh tears as she stared into the eyes of her attacker. Where before there had been feral hunger, there was now something akin to fondness. It did nothing to quell the horror curdling in Medusa's gut.

Poseidon smiled down at her, as one might smile at a beloved pet. 'Don't stray too far, sweet priestess.'

Before Medusa could react, his lips pressed against hers. She tried to pull back, but his strong fingers held her face in place as he forced his tongue into her mouth. Medusa closed her eyes and tried to choke down the bile rising up her throat. When Poseidon finally drew back, she could breathe again.

'Stay close. I like to be able to find my lovers easily.' Poseidon kissed Medusa's forehead and returned to his feet. He opened his mouth to speak again, but stopped, tilting his head as if hearing a sound beyond Medusa's comprehension. 'My niece approaches. Until next time, my sweet.'

Medusa blinked, and he was gone. If not for the burning pain between her thighs and the disgust and shame coiling through her insides, she wouldn't believe he had ever been there at all. She brought her knees up to her chest, wincing as pain shot through her lower abdomen, and let the tears fall.

Aching sobs wracked her body. She could barely breathe, barely think. Everything was a terrible blur, Poseidon's words already fading from her memory, but that disgusting feeling of violation, of pain, of degradation... it only grew with each passing moment.

Something creaked beside her, but Medusa didn't move. She shivered on the cold stone floor, drained and hollow. The next creak was louder, followed by an almighty crack which echoed around the naos and forced Medusa to raise her head. She blinked, her eyes stinging and swollen, and could not believe what she saw.

The statue of the Goddess Athena was moving.

Cracks spread over the goddess' face and body as the statue stepped down from the dais upon which it stood and set its stony gaze on Medusa.

'My Lady,' Medusa breathed, drawing her ruined clothing further over her body. 'Thank goodness you are—'

'I am *not* your Lady!' Athena's voice thundered through the air, shattering the stone that encased her and revealing the goddess in all her glory. She stood tall and strong, garbed in a shining bronze helmet and a finely embroidered chiton which gleamed as if spun from pure gold. Stern grey eyes swept over Medusa's crumpled form, and a look of distaste twisted her lips. 'You have desecrated my most holy of places.'

'W-what?' Medusa looked up at her goddess, astounded. 'I didn't... I couldn't...'

'You are a priestess of my order, are you not?' Athena's voice was as hard and cold as a mountain peak during the darkest winter.

Medusa swallowed. Why was her goddess speaking to her in this way, at a time when she needed her comfort and protection the most?

'Yes...' she replied, her voice barely more than a whisper. 'I have been a loyal serva—'

'And in doing so, you vowed to abstain from the touch of any man, did you not?'

Medusa's stomach knotted. 'Of course, Lady Athena, but this...' Medusa gestured at her torn clothing, struggling to find the words to convey the horror of what just happened. 'This was not my choice. I tried to stop him!' Desperate tears filled Medusa's vision. She approached the goddess on her knees and grasped at the hem of her chiton. 'Please, don't exclude me from your blessings. I didn't want it. I didn't!'

Athena stepped back, her expression one of pure disgust. 'Do not *touch* me, mortal.' She brushed off her clothing, as if Medusa's fingers had soiled the fabric. 'What you did or did not want is of no interest to me,' she continued. 'You, one of my own priestesses, were defiled in my own sanctuary. Such sacrilege must be punished.'

Eyes darting around the naos, Medusa searched for who the goddess planned to punish. It was absurd, and the rational part of her mind told her that, but the desperate, panicked part told Medusa that it couldn't be her. That Poseidon must be behind her – the true culprit. The one who deserved punishment.

'Do you consider yourself beautiful, young Medusa?' Athena sneered, drawing the priestess' gaze back to the goddess.

Medusa blinked. She had been told she was fair to look upon her entire life. Her mother had praised her plump lips, her large eyes and her ample figure, reminded her how valuable those assets were. After all, it was Medusa's purpose in life to be desirable, to be admired and coveted so that she would attract a high-status husband and keep the family line strong. In truth, she had never questioned her appearance. Beauty was an expectation – like her skill with the loom, her theological knowledge, and her articulate speech. But the way Athena spoke of it... It was as if it was a sinful vice. Something to be ashamed of.

The goddess stared down at Medusa, eyebrows raised. She expected an answer.

'I... I suppose so, Lady Athena,' Medusa murmured, choosing her next words carefully. 'At least, I have always been told as much.'

An unkind smirk twitched at the goddess' lips. 'You suppose so.'

Athena stretched a slender arm out towards Medusa. For an un-believable moment, it seemed she was offering a helping hand to the priestess. Then she snapped her fingers and, coiled around the entire length of her arm, a large black viper appeared.

Medusa gasped and fell back, scrabbling to put distance between herself and the deadly beast. Its small black eyes locked onto her, and an involuntary whimper fell from her lips. It was known that serpents were under Athena's dominion – their earthly wisdom and propensity for renewal were aligned with her own divine abilities – but this otherworldly creature emanated danger, and the threat of death. Athena's eyes shone with dark satisfaction; she was enjoying Medusa's fear.

'And what about this serpent, Priestess? Is she beautiful?'

The snake reared up and hissed at Medusa, sending her scurrying further back.

'No?' Athena advanced on the priestess, looming over her with the deadly viper outstretched. 'You see, Medusa, a serpent does not hide its nature behind a pretty face. The danger it poses is plain to see. Its hiss alerts those who stray too close, its sharp fangs are a final warning not to touch. Perhaps you need to learn something from it.'

Before Medusa could respond, a great, piercing pain shot through her skull. She tried to rise, but fell forward onto her knees as the pain seared across her scalp, a deep burning as if her brain was about to burst out of her head.

'What...' she forced out through gritted teeth, 'what are you doing... to me...'

Athena's voice reverberated around the naos, deep and resonating and powerful. 'Your beauty will no longer be a mask for your venomous nature.'

A fresh wave of agony flared through Medusa's skull. She clutched her head, horror washing over her as she felt something moving beneath her fingers. Not just something – *many* things, squirming and thrashing just below the skin of her scalp.

'What... what...' She couldn't get the words out; the pain was too great. Spots darkened her vision and she squeezed her eyes shut, gulping for air in a vain attempt to ease the agony.

'You will be forever marked as a danger,' Athena continued, her thunderous voice shaking the ground beneath Medusa's knees. 'No man will dare to look upon you, nor desire to indulge in your flesh.'

A terrible, scalding heat erupted behind Medusa's eyelids. She crashed forward to the ground, her palms pressed into her eyes, her back arching as the pain almost overwhelmed her.

'From this day forward,' Athena's voice rumbled, distant and warped as it found Medusa through her agony, 'you are a monster.'

Medusa's head burst open, and she screamed until the blackness took her.

Head down, headscarf pulled tight around her face, Ismene strode quickly and with purpose.

People bustled around her – shoppers hurrying to the agora, labourers carrying tools and masonry, servants scurrying after their masters – but all she heard was the *thud* of her father's body hitting the ground.

Over and over again.

A surly merchant barged past Ismene, knocking her back with his large shoulder, snapping her out of the memory and back into the present. There was no use thinking about her father anymore. She did what she needed to do to get away, and one way or another, she would never see him again.

She just hoped her mother would be all right.

Shouts erupted from up ahead – sailors, by the sound of their colourful language – and Ismene picked up her pace. She was almost at the docks, where Medusa was hopefully waiting.

They had planned their escape in meticulous detail, and Ismene knew from the height of the sun in the sky that the ship that would give them passage to the island of Lade was due to depart very soon. There would be no time to go to the temple first; she just had to hope Medusa had gone ahead with their plan without her. They hadn't wanted to entertain the idea that Ismene wouldn't be able to escape in time, but they both knew that if she should be held up too long, Medusa had to continue with their cover story and visit her family home.

She walked as quickly as she could without attracting attention, her face covered as much as possible. Thaddeus might not be hunting for her, but Ismene couldn't risk any of his associates recognising their friend's unescorted daughter and dragging her back to the family home. It didn't matter that her whereabouts were none of their business – she was an unmarried woman, and they had authority over her.

Finally, the Miletus dockyard came into view, and Ismene's heart leapt into her throat. So close. She was so close to leaving it all behind. The loneliness, the shame, the utter contempt... it would all be washed away as they crossed the Ionian sea.

She couldn't wait.

Ismene almost broke into a run when she spotted the ship Medusa had chartered for their voyage, with three rows of oars along its side and a shabby, off-white sail piercing the cloudless sky.

*She's still here!*

It was a small, unimpressive vessel which blended in easily with the other trading ships moored at the harbour. Perfect for escaping the city unnoticed.

The ship's captain stood on the dock, his arms crossed and a look of annoyance creasing his round face. When he noticed Ismene approaching, he called out in a stern voice.

'You, girl!' Heat flushed Ismene's cheeks and she hurried up to him, hoping a closer proximity would force him to lower his voice. It didn't. 'Are you one of the passengers?'

'Yes,' she breathed, heart pounding from her dash to the docks. 'Is the priestess already on board?'

The captain's brow furrowed in confusion, and unease stirred in Ismene's chest.

'What is it?' she asked, peering around him to see if she could spot Medusa on deck. 'Where is she?'

'I was hoping you'd answer that,' the captain replied gruffly, hands on hips. 'She hasn't turned up, and we're waiting to push off.'

Ismene's heart dropped. This wasn't the plan. A sudden cancellation would draw suspicion on the priestess, and jeopardise any future escape for the pair of them. Ismene chewed her lip, her mind racing.

Had Medusa changed her mind?

Had she been relieved when Ismene didn't make it to the temple, and decided to carry on as normal, without her?

Ismene shook her head. No, that wasn't possible. She knew Medusa – knew her on a level deeper than anyone she had ever interacted with – and she knew she wouldn't shrug off her plans so quickly.

Something must be wrong.

Images flashed through Ismene's mind, each scenario worse than the last. Medusa injured with no one coming to help, Medusa unconscious floating in the courtyard pool, Medusa attacked on her journey to the harbour and left for dead in the streets.

Panic flooded her, and without saying another word to the captain, Ismene raced off towards the temple.

Raging agony dulled to a lingering ache, and Medusa was finally able to open her eyes again.

She was alone, curled up in the corner of the naos where she had cowered until the pain overwhelmed her senses. Medusa sat up and her vision rocked. She had to breathe deeply for a few moments while it settled to prevent herself from vomiting over the stone floor.

She turned towards the statue of Athena, dread curdling in her gut. It stood still and silent, as it always had, the goddess staring out into the empty room impassively.

As if nothing had happened.

But it had... hadn't it? She remembered it so clearly: the anger in Athena's voice, the fear as Medusa realised she would be punished, the blinding pain that still throbbed through Medusa's skull. It was real. It had to be.

Her head felt oddly thick, and heavy, as if some great force was pushing and pulling on her scalp. When Medusa brought her fingers to her head to investigate, she screamed.

Snakes.

*Live* snakes, at least a dozen of them, and they seemed to be coming directly out of Medusa's scalp.

She screamed again. And again. She screamed until her throat was raw and she felt light-headed. She screamed until hot tears streamed down her cheeks and she was out of breath, and choked out a final, gasping sob.

What had the goddess done to her?

'Priestess?'

The voice was distant, warping as it reached Medusa through the mists of her panic.

'Priestess? Are you all right?'

It was Kephissa, alerted by Medusa's screams.

'Help me!' Medusa cried out, her voice cracked and strained. She knew Kephissa couldn't do anything – no one could reverse the power of the gods – but Medusa needed validation that this was really happening. That someone else could see it.

Hurried footsteps approached the naos, and Medusa's pulse quickened. Kephissa rushed through the doorway, face flushed and eyes darting around the small space for the source of Medusa's panic.

'Priestess?'

Medusa looked up, bracing herself for the reaction to her monstrous appearance. The two women locked gazes, and Medusa's stomach dropped as a look of abject horror grew on Kephissa's face. The senior acolyte's eyes widened into an unblinking stare as she stood frozen in place, petrified.

'Kephissa,' Medusa sobbed, 'I can explain, please, just... Kephissa?'

The other woman still wasn't moving. Her expression was locked in a terrible silent scream, her arms partially raised at uncomfortable angles.

'Kephissa?'

Medusa rose on unsteady feet and took several tentative steps towards the other woman. As she entered the dappled light coming through the doorway, she noticed the unusual pallor of Kephissa's skin. Where her hands and face were usually bronze, she was eerily pale, almost like…

Stone.

Terror creeping through her insides, Medusa lifted her trembling fingers and brushed Kephissa's cheek. Cold marble greeted her touch, and Medusa's heart shattered into pieces.

'Kephissa!' she sobbed, knowing the other woman couldn't hear her, but at a loss for what else to do. 'Kephissa, please…' Fresh tears rained down Medusa's cheeks as she grasped the frozen woman's shoulders. 'Kephissa!'

Medusa's shriek echoed off the walls of the naos and out into the temple proper.

She had done this. Kephissa was lifeless, her soul frozen in time or else condemned to the darkness of Hades, and it was Medusa's fault.

'I'm sorry…' she sobbed, wrapping her arms around the senior acolyte's petrified body. 'Gods, I am sorry!'

'Priestess?'

Medusa's heart pounded. Another acolyte, coming to check on their priestess. She could not let them suffer the same fate as Kephissa. She had to get away from the temple, away from these innocent women who had served Medusa so faithfully, before it was too late.

Medusa hastened to wrap her torn clothing around herself, tucking in and tying the linen where she could, and dashed out of the naos.

'Stay back!' the priestess shrieked as she barrelled through the doorway, arms held up to hide her hideous visage. 'Do not look at me!'

Medusa stumbled blindly through the temple, relying on her feet to guide her through the once-familiar surroundings, but panic clouded her memory. She staggered and circled while a flurry of anxious questions bombarded her.

'Priestess, what's wrong?'

'Are you unwell?'

'Please, let me help you!'

Medusa bumped into a plinth that should not have been there, sending a vase falling to the ground and shattering at her feet. She sprang back, and did not realise she had lowered her arms in surprise until she looked up from the scattered shards and her gaze met with that of another young woman, a new acolyte whose name Medusa had not yet learned.

'NO!' Medusa screamed, but it was too late. The woman's face froze and hardened, a dull white-grey spreading from her wide eyes over her face and down her neck, her once-olive skin paling until she was petrified – not in terror, but in actual stone.

Screams and shouts erupted throughout the temple. What were once offers of help became cries of terror.

'Monster!'

'Demon!'

'Goddess, help us!'

Panic flooded Medusa's body. She stared into the lifeless eyes of the girl she had destroyed, horror clutching at her heart. 'No,' she murmured, inaudible over the din. 'I am not...'

'Out, demon!' Something flew past Medusa, narrowly missing her head and clattering to the ground behind her.

'Begone, monster!'

Something else was thrown, bursting into flame ahead of her – an oil lamp, still lit. It had been meant to hit her.

'Monster!' another woman shouted, rallying the others into a horrible chant.

'Monster! Monster! Monster!'

'You... You do not understand...' Medusa stammered, knowing she must flee, but unable to tear her gaze away from the frozen young woman. 'You... You do not...'

Her mouth was dry, her heart hammered in her chest.

'Monster! Monster!'

Another lamp erupted by Medusa's feet, so close she felt the flames singe the hem of her tattered clothing. Hot tears welled in her eyes.

'I... I...'

'Monster! Monster! Monster!'

A surge of emotion pulsed through the priestess.

'I AM NOT A MONSTER!'

Her desperate shriek echoed off the marble walls, ricocheting and reverberating until it seemed to scream back at her from all angles.

And then... silence.

Terrifying, bone-chilling silence.

Medusa turned, and ran.

Screams echoed in the distance, and a terrible dread seized Ismene's insides.

*Medusa!*

She quickened her steps, practically sprinting through the winding Miletus streets, not caring who she pushed or barreled into in her hurry to reach the woman she loved. Her rational side told her she had no evidence the commotion was linked to Medusa, but she knew from the horrible feeling in her gut that it was.

Ismene rounded the corner onto the broad roadway leading to the temple, and she realised the shouts and cries were not coming from the temple itself, but the streets beyond. A cacophony of terror lay ahead, with men and women alike shrieking as if confronted with the Titans of Tartarus themselves.

Ismene allowed a glimmer of hope to bloom in her chest.

*Perhaps Medusa and the temple have been spared whatever this horror is.*

She finally neared the temple entrance and the screams stopped. The sudden, deafening silence halted Ismene in her tracks. She stood and listened, the complete lack of sound chilling her to the bone. If whatever this threat was had been destroyed, where were the shouts of triumph? The cries of unsettled children? The clangs and crashes of wreckage being repaired?

*Something isn't right.*

Ismene crept to the temple entrance, unease creeping up her spine. The quiet was oppressive. Where usually there'd be the sounds of acolytes passing through the grounds attending to their duties, or worshippers offering prayers to the goddess, there was nothing. Ismene almost didn't want to pass beyond the columns into the temple itself, afraid of what she might find, but she forced herself to walk forwards.

What she saw was incomprehensible.

Statues, dozens of them. They were scattered throughout the temple in strange positions, all facing a single point as if placed there for some bizarre ritual Ismene had never come across in her training.

Ismene stepped towards the nearest figure, cringing as each footstep shattered the fragile silence.

'Hello?' she tentatively called. Her voice ricocheting off the many statues was jarring, and extremely unpleasant. Everything about the scene around Ismene felt wrong.

She reached one of the statues, looked up at its granite face and swallowed a scream.

*No, no, no, no. It can't be!*

Ismene knew that face. Evadne. The girl was quiet but studious and helpful, and had offered to assist Ismene with her first libation ritual when Medusa had been called to attend to other duties. She had been so patient and kind, never once scolding Ismene when she poured clumsily and spilled the wine. And now... Ismene could hardly believe it.

A cold dread pooled in Ismene's gut. Evadne wasn't the only statue here. She tore her eyes away from the frozen acolyte and turned around.

*Oh gods, oh no.*

Bile burned up the back of Ismene's throat. She recognised all of these faces. Each woman had served alongside Ismene during her training, offering gentle advice or a reassuring smile when she struggled through a new activity. Not one of them had ever given her a harsh word or unpleasant look. What sort of monstrosity could have done this to these innocent people?

A fresh pang of panic struck Ismene as her eyes flitted from one frozen face to the next. Someone was missing – someone very important.

*Where is Medusa? Is she...?*

No. She couldn't bring herself to finish the thought. Medusa had to be all right; the alternative was too unbearable to even contemplate.

Ismene had to find her.

Heart thundering in her chest, Ismene sprinted through the temple and into the courtyard. It was empty, not even a breeze to disturb the glassy surface of the pool. Ismene's pulse throbbed in her ears, and her breathing grew rapid.

*Medusa, where are you?*

Ismene chewed her bottom lip, her stomach roiling. This was their favourite spot; she had desperately hoped she would find Medusa there. She glanced back into the temple, her chest tightening at the silhouettes of the poor petrified women within, and a thought occurred to her.

*This was* our *favourite spot, but it wasn't Medusa's. Not when she was alone.*

The naos. That had to be where she was.

The silence was stifling as Ismene crept through the temple to the naos. The building had always had a quiet serenity to it, but there had also been an undercurrent of activity, the bustle of worshippers and acolytes moving to and fro and offering soft prayers to the goddess.

For all of that to be silenced was unsettling at best.

'Medusa?' Ismene called softly as she approached the doorway. 'Are you in there?'

Nothing.

Heart crawling up her throat, Ismene slipped into the naos, and was struck by a wave of despair.

Medusa wasn't there, but someone else was, someone Ismene cared for greatly.

'Kephissa...' she murmured as she walked on unsteady feet to the statue of the woman she had been speaking to just a day prior. A grotesque mask of terror twisted the senior acolyte's face, sending chills through Ismene's body. The surrounding oil lamps cast undulating waves of warm light and dark shadow across Kephissa's features, so they appeared to warp and shift. It was as if the woman inside was trying to break free, to undo the horrific curse something had bestowed on her.

Ismene traced an uneasy finger down the other woman's stony cheek, barely believing what was in front of her. 'What did this to you?' she whispered, blinking back tears. 'What happened here?'

Ismene tore her eyes from Kephissa's frozen face as something else caught her attention. The flickering lamplight glimmered off something on the ground. Something small, and shiny.

She knelt on the cold floor, and a rush of emotion swept over her. There, glinting in the wavering light, was a single silver obol, decorated with the head of a horse.

*Is it...?*

Ismene plucked the coin from the ground and was surprised to find a thin golden chain follow it. It coiled in Ismene's palm, a delicate, fine thing that could only have belonged to her beloved priestess. She placed the obol gently on top, and ran her thumb over the raised equine image, tears springing into her eyes once again. This lost coin – a simple token that Medusa had kept close all this time – had been transformed into something beautiful.

*But why is it here?*

Whether this was a gift for Ismene or a trinket for Medusa to keep herself, it wouldn't be something the priestess would discard like this.

Ismene cast her eyes over the floor in front of her, and a few other items came into focus in the dappled lamplight. Painfully familiar objects were scattered about: a small wooden comb, a copper hand mirror, and, as Ismene looked closer, she noticed a few loose beads. She scooped them up, her chest fluttering as she studied their design.

Polished gemstones. Simple and understated, but fine and elegant. The kind Medusa sewed into her clothing.

*Oh, gods.*

The room swayed as a horrible realisation swept through Ismene. Whatever monster had done this, wherever it had gone to – it had taken Medusa.

Ismene's stomach churned and a great wave of nausea crashed over her. Medusa – her strong, smart, wonderful Medusa – had been taken. She was gone. It was almost too terrible to comprehend.

Ismene's chest constricted, and her breathing became rapid. Her heart hammered so hard she felt it might burst. Medusa was her shining light, her guiding star... Without her, Ismene was lost.

'I should have been here,' she whispered, choking back the sob threatening to erupt from her trembling chest. 'I should have been with you.'

The dam burst, and hot tears flowed down Ismene's cheeks. She felt numb, adrift; unanchored without Medusa by her side.

'I should've known it was too good to be true,' she sobbed, clutching the beads in her palm so tight it hurt. She welcomed the pain. 'Father always said I had no future outside of his damned house.' She scrubbed the tears from her eyes with the back of her hand as Thaddeus' words echoed in her mind.

*Defective.*

*Broken.*

*Useless.*

*Shameful.*

A rush of anger and pain overwhelmed her. Ismene threw her head back and screamed into the silence.

'Are you happy now?' Her voice ricocheted off the stone walls, shrill and almost inhuman, like the shrieking of a dozen harpies. 'I've got nothing,' she howled, her throat raw. 'Nothing!'

She slumped forward onto her hands, trembling as great, heaving sobs wracked her body. 'I can't...' she whispered, her voice hoarse and near-silent.

A shadowy image of her father flashed into her mind, lying still on the ground, blood pooling all around him. It shifted, and Thaddeus was gone, replaced by Medusa. She lay broken and bleeding, her large eyes wide and staring, pleading – no, *begging* – for help. Medusa was out there somewhere, captured or injured or worse, with no one to save her.

No one, except for Ismene.

She pushed herself up to her knees, a fresh fire kindling in her gut. Medusa had risked everything to rescue Ismene from her suffering, and Ismene would be damned if she didn't at least try to do the same.

She rose to unsteady feet, the horse-head pendant clutched tightly in one hand and the gemstone beads in the other.

'I'll find you, Medusa,' she said, her voice weak and broken, but firm. Resolute. 'I swear, even if it takes a lifetime, I will find you, and I will save you.'

Silence. Sweet, blessed silence.

Medusa collapsed against the wall of the barn, relief draining her body of what little energy she had left. Her chest heaved as she gulped for air, her lungs burning from the exertion forced upon her body. She did not know how far she had run, arms over her face as she stumbled blindly through the city, seeking solitude and finding only more and more people.

They had screamed at the very sight of her. They fled as she approached, shouting for the gods to intervene, to destroy the monster that had been set upon them. If only they knew that it was the gods themselves who were responsible.

Medusa tried to push the memories out of her mind, but each time she closed her eyes they returned. Poseidon pinning her to the ground, feral lust burning in his eyes. Athena, incandescent with rage, striking down the woman who had obeyed and worshipped her. Medusa's heart shattered again and again with each image.

Her trembling knees gave way, and Medusa crumpled to the ground. For several long moments, she simply lay there, drained and desolate. She couldn't move, couldn't think, couldn't breathe. She was paralysed, crushed under the weight of all that had happened.

A thud sounded outside, and Medusa was brought back to her senses. Her aching limbs screaming in protest, she pushed herself up into a seated position, and listened.

She did not know who owned this old barn – she had simply ducked into the first empty structure she had found once she had escaped the crowded inner city – and she did not want to find out. Dread chilled her veins as she pressed herself against the wall and drew her knees up to her chest, making herself as small as possible. The thought of coming face to face with one more human being made her want to vomit.

A second thud, from the same direction as the first. Medusa's heart pounded in her chest. They had found her. They thought her a monster, and they sought to destroy her. She shrank further into herself, shrivelling into the shadows. Praying would be futile; the gods would not save her – she knew that for certain, now.

Medusa held her breath as something akin to footsteps scraped the dirt outside the barn. It was an odd sound, as if the person carried a lot of weight, but there was no thud of heavy boots, no strike of sandal leather against the ground. It was almost otherworldly, inhuman.

'Oh gods,' Medusa whispered, her breath shuddering. 'What new punishment is this?'

Something slammed into the barn door, and Medusa jumped, swallowing down a cry before it burst through her lips and gave her location away. It slammed again, and again. The door groaned under the force, and the wooden bar holding it shut began to bow and splinter. It would not keep the intruder at bay for long.

Medusa squeezed her eyes shut as silent tears rained down her cheeks. She curled in on herself, trembling. What further horrors did the gods have in store for her? Had she not suffered enough?

A terrible crash echoed through the barn – the doors had finally broken, and whoever hunted Medusa had gotten inside.

Those scraping footsteps resumed. Medusa pressed her forehead into her knees and tried to suppress the sobs building in her chest. The serpents atop her head writhed and softly hissed, and Medusa willed them to be quiet. A small voice in the back of her mind screamed at her to run, to take a chance and attempt an escape, but she could not summon the energy to move. Her limbs were lead weight, her lungs stung with every breath. She was spent.

The heavy footfall drew closer and Medusa's heart galloped in her chest. She inhaled slowly, forcing the air through her tightening chest in an attempt to calm herself. She might be hiding in the shadows, but if she was to meet her end here, she would face it with the strength and dignity of a priestess of Athena.

The footsteps stilled, and Medusa braced herself. A large hand grasped her shoulder and she started, but rather than rough and forceful, it was soft, and gentle.

'Sister,' a strange, melodic voice murmured from somewhere above her, 'do not be afraid.'

Medusa opened her eyes and raised her head. Two creatures loomed over her, as incredible as they were terrifying. Women, dressed in simple robes, and taller and more muscular than any Medusa had seen before, stood looking down at her. Medusa stared at them, and her heart leapt as she took in the writhing serpents which adorned their heads. One woman sported a head of long, slim golden snakes, while the other had thick mottled-green vipers with sharp, triangular heads all turned in

Medusa's direction. Medusa's own serpents seemed to react to their presence, calming and settling into place.

The woman with the golden snakes held out a hand to her, thick, pointed claws at the end of each long finger. 'Come, sister.'

'Sister?'

Aside from the serpents, these two women did not resemble Medusa in any way. They looked strong, even dangerous, but as they looked down at her trembling form, she did not see aggression. There was compassion in their large, dark eyes. Perhaps even sympathy.

The golden-haired woman nodded. 'You are kin. We sensed you come into being, and sought you out.'

'The humans do not tolerate our kind,' the green-haired woman added. Her voice was cooler, sharper, but no less cordial. 'If you come with us, we will keep you safe.'

Safe. Medusa had thought she was safe at the temple. Safe under the protection of her goddess. Safe in the privileged position of priestess. But none of that mattered when a powerful god took what he wanted whether she liked it or not, and left Medusa to suffer the consequences.

'How?' she breathed, barely able to force the words out as fresh tears brimmed in her swollen eyes. 'How could I ever feel safe again?'

The golden-haired woman rolled her shoulders and Medusa gaped as she shook out a great pair of feathered wings. 'We have our ways.'

The green-haired woman stepped closer, shaking free her own wings. They reached several feet above her head and almost touched the ground. Medusa had no doubt they could carry the woman high into the sky with ease. 'They call us the Gorgons,' she sneered. 'Monsters. But we are Phorcydes, the daughters of gods, granddaughters of Mother Earth, of Gaia herself, with powers befitting our lineage. And you, little sister,' she continued, a smile softening her sharp features, 'you are now one of us. We know our kin; our powers call to each other, and we knew you the moment you were created. You are family.'

'Come,' the golden-haired woman repeated, taking Medusa's hands in her own and raising her to unsteady feet. She was strong – unbelievably so. It was as if Medusa was nothing but a tiny kitten in her grasp. 'I am Euryale,' she muttered softly, drawing Medusa close and wrapping gentle arms around the shorter woman. 'I will lead you home, where no one who means you harm can find you.'

'And I am Stheno,' the green-haired woman said, placing a strong hand on Medusa's shoulder. 'I will carry you, and you will always be safe in my arms.'

Medusa pulled back and looked up at the two women, tears freely streaming down her cheeks now. Family. These two god-daughters – these stunning, terrible divine beings – did not know her, yet already considered her family. Her affliction did not elicit fear, but instead bound them to her in a way she did not yet understand. If she went with them, she could be safe. No more screams, no more shame, no more fear. But...

An image flashed in her mind. A beautiful face. Golden eyes and honey-coloured curls glinting in the sunlight.

If she went with Euryale and Stheno, Medusa would likely never see Ismene again. It broke her heart to even consider, but what pained her more was the thought of Ismene meeting the same fate as those poor women in the temple. She could not bear to see Ismene's face frozen in stone, disgust twisting her features as she looked upon Medusa, transfigured and monstrous. It would shatter her completely, and she would not be able to go on.

Ismene's safety was more important than her own, and Medusa would not put the woman she loved more than anything in creation at any further risk.

'All right,' she said, taking a deep, shuddering breath and grasping one of each of their hands in hers. 'I will come with you, sisters. Take me home.'

# Part Two

A cacophony of revelry assaulted his senses. Flute and lyre music competed for dominance as scores of aristocrats chattered, guffawed and called out for more wine. They were no doubt regaling each other with exaggerated tales of political genius or athletic performance, their voices strategically projected towards the king as he passed by each group.

Perseus scowled as King Polydectes strutted through the fawning crowd, soaking up every drop of false praise. The man was a pompous fool; the only people more foolish than he were the noblemen tying themselves in knots to earn his favour. Between them they held almost enough riches to rival the king himself, yet it seemed that their tremendous wealth was nothing if they could gain a modicum more power from being his current favourite.

Perseus shifted, and cringed as the rough linen of his formal chiton scratched at his back and chest. It was the best he could afford without taking money from Dictys – who barely had an obol to spare himself – and yet Perseus knew he stood out like a beggar amongst gentlemen. He stood alone, busying himself with drinking the too-heavily spiced wine.

The strong flavour overloaded his simple palate, but he forced it down. Was it not enough that Polydectes was king, and that he was hosting this banquet in his opulent palace surrounded by gilded statues and a host of servants and slaves? Did he also have to demonstrate his wealth by being heavy-handed with exotic spices that likely cost more per jar than Perseus earned in a year? It was vulgar, but Perseus expected nothing less from the man who had been stalking his mother like a ravenous lion for as long as he could remember, waiting for the moment Perseus left her vulnerable so he could finally pick her off and have his way with her.

Thank the gods Polydectes had now set his sights on a grander prize, and the man's vast pride would soon lead him to his downfall. Perseus could not wait to hear word of the older man's eventual execution.

A horn sounded, and all heads turned towards the king, who had raised his cup as if ready to make a speech.

'Esteemed guests!' Polydectes announced from the far end of the room, where he stood behind a high table adorned with a luxurious feast. 'You are very welcome in my home. Thank you for joining me to celebrate my decision to challenge Oenomaus of Pisa and win the hand of his fair daughter.' A roar of applause erupted from the intoxicated crowd of sycophants, and Perseus resisted the urge to roll his eyes. A broad smile spread across Polydectes' bearded face as he lapped up the cheers and assurances of victory. The display made Perseus want to vomit.

'Please,' Polydectes continued, waving for quiet without sincerity. 'Eat and drink your fill. We have the finest meats and fruits in all of Greece, enough wine for each man many times over, and the most beautiful serving girls in Seriphos!' Thunderous cheering was the response, which Polydectes cut short by raising his hand. 'But first, dear guests, before we lose ourselves to the revelry, please approach, one by one, and present to me your gift – or your promise of a gift – to celebrate my upcoming marriage!'

Another cheer, followed by excited murmuring and the shuffling of feet as the guests lined up to kneel before Polydectes. Perseus stood frozen, his heart in his throat. A gift? The invite had said nothing about a gift! Damn that self-serving, self-absorbed man to Hades!

The crowd thinned and Perseus drifted to the back of the line so as to remain inconspicuous. He was already clearly the poorest man in the room; he could not face Polydectes without the promise of a substantial gift.

But what could a young fisherman possibly have to offer an ostentatious king? Perseus was only welcomed into these social events because he had been raised by the king's brother, and Polydectes had subsequently taken a fancy to his mother. Dictys was a good man, but he had welcomed the king into his home and did nothing to deter his piggish brother's advances on Danaë, which rankled Perseus.

The line shifted forward and Perseus rubbed his temples as he tried to conceive of a suitable gift for Polydectes. Why had he drunk so much of that hideous wine? It had addled his brain and dulled his senses, and he was running out of time.

Polydectes embraced a grinning nobleman, proclaiming him blessed by the royal house for his gift of four of the finest racing horses for the king's upcoming chariot race to win the hand of Hippodamia.

Horses! How could Perseus possibly compete with such gifts? He was blessed with certain exceptional qualities – he was strong, he had exceptional reflexes, he proved popular with men and women alike – but what use was all that to the King of Seriphos?

'Ah, young Perseus!'

Perseus blinked, his stomach dropping as he realised he was next to face the king. Polydectes opened his arms to greet the younger man, a grin spread across his face which did not reach his dark eyes. Perseus knew the king had no love for him, but he would not be one to drop the pretence in front of the gathered nobility.

Perseus dropped to one knee. 'My king,' Perseus muttered with as much sincerity as he could muster, 'I am at your service.'

'Rise, my boy, and share your gift.'

Perseus cringed at the tone in the king's voice. He knew. He *knew* Perseus had no gift to offer, and he was going to force him to admit it in front of the entire congregation.

'King Polydectes.' Perseus strained to keep his voice firm, confident. 'My gift to you is a promise.'

Polydectes laughed. 'A promise?' He turned to the crowd. 'The boy offers a promise!'

The crowd of snivelling puppets cackled, and Perseus felt heat rise up the back of his neck. He retained a mask of neutral conviction. He would not let these grovelling worms shame him. He thrust out his chest and held his head high, and waited for the forced laughter to settle before speaking.

'Yes, your highness, a promise I can guarantee no other guest here could fulfil.' That quietened the fools. 'Name any prize that you desire – the thing you covet above all else – and I swear I will retrieve it for you.'

Polydectes raised an eyebrow. '*Any* prize?' There was a scepticism in his voice which raised Perseus' hackles. 'There is something, but... it would be quite the feat, even for a strapping lad such as yourself.'

'I will do it.' Perseus met Polydectes' dark gaze with his own. 'I swear.'

A fiendish smile lit up the king's face. 'In that case,' he said, clapping a hand on Perseus' shoulder, 'stand up, my boy, and accept your charge.'

Perseus rose to his feet and waited, certain he could manage any task he was given.

'I have had word of a woman,' Polydectes began, directing his speech to the crowd as much as to Perseus himself. 'A monstrous woman. An unholy being borne of the horrors of Tartarus herself, with serpents for hair and a visage so hideous she turns men to stone with just a look. She has been terrorising our brethren on the Ionian coast, leaving swathes of petrified men, women and children in her wake.' Polydectes drew himself up to his full height and fixed Perseus with a fierce stare. A challenge. 'I want her head.'

Murmurs rippled through the audience, and all eyes settled on Perseus. They awaited his response.

Perseus drew his fist to his chest, and forced a self-assured grin. 'It will be done.'

The hot midday sun beat down on Medusa's face, so bright it burned through her closed eyelids. She clenched them shut tighter, refusing to allow the allure of the beautiful day to tempt her.

'You must open your eyes, little sister.'

'I will not.'

'You know you must.'

Euryale's voice was gentle, but Medusa could hear the hint of frustration her new sister was trying to hide. They had only been in each other's company for a few weeks, but Medusa had learned the key differences between the two women who had welcomed her into their home. Where Stheno was direct, forceful and protective, Euryale was patient and caring. She eased Medusa into her new life gently, but with a quiet insistence that she embrace her new form, and learn to wield it.

'Just once more.' Euryale's plea was firm. She would not relent and give up on today's lesson just yet. 'If you are unsuccessful, we will let you rest. Agreed?'

Medusa sighed. She knew her sisters meant well, but each failure broke her heart further. Unlike them, she was no demi-god, no descendent of powerful primordial deities. The likelihood that she could wield a fraction of their potential was infinitesimally small. And yet, they continued to try to teach her, for no benefit other than her own happiness. Their kinship was beyond anything Medusa could have expected. She owed them some willingness to learn, at the very least.

'All right,' she relented. 'I will try once more.'

'Thank you, little sister.' Medusa could hear the smile in Euryale's voice, and her tension eased a fraction.

'Relax yourself,' Stheno's stern voice instructed from somewhere ahead of them. 'Calm your mind and body, and you will not fail.'

Medusa took a deep breath and slowly released the air through her nostrils. She wanted more than anything for this to work, but doubt tugged at the back of her mind. The price of failure was irreversible, they all knew that. But she had promised to try, so she took another breath and opened her eyes.

Her gaze met Stheno's, standing a few feet ahead of her. With tremendous reluctance, she lowered her eyes to the woman's hands, where she held a struggling shrew. The rodent twisted in Stheno's grasp until its gaze locked with Medusa's. She fought to remain calm, but as the shrew shrieked in alarm, her heart pounded in her chest. For a fleeting moment she allowed herself to hope, but her stomach dropped as the creature's small body stopped moving, and it became cold, hard stone.

Soft fingers stroked Medusa's shoulder. 'I am sorry, little sister. I know it pains you.'

Stheno moved to place the petrified shrew on the ground, but Medusa rushed forward to prevent her. 'Don't!' she urged, pulling the animal from her grasp. 'Please, I have to keep it. To remember.'

Stheno frowned, but there was understanding in her onyx eyes. 'It does you no good, little one.' Her voice was deep and sombre, reminiscent of a funeral dirge. 'Reminding yourself of your failures will not help you succeed. You torture yourself.'

'She is right.' Euryale approached her sisters. She reached down and coaxed one of the snakes atop Medusa's head into her large, clawed hand, so that it rested on her palm. Medusa wanted to look away – she hated being reminded of their existence, of what had been done to her – but resisted. The beast's scales were darker than the blackest night, but its thick body glittered in the sunlight as it undulated on Euryale's hand, hissing quietly. 'Your serpents are unsettled,' the taller woman continued. 'They should not be like this.'

'I *am* trying,' Medusa insisted, watching Euryale release the serpent back into its nest atop her head. 'I hope you know that.' She looked to Stheno, who continued to frown. 'Both of you.'

Stheno smiled then, perhaps realising that further admonishment would not prove helpful. She placed the petrified shrew in Medusa's hands. 'We know, little sister. Come, Euryale,' she called, stepping away from Medusa. 'Let us leave our sister to her thoughts. There is dinner to prepare, and I am sure Medusa would benefit from a moment without being observed.'

A shy smile pulled at Medusa's lips. These extraordinary women were not related to her by blood, but they always seemed to know what she needed from them. 'Thank you,' she whispered, but Stheno was already leading Euryale away from the clearing they had gathered in for their practice.

Medusa looked down at the shrew in her hands, frozen in a moment of pure terror as it beheld her hideous visage. She blinked back tears as she ran a hesitant finger over its stony back. It was perfect, each hair and whisker captured in such exquisite detail even the most skilled sculptor could only dream of matching it.

Another wasted life, because of her.

Medusa took a shuddering breath. She wanted to do as Stheno asked and steady her emotions, but it seemed impossible. She had been rescued from the chaos of Miletus, but had left a swathe of destruction in her wake. All those people, petrified in stone, frozen in time forever – how could she ever be calm again when she knew what she had done to them, knowing she had condemned them to a fate worse than death?

And there was something else, some*one* else, who haunted Medusa's dreams and whose face stared back at her every time she closed her eyes.

Ismene.

She had done the right thing by leaving Ismene behind – in that Medusa was absolutely certain – but she missed that woman with every fibre of her being. She longed for the feel of Ismene's hands in hers, for the warmth of her body beside her, for the glint in her golden eyes each time she looked at her. For that sly smile Ismene reserved for Medusa when they were alone.

The tears she had been suppressing trickled down Medusa's cheeks. 'Gods, Ismene,' she whispered, staring out over the island she now called her home. 'I hope you are well, and I hope you are safe. I hope you escaped your father's bindings.'

She took an uneasy breath, swallowing down the sobs that threatened to surface. 'I hope you forget me, and find happiness.'

With that, she turned to follow the path taken by her new sisters. There was an emptiness within Medusa that ached constantly, and it would never be eased without Ismene.

Pulling her headscarf further over her face, Ismene lingered in the shadows, and waited.

The agora thrummed with its usual hustle and bustle, making it easy to remain unnoticed in her hiding place within the colonnade. She had seen no sign of her father since she'd fled her family home, but Ismene could not shake off the habit of hiding from the threat of his wrath. If she was truly honest with herself, Thaddeus likely would not be seen in the city again, but if she let her thoughts linger on what she had done to him for longer than the briefest of moments her resolve might unravel completely. Now was not the time; she had to focus.

Ismene eyed each man as he walked past, scanning each face for the tell-tale scar that would confirm it was who she sought. It had taken days to even get this one small lead as to what might have happened to Medusa, questioning every man and woman who would entertain her rambling questions. Many ignored her, some even threatened her, and so Ismene had taken to lurking in the shadows, and only speaking to those most likely to have seen something useful to say.

Finally, a potential candidate came into view. A thickset middle-aged man meandered through the crowd. He wore the flat, broad hat of a farmer, but even with the brim obscuring his face a deep scar running across his nose and down into his dark beard was clearly visible. When he neared Ismene's hiding place, she stepped out in front of him.

'Harpalion?' she asked, holding up her palm so he stopped in place.

The man halted, but his face twisted into a scowl as he faced Ismene. 'Who are you?' he barked, annoyance evident in his rough voice. 'What do you want?'

Ismene stood up straight and met Harpalion's gaze. She had seen Medusa use her words to influence strong-willed men before; she could do the same. She had to.

'I hope you are the man I seek,' she began, hoping her tone was more flattering than desperate. 'A man of great importance to me. I heard tales of a strong, strapping farmer who saw something incredible, and he could only be you.'

Harpalion's face softened a little at that. 'I am him,' he said slowly, glancing over his shoulder as if to check if they could be overheard. 'Why is it you want to know what I saw?'

'The creatures you saw stole something very important to me. It's critical you tell me what you saw, and where they were headed.'

Harpalion raised a sceptical eyebrow. He studied Ismene for a moment. She resisted the urge to shrink into her headscarf and avoid his intense stare. This wasn't the time to hide. She set her jaw, squared her shoulders, and met his gaze.

'Please.' She leaned closer and placed a hand on Harpalion's arm. 'This is important.'

His frown flattened, and a glint of sympathy briefly glittered across his eyes. 'Fine,' he huffed, his voice a little lighter now. 'But come, let us speak somewhere quieter.'

Pressing a firm hand on her elbow, Harpalion steered Ismene through the crowded agora. The press of so many people so close together was overwhelming, but Harpalion guided them through with confidence, and the mass of traders, travellers, and officials parted to let them through willingly. Many of them nodded at the farmer in acknowledgement, or offered a short greeting.

'You are well-known here,' Ismene commented as they approached a quiet corner of the open-air region of the agora. A handful of politicians milled around between the government buildings, wealthily-dressed men who wouldn't look twice at someone such as her, but otherwise there was relative privacy.

'I often sell my crops here.' Harpalion shrugged, and gestured to a nearby stone bench.

Ismene sat in silence, anticipation bubbling in her chest. This was it. After many days of unanswered questions and half-heard gossip, she would finally know her path.

Harpalion sat beside her, a respectful distance away. 'So, you want to know what I saw, Miss…?'

'Ismene.'

He nodded. 'Not many have believed my account – they called me mad, said that I was seeing things – and I have a respectable reputation to uphold, so I would ask for your discretion, Ismene.'

'Of course.'

Harpalion glanced around once more before continuing. 'Monsters. Two of them. Hideous winged creatures flying over Miletus with a woman in their arms.'

Ismene's chest tightened. 'A woman?' She leaned closer, her heart pounding. 'Describe her, please.' Harpalion frowned and Ismene tried to steady herself. She didn't want to frighten him away by appearing too eager. 'It might be the person I'm looking for. Please, go on.'

Harpalion rubbed his chin, his thick, calloused fingers picking at his curled beard. 'I did not get a good look at her,' he mused. 'Her captors were large, inhuman things, and she was like a babe in their arms. This part may sound mad, but even from my farm I could make out a head of snakes on each of them.'

*Snakes.*

The few witnesses who had been willing to speak to Ismene had told panicked tales of a dreadful snake-haired woman turning innocent people to stone. Perhaps she had been one of these two winged monsters.

'Do you remember anything about the woman they carried at all? Any detail, however insignificant, might help me recognise her.'

Harpalion's eyebrows furrowed. He seemed to be genuinely trying hard to remember what he could for Ismene. It was the first real act of kindness she had experienced since she last saw Medusa, and that thought warmed and broke her heart in equal measure.

'I seem to remember she did not wear the clothes of a peasant,' he considered. 'Like I said, I saw little of her, so do not take this as truth, but I swear I noticed the glint of beads and jewellery. Fine things, you know. What the upper classes wear.'

Ismene's pulse quickened. Medusa had been wearing beads that morning – she had seen them on the naos floor.

*It's her – it has to be!*

'And where were they going?' she asked, her words coming out in a frantic rush. 'Which direction?'

'South-west.' Harpalion responded almost as quickly. 'I studied them for some time, until they disappeared on the horizon over the sea. From the direction they were going... I would say they were headed to Krete.'

*Krete?*

It was farther than Ismene had ever dreamed of travelling, but not impossible. Krete was a place of legend itself. It was the birthplace of Zeus and a hive of commerce and political manoeuvring; Ismene had heard many of her father's customers speak of its bustling ports and magnificent palaces. If Medusa herself couldn't be found there, no doubt there would be witnesses to the flight of her two monstrous captors.

'Thank you.' Ismene grasped Harpalion's hands in hers, not caring who saw or what they thought. 'Thank you so much! You've done more for me than you know.'

Harpalion pulled his hands back but Ismene noticed the flush of pink in his cheeks and the shy smile curving his lips. 'You are most welcome. I hope you find what you seek.' He cleared his throat and some of his previous rough demeanour returned. 'Now, if you don't mind, I have several traders I need to see before I return to the farm. Good day, and gods bless you.'

Before Ismene could respond, Harpalion stood and marched off, melting back into the crowd as if he had never been there to begin with. She stared after him, a thousand butterflies fluttering in her chest.

*Krete.*

She would find a ship, sail to Knossos, and begin her search.

Ismene knew she had less than a one in a million chance of finding Medusa, but as long as a chance remained, she would chase after it.

A brisk wind blew from the sea, swirling up the cliff and whipping the fabric of Medusa's chiton around her legs and ankles. She took a deep breath, feeling the sharp salt sting the back of her throat, and shuddered. How long would it take for the memories to fade, for Medusa to taste the tang of sea air without feeling Poseidon's body pressed against hers, his hot breath creeping across her skin? She shook her head, forcing her mind back to the present. Holding her arms out wide, she stepped closer to the cliff's edge and felt the wind wash over her. The cold bit into her flesh, but it reminded her she was alive, and that was something to be grateful for, at least.

The sun was setting, its oranges and pinks bleeding over the tumultuous waves. Her sisters would be expecting Medusa back for supper soon, but she could not bring herself to go back. Her quarters in the small ruined temple they called home had become a testament to her failure, littered with petrified creatures she had been unable to save from her evil gaze. They seemed to watch her, reminding her of the vile creature she had become, of her weakness in not being able to harness what limited power she possessed.

Until she could control herself, Medusa could not join her sisters when they ventured from the island to hunt or forage. If she turned an unsuspecting farmer or one of his animals into stone, their presence would be revealed, which could bring danger to their secluded home. The sisters were powerful, yes, but greater powers existed beyond their island, and they would not risk leading anyone here. Until the day she mastered her sight, Medusa was trapped, like an animal too unruly to be allowed out of its cage.

But it was not just her confinement that weighed on Medusa's shoulders. Every time she stole the life from another living creature, her heart broke a little more. She was no longer the acclaimed priestess, offering the comfort of prayer or the wisdom of the Goddess to whoever needed her most; she was a monster. An unholy demon even her divine sisters could not save. She was not sure how much longer she could bear it.

A pang of sharp pain struck her abdomen, and Medusa bent over almost double. Ripples of nausea rippled through her gut.

'Gods…' she whispered to herself, sucking in air in a vain attempt to soothe the sudden cramps. 'What new curse is this?'

She tried to straighten, but hot pain wormed through her insides, and she folded in on herself, breathing heavily.

Something was wrong – whether she liked it or not, Medusa needed to return to her sisters.

She turned away from the clifftop and stumbled inland, towards their temple home. Each step sent a wave of pain crashing over her until she could barely walk. Black spots flared in her vision, growing larger until everything went dark. She fell to her knees and crashed onto the ground, grasping at the soft grass under her fingers.

'Sisters...' she managed to whisper before unconsciousness claimed her completely.

Something cold pressed against Medusa's forehead, and her eyelids fluttered open. The shining, almost-black eyes of Euryale met hers, and relief flashed across the Phorcydes' face.

'You are awake,' Euryale said softly, brushing gentle fingers across Medusa's cheek.

'What happened?' Medusa's head felt thick, and heavy. The pain in her core was now a dull ache. Unpleasant, but manageable.

She eased herself upright and realised she was back at the temple, on the makeshift cot in her quarters.

'We found you out by the cliffs,' Euryale responded, passing a cup to Medusa. It was full of cool water, and Medusa drank deeply, relishing in the soothing coldness as it slipped down her throat. 'You had collapsed.'

'What happened, little sister?' Stheno stood in the doorway, concern creasing her brow. 'Did something hurt you?'

Medusa raised a hand to her head, quickly pulling it back as her fingertips brushed a writhing serpent. She was still unused to them, and she still hated them. 'No...' she said slowly, recalling the circumstances of her fall. 'I was struck with a sudden pain and sickness, and could not make it back to you both.'

'Pain?' Euryale asked, motioning for Medusa to keep drinking. 'Where is this pain?'

Medusa waved a hand across her abdomen, and Euryale frowned. A silent look passed between her and Stheno.

'What?' Medusa asked, unease creeping up her spine. 'What is the matter?'

Euryale opened her mouth, but Stheno spoke before she could.

'Nothing.' Stheno strode to the cot and gently pushed Medusa's shoulders so she was lying down again. 'You need rest, that is all.' Stheno smiled, but it did not quite meet her ebony eyes. Her soft lips brushed against Medusa's forehead, and she whispered softly in her ear. 'Please try to sleep.'

Stheno blew out the candle by Medusa's cot, and darkness flooded the room. A whisper sang in the dark, not meant for her ears but impossible to ignore.

'Sister, I need to speak with you.'

The two sisters swept out of Medusa's quarters, leaving her alone, and unsettled.

Sleep came very slowly.

Knossos was overwhelming.

Miletus was a thriving port city – one of the greatest in Ionia, by all accounts – but Knossos was *grand*. Crowds of people milled about the streets, weaving between impressive multi-storey buildings adorned with colourful frescoes depicting scenes of revelry and ritual, often including fantastical animals Ismene had never heard of before. There seemed to be as many women as men milling about the narrow streets. They wore strange patterned dresses and did not cover their heads and hair as most women did in Miletus. The Palace of Knossos itself towered over everything, a great sprawling complex of buildings, colonnades and courtyards on the hill which overlooked the city.

Ismene had been in the city for a few days, and the currency she and Medusa had stashed away for their escape was beginning to dwindle. Finding lodgings and food in such a large city was simple enough, but if she didn't find Medusa soon, she would no longer be able to sustain herself.

As the sun dipped towards the horizon on her fifth day in Knossos, Ismene wandered down the cobbled street towards the cramped boarding house she would be calling home that night. Hunger growled in her gut and a dull ache throbbed in her feet, but she would not find much comfort that night. A long day exploring for rumours in and around the bustling Knossos marketplace had been fruitless, and as yet another day drew to an end with no success, the determination that had driven her to this unfamiliar island was beginning to waver.

Ismene forced herself to keep moving. There was food in her room, and though stale bread and old goat's cheese was not a very appealing prospect, she needed to eat. She walked on, distracting herself from her aches and pains by looking at the great stone walls rising up on either side of her. Even in this unassuming area of the city, brightly coloured plaster decorated the stone, repeating patterns of blue, red and yellow. Ismene swept her gaze over them, following a beautiful series of intricate circles upwards until she found herself staring up at the sky.

Despite the lingering dusk, an array of stars was already beginning to wink into existence. Astraeus must favour the people of Krete, blessing them with starlight before night had truly arrived. In any other circumstance, Ismene would be enchanted by her surroundings. Knossos was truly beautiful, and the Kretan way of life fascinated her, but time was slipping by, and her current tactics were bringing her no closer to finding Medusa.

She needed to be bolder.

So far, Ismene had been sticking to the shadows, listening to groups of citizens as they browsed the marketplace, or left the temple following worship, or gathered for discussions. So far, all she had gleaned was that there was no public outcry from witnessing two winged monsters tear across the sky. It was tempting to assume Medusa's captors had not passed by the Kretan coast as Harpalion had hypothesised, but something in her gut told Ismene otherwise. If she had learned one thing from her investigations in Miletus, it was that these rumours were not always rife amongst the upper classes. It was in another area of society where she would find the information she needed.

A fresh sense of purpose swept over her, and Ismene's steps quickened, a plan already forming in her mind.

The midday sun beat down on Ismene's head, her scarf doing nothing to protect her skin from the heat, or her nose from the acrid dry dust being kicked up off the road. The mule she was struggling to ride lurched to a stop, and she had to cling to its short mane to prevent herself from toppling over its head and onto the ground.

'This is far as I go, miss,' the old farmer beside her announced gruffly, coming to a stop on his own mount. 'The quarry is another mile or so onwards. Follow the road on foot, and you'll find it, no problem.'

'Thank you so much.' Ismene knew she had been lucky to negotiate this much from the only stranger who would entertain her questions at the market, and didn't try to push for further assistance. She tried and failed to gracefully dismount her mule, struggling against the bags of supplies pressing up against her back. The farmer hopped down with no difficulty and offered an arm up to her. She accepted it gratefully, clutching against it as she tumbled to her feet.

'Take care now,' he said as Ismene found her balance and released him from her grip. 'I hope you find what you're looking for.'

Before she could respond, he turned away and led his two mules off the road onto a dirt track towards a small farmhouse surrounded by olive trees. Ismene took a deep breath, and a luxurious woody and earthy scent flooded her nostrils. Beyond the olive trees there must be fields of herbs growing nearby. Ismene could pick out hints of thyme, wild sage, and something else she couldn't quite identify. It was no surprise; Krete was known for its vast array of medicinal herbs and flowers, and she didn't doubt there was a wealth of flora she didn't even know existed that flourished on this island. It saddened Ismene to leave the relative lushness of the farmer's grove for a barren limestone quarry, but it was necessary to find the answers she desperately needed.

Ismene was dead on her feet by the time she reached the quarry. True, it was only a mile's walk, but with the hot sun bearing down on her, and the sandals on her feet being entirely inappropriate for such travel, it was a slow and uncomfortable trek.

The dry earth opened up ahead of her into a huge plateau of white stone. Diggers scurried over its surface like lines of ants, carrying freshly cut blocks which Ismene supposed would be piled up and transported to Knossos or some other great town, where a wealthy landowner would build himself a palace or grand villa.

Small groups of workers rested by the quarry's edge under the shade of a tree, enjoying a brief moment of respite before their next shift. Wearing only ragged loincloths, most bore the sun-darkened skin of workers used to labouring outdoors, but some appeared lightly burned and swayed a little on their feet, unused to such extended periods under the sun. These must be the servants sent from Knossos itself that she had been told about, plucked from the workshops and merchants' stores and forced to labour at the quarry, where the need was greatest.

Such people had no choice in where they worked – they held no rights of their own and would go wherever their masters sent them. And if the king or some other powerful man directed their masters to have their servants work at the quarry, that's where they went.

Ismene felt for them. Life under her father's rule had not been easy, but she'd always been comfortably housed and well-fed as an artisan's daughter. These men had likely never known comfort. They were the lowest-status members of society, and yet without them, society itself couldn't function. They kept every aspect of life running, quietly going about their work on the periphery of the wealthy and powerful, and in doing so, they knew things no one else did.

Ismene had tried to speak to servants within Knossos, but with so many sent to the quarries, what few workers remained in the city were either too busy or too close to their masters to speak with privately.

The quarry, however, was a place thrumming with conversation. People spoke to each other as they dug, chatted as they rested and ate, and slept side by side in the make-shift campsites encircling the site.

If anyone had seen two supernatural beings flying over Krete recently, it was likely one of these men knew about it.

Ismene hurried towards the nearest cluster of workers, but was almost immediately halted as a gruff voice called out to her.

'You there! Woman!'

A sturdy, bare-chested man wearing a rough, dirt-stained perizoma sauntered over to Ismene from where he had been standing in a small group of other men. As he drew closer, a pang of anxiety struck Ismene when she spotted the cruel smirk on his face.

'What is a respectable-looking woman like you doing here?' he sneered, stroking his thick, dark beard. Ismene drew her headscarf further down her face as the stranger looked her up and down. 'Looking for a strong man to show you a good time?'

'No,' she replied, cringing at the meekness of her voice. She had not come all this way to revert back to cowering before an overbearing man. 'I'm here to ask some questions to the workers.'

'Questions?' The man barked a harsh laugh that turned Ismene's stomach. 'Hear that, boys?' he called to his gaggle of comrades lurking nearby. 'The woman has questions for us.'

A gangly man with a bald head and a scar running down the side of his skull approached, his dark eyes fixed on Ismene. 'I bet I've got some answers for her.' He laughed, licking a thin pair of lips that were cracked from many days working under the sun.

'What's your name, girl?' the first man asked, grabbing Ismene's arm before she could move away. His grip was strong, his thick fingers digging into her skin so hard it hurt. 'I bet me and Nikandros can give you everything you need.'

'Let go of me,' Ismene demanded, pulling back and wincing as her skin tugged against the man's vice-like grip. He raised his hand and yanked her closer, grinning at how easily she fell forward.

'Don't go damaging her, Timon,' the man Ismene assumed to be Nikandros spat, taking hold of Ismene by the shoulder and tugging her towards himself. 'She'll be no good if you've broken her before we've even started.'

Ismene's blood ran cold.

*Started what?*

'I saw her first,' Timon growled through gritted teeth. 'I'll do what I like.'

'That so?' Nikandros retorted, drawing himself to his full height so he stood above the shorter, stockier man. 'Fancy trying it?'

The two men glared at each other, two predators ready to fight over their captured prey. Ismene's skin crawled where she felt their fingers digging into her flesh, neither ready to relinquish their grip on their prize.

Ismene seized her chance, swinging her leg forward with as much force as she could muster, and striking Timon between his legs. He buckled, groaning, and Ismene twisted out of the other man's grasp and ran.

A jolt of pain tore through her scalp as she was jerked back by the hair and thrown onto the hard ground, a plume of dust billowing around her.

'Where do you think you're going, girl?' Nikandros snarled, grabbing Ismene by the wrist and pulling her roughly to her feet. 'You've got fight in you, I'll give you that. I reckon you'll be a lot of fun.' He winked, and cold dread slithered up Ismene's spine. 'You can go second,' he said to a winded Timon, who was bent over double, gasping for breath. 'I don't think you're up to much right now, are you?'

Nikandros tugged at Ismene, dragging her towards where a few men were still gathered by the quarry's edge, chattering excitedly amongst themselves when they saw their friend had a woman in tow. She struggled in his grip, twisting and pulling with all her strength, but time working in the quarry had given this man power far beyond what Ismene could muster.

'Halt!' an authoritative voice called out, and Nikandros stopped dead. 'What do you think you are doing?'

Nikandros turned and stood frozen in place as another man approached. Unlike Ismene's attackers, this man wore a fine linen chiton pinned at the shoulders, and Ismene's stomach leapt as she spotted a multi-tailed scourge tucked into the belt around his waist.

'Well?' the man asked, hard eyes moving between Nikandros and Timon, one sceptical eyebrow raised. 'Can either of you explain why you worms thought you could lay your hands on my *wife*?'

*Wife?*

Nikandros blanched. 'Apologies, Master Belos.' He let go of Ismene as if her touch scalded him. 'We didn't know, I swear we didn't.'

Belos stepped forward, placed a firm but gentle arm around Ismene's shoulders, and pulled her close to him. 'You shouldn't *have* to know.' His tone was dark, completely at odds with the tenderness of his fingers clutching Ismene by his side. With his other hand, he drew the scourge from his belt, and Nikandros and Timon both dropped to their knees.

'Please,' Timon begged, all his prior bravado gone. 'Have mercy.'

Ismene stiffened as Belos held up the scourge as if inspecting the plaited leather ropes. 'Would you have shown this woman mercy?' he asked, his words hard and dripping with venom. 'Would you have released her if she begged, as you do now?'

The two kneeling men looked at each other, grimacing as if measuring up the punishment they might receive if they told a blatant lie or admitted to their planned cruelty.

'I did not think so.'

Belos raised his arm high and Ismene clenched her eyes shut. An ear-splitting crack, followed immediately by a gut-wrenching scream. And then another, and another. Ismene trembled as Belos doled out his punishment, not daring to open her eyes even when she heard the hurried footsteps of the two whimpering men fading away.

'It is all right,' a much warmer iteration of Belos' voice murmured into her ear. 'They are gone.'

Belos released her from his embrace, and Ismene looked up at the man who had saved her, the man who had unleashed cruel discipline on two men, and yet regarded her with kind eyes and a sincere smile.

'Why did you do that?' she asked, her heart still pounding.

Belos shrugged. 'I had to punish them. It would do no good to let thugs like those two think they can behave however they like.'

'No,' Ismene replied, her stomach turning from how flippantly Belos referred to his brutal actions. 'Why did you call me your wife?'

'Oh.' A shy laugh escaped Belos' lips, and his bronze cheeks seemed to flush. 'It was the first thing I could think of to get them to release you. I hope you are not offended, Miss...?'

'Ismene. And... no, not offended at all.' She felt her own face heating. 'Thank you.'

Belos smiled, and Ismene could not believe those kind eyes were the same ones that had  instilled such fear in two strong, dangerous men. 'Let me escort you back to the road,' he said, offering his arm for Ismene to take. 'It is not safe for you here.'

'No.'

Belos raised an eyebrow at Ismene's response, but instead of arguing, he simply crossed his arms and waited for her to continue.

'I'm sorry, your protection is appreciated, truly, but I have questions I must ask your workers urgently. I can't leave yet,' she said.

'I must insist.' Belos' voice was firmer now, more akin to the quarry master Ismene had seen addressing his workers. 'You have seen what happens to lone women in places such as this. Naming you as my wife will only do so much for so long, and the other foremen are not as kind as I am.'

'I'm afraid *I* must insist,' Ismene replied, instilling as much authority into her own voice as she could, although it was nothing like she had heard Belos manage. 'I'm looking for someone, someone more important to me than anything else in the world, and I think your workers could help me find them. Please, Belos,' she pleaded, taking his calloused hand in hers and looking deep into his umber eyes. 'I will do this with or without your help, but without will be much harder.'

Belos took a deep breath and raked a hand through his dark cropped curls. Ismene held his hand tight, her pulse racing. She was too close to be turned away now. He had to help her, he just had to.

'Fine,' he muttered, and Ismene's heart leapt into her throat. 'But as soon as you get what you need, you will leave and get far away from this place, all right?'

'Oh, thank you!' Ismene practically jumped with delight, still clinging on to Belos' hand. 'Thank you so much.'

Belos nodded and hooked his arm through hers. 'Come, I think I know someone who will prove useful to you.'

Acrid liquid burned down Medusa's throat and every instinct in her body screamed at her not to swallow, but she forced it down.

'Good, little sister. Keep drinking.'

The foul-tasting tea sent Medusa's stomach roiling, but Euryale insisted she drink it twice daily to soothe her cramping and stave off her fainting spells. It helped a little, but Medusa could tell from the concerned looks that passed between her sisters every time she drank it that it was not working as well as they expected. Each day she grew weaker, and although she continued attempting to control the power of her gaze, the two sisters kept a close watch on her at all times, and ushered her home at the first sign of fatigue. She was ravenously hungry most of the day, but each time she ate, the food tasted like ash and swallowing just a mouthful tied her stomach in knots.

'I detest this drink,' she grumbled as Euryale withdrew the empty cup from her lips.

A small smile tugged at Euryale's lips. 'I know you do, but trust us, sister, it is good for you.'

'Is it?' The heat in Medusa's words made Euryale recoil, but she continued regardless, her frustration finally bubbling over. 'I am not blind, sisters. Nor am I stupid. I know you worry about me, and I know your remedies are not curing me of whatever ailment I carry.'

'Medusa, please.' It was Stheno's turn to speak, now. She strode into the room from where she had been lurking by the doorway, and knelt beside Medusa's seat. The three sisters had taken to spending their evenings in the central hall of their dilapidated temple, seated on simple benches around the hearth. 'If you continue to drink—'

'No.'

Stheno raised an eyebrow. 'No?'

Medusa sighed. 'Forgive me, sisters, but I would like to know the truth. I know I am deeply indebted to both of you. You rescued me in my time of need, you welcomed me into your home, and even now, you care for me and protect me as one of your own. For all of that I am truly, deeply grateful. Please believe me when I say that.'

Stheno's face was neutral, but she nodded, appearing to appreciate Medusa's thanks.

Euryale took Medusa's hand in hers, wrapping her long fingers around and squeezing it tightly. 'We *do* consider you our own, little sister. We love you as if we had been sisters always.'

Medusa could not help but smile at that. She did not know what she had done to deserve such kindness and affection from these two remarkable divine beings. 'As do I.' She blinked back the tears pricking the backs of her eyes. 'But if you truly believe me to be your sister, I beg of you to be honest with me. My illness is not what it appears, is it?'

Euryale and Stheno looked at each other, Euryale's eyes shining with what Medusa thought could be a request for permission. Finally, Stheno nodded, and Euryale's gaze fell back on Medusa.

'You are right,' she said slowly. Medusa could tell she chose her next words carefully. 'Your... *illness* is not dissipating as we would expect, even with our herbal remedies and our divine influence on them. We are concerned, but...'

'We did not want to worry you any more than was necessary.' Stheno cut in. 'Without knowing the full nature of the malady, it could be dangerous to put you under additional stress.'

Medusa sighed. She wanted to be angry with her sisters, but how could she, when they only had her best interests at heart in everything they did? 'Is there nothing you can do?'

Euryale frowned. 'There may be *one* thing we can try. A ritual that—'

'Euryale!' Stheno hissed, her dark eyes wide. 'Be quiet!'

'What?' Medusa asked, her gaze flitting between the two sisters. 'What is it?'

'A ritual,' Euryale continued, ignoring Stheno's protestations. 'We can push a fraction of our magic into you, and probe for signs of supernatural injury or sickness. It should work, but it is somewhat dangerous.'

'Highly dangerous!' Stheno shouted, her usually low voice becoming shrill. 'Such magic is difficult to control, and if we infuse you with just a fraction too much of our power it could do irreparable damage. Unlike us, you are mortal, little sister. We do not know if you could handle such power. It might even kill you.' She shook her head and crossed her arms in defiance. 'No. I will not allow it.'

'*Please*, sister,' Medusa pleaded. She rose from her seat, but before she could take a single step towards Stheno, her vision began to sway and her knees buckled beneath her. She crumpled into Euryale's arms, who gently returned her to her seat. 'I cannot carry on like this,' Medusa whimpered, her energy already drained from the small amount of effort expended. 'I would rather risk injury than remain ignorant and gradually waste away into nothing.'

Stheno stared down at Medusa, her mouth a grim line but her eyes flashing as emotions warred within her.

'Stheno,' Euryale murmured, moving to her sister's side and placing a hand on her arm. 'She has made her choice. We should at least try to get answers for her.'

Stheno closed her eyes and took a deep breath, the green vipers atop her head hissing softly in the silence. 'I know you think me stern, even unreasonable at times.' Her eyes opened, and Medusa was surprised to see them glistening with tears. 'But it is only because I could not bear to lose you.' Her gaze shifted between Medusa and Euryale. 'Either of you.'

Stheno strode to Medusa and knelt so they were eye to eye. 'Euryale and I are not the only progeny of our divine father, but his children are spread far and wide, and we are not immune to loneliness. When we sensed you come into being, it filled our hearts with joy to learn we had a new sister to welcome into our small family here, and it would break my heart to lose you just as we have gotten to know you.'

Tears fell freely down Stheno's cheeks now, and seeing her usually stoic sister so troubled tore Medusa's heart in two. She cupped Stheno's face and brushed a tear away with a small thumb. 'Thank you, sister,' she whispered, swallowing down a sob of her own, 'but you do not need to fret. I trust you both completely, and I know you will keep me safe in this ritual. You won't lose me, I promise.'

A small chuckle fell from Stheno's lips. 'While I wish I could hold you to that promise, it will be on our shoulders to make it so.' She took Medusa's hand from her cheek and pressed her lips against the back of it. 'But I know you seek answers, and I will deliver them to you, if that is what you desire.'

Medusa smiled. 'It is. Thank you, sister. And thank you for your faith – it means everything.'

'No harm will come to you while I am by your side, little sister. I will ensure it is so.' Stheno rose and stepped back, her usual controlled demeanor returning. 'You should rest now. Tomorrow we will conduct the ritual.'

Soft candlelight flickered in the darkness, casting eerie shadows on the marble walls surrounding them. Medusa lay in the centre of the chamber on a bed of cypress and cyclamen, their fresh scents bringing new life to the forgotten temple the sisters called home.

Stheno and Euryale knelt at either side of her, eyes closed and fingers pressed gently against the flesh of her arms.

'Are you ready, little sister?' Euryale said softly, her voice soothing and honey-sweet. 'We will soon infuse you with our magic.'

Medusa's heart raced in her chest, but she nodded. 'Yes.' Her voice was barely a whisper, but her sisters heard it, and nodded in turn.

'Remain still,' Stheno instructed. 'This will hurt a little, but you must not move.'

Medusa steeled herself as her sisters' fingers pressed harder into her arms. Their long nails broke into the flesh, and she fought the urge to cry out at the sudden, sharp pain.

'Be calm,' Stheno murmured, trance-like.

The pain in Medusa's arms was overwhelmed with a new sensation. A strange heat blossomed from the small wounds and travelled up towards her heart. It pooled in her chest before spreading further, seeming to probe every inch of her. She tried to remain motionless as liquid fire explored, snaking down her torso and burning down her thighs.

Euryale and Stheno's brows creased in confusion, and Medusa felt the heat gather in her abdomen. It swirled in her gut, prompting a surge of pain in the depths of her core. The two sensations warred against each other, and Medusa fought to not cry out as the pain swelled to a new level of agony. She gritted her teeth and closed her eyes, reminding herself over and over again that she trusted her sisters; they would not harm her.

The heat winked out, and Stheno and Euryale gasped in unison, as if they had just surfaced from deep underwater and were desperate to refill their lungs. Medusa remained still, her own chest heaving as the pain in her abdomen slowly dissipated. Her eyes flickered open and she saw her two sisters unmoved, still kneeling by her side, staring at each other with unreadable expressions.

'What is it?' Medusa asked, easing herself into a sitting position. Her sisters didn't seem to hear her. 'Euryale,' she said, putting a hand on her sister's arm to pull her out of her stupor. 'Please, you're frightening me.'

Euryale's attention snapped to her, then, and Medusa recoiled at the alarm blazing in her large, dark eyes. Her golden-haired sister was the one who calmed her, who reassured her all would be well when things appeared most bleak, and to see her so shaken turned Medusa's blood cold.

'What?' she repeated. 'Tell me, please!'

Stheno cleared her throat, drawing both her sister's focus. 'We sensed something,' she began.

'Some*one*,' Euryale interjected.

A shiver ran down Medusa's spine and she wrapped her arms around her torso. 'What do you mean?'

'Poseidon.'

The name hung in the air like a spectre. A torrent of memories flooded Medusa's mind. She could feel his breath on her neck and the cold seeping into her skin as she lost everything to him.

The chamber seemed to shrink around her as Medusa's throat tightened, panic building in her chest. 'What... what...' She could not breathe, she could not think. Darkness encroached upon her vision, threatening to swallow her.

'Medusa.' Euryale's gentle hand on her arm brought Medusa back to the present. 'You are with your sisters. You are safe.'

She blinked, and her surroundings fell back into their rightful place. The candlelight returned, the shadows withdrew to the corners of the chamber, and Medusa beheld the concerned faces of her dear sisters.

'Here.' Euryale handed her a cup of water. Medusa took it with trembling hands and took a small sip. It was tepid, but she welcomed the distraction.

'Take your time,' Stheno murmured, rubbing a hand on Medusa's upper back. It soothed her somewhat, but did not still the roiling in her stomach. Poseidon was there, inside of her... it was almost enough to make her vomit. She needed to know more; there must be a way to purge herself of him.

'What...' She paused, struggling to verbalise the confusion swirling in her mind. 'How is... *he* within me? Am I cursed? Did he poison me with his magic?'

A look passed between Euryale and Stheno which flooded Medusa with anxiety. Whatever they knew, they did not want to reveal it to her. A small spark of irritation ignited in her gut. While she treasured the relationships she had developed with her sisters, and welcomed the protection they offered, they did not need to handle her like she was a child, too naive and innocent to receive bad news.

'Tell me,' she demanded, staring intently at each sister in turn. 'I know you care for me, sisters, but I am not so fragile I cannot hear the truth.'

Silence stretched between the three women, but Medusa did not relent. She would wait as long as was necessary to get an answer. Finally, Stheno relented.

'Medusa,' she said quietly, taking her hand and squeezing it tight. 'You are with child.'

Eyes closed and standing perfectly still, Perseus listened.

A brisk northerly wind blew through the trees, shaking the branches. He strained to hear the whispered wisdom in the rustling leaves, but he could make out nothing more than noise.

'Concentrate,' he whispered to himself, remembering the advice he had received at Delphi. In the fabled oak grove of Dodona, he would find the answers he sought. He simply had to listen to the words of the trees.

Perseus took a deep breath, let it out slowly, and listened.

Still nothing.

'Damned trees!'

Perseus opened his eyes and glared at the ring of mighty oaks that surrounded him. The priestess at the Oracle of Delphi had been unable to disclose the location of the monster he sought, but assured him the divine oaks of Dodona would reveal his path. If only they would speak to him!

He tried once more to listen to the voices of the trees, but could only hear the same rustling as the breeze passed through their branches. Boiling frustration pulsed through him, and he threw back his head and cried out, 'Gods above, tell me how to find this snake-haired woman!'

The wind dropped, and the quivering leaves grew still. A dense silence fell over the grove, raising the hairs on the back of the young man's neck. He stood motionless, unwilling to break the unsettling quiet, until he noticed movement amongst the tree trunks.

A figure slipped between the mighty oaks, flitting between the trunks too quickly for Perseus to identify any details.

'Who goes there?' he called out, irritation lacing his voice. The priests had promised he would be undisturbed while he consulted the oracle. 'Show yourself!'

A low laugh resonated through the grove. It echoed from all directions. Perseus turned, eyes darting between trunks and through branches, searching for the elusive intruder. The laughter only grew louder as he moved, as if mocking him.

'Face me, you coward!'

The laughter receded, and a man stepped out from amongst the trees. He was tall, slender and smooth-faced, with a light mop of curls atop his head and wearing a finely embroidered chiton of green and gold.

'Greetings, brother,' the man announced, his voice smooth as silk. A small smirk twisted his lips, as if he was in a constant state of amusement. 'I believe you are in need of assistance.'

Perseus stared at this strange visitor. He bore the features of a man, but even from this distance, Perseus could sense a great power emanating from him.

'Who are you?'

That low laugh again. Now it was centred in one place, it was almost musical. 'You wound me, young Perseus,' the stranger said, clutching a hand to his chest. 'You do not recognise your divine kin?'

Perseus frowned. What was this stranger talking about?

'Here,' the man offered, with a sly wink. 'Let me help you.'

He waved his hand, and to Perseus' surprise, a golden staff appeared. Atop it were two magnificent wings, and around it were entwined two great, golden snakes. Every single Greek alive would recognise such a thing. There could no longer be any doubt as to the identity of its bearer.

'Hermes,' Perseus gasped. He dropped to one knee, bowing his head.

'Correct.' Hermes chuckled, and the crunch of acorns and fallen leaves signaled his approach. 'Good to see you have some reverence for your immortal family.'

Perseus raised his head at that. 'What do you mean?'

Hermes scoffed and looked off to his side, into the trees. 'Really, sister, you think this one is worthy of our aid?'

Sister? Who else could be—?

A woman stepped out from behind one of the great oaks, and Perseus gaped as he beheld her. Even taller than Hermes, bearing a gleaming shield and wearing a helmet of finely-polished bronze, it could only be the goddess of wisdom and warfare herself: Athena.

'Yes,' she responded, her tone stern. 'Although with the way he is gaping at us, I may begin to have doubts myself.'

'Lady Athena,' Perseus breathed. He cleared his throat and summoned a stronger voice. 'How may I be of service?'

Athena raised her eyebrows and approached slowly, appraising Perseus as she did so. 'You may stand, brother, for today it is we who will serve you.'

Perseus rose, his heart pounding. Two gods, offering to aid him – it was more than he could ever have imagined! One question tugged at the back of his mind, however.

'Forgive me, both of you, but why do you keep calling me brother?'

Athena frowned as Hermes let out another wry chuckle. 'Your mother did not tell you about your father?'

He shook his head. 'She told me very little,' he mused, 'only that he was with her for a brief time before departing, and that she never saw him again.'

Hermes cackled at that. 'She is no liar, at least,' he laughed. 'Father never did linger with his consorts for long.'

Father?

'Hermes!' Athena scolded, her grey eyes darting to the messenger god. 'You must show respect for the god-king.'

Realisation dawned on Perseus, then, and his heart leapt into his throat. 'You cannot possibly mean...' he choked out, barely daring to speak his next words aloud, 'that Zeus is my father?'

'Yes.' Athena nodded. 'He coupled with the mortal woman Danaë when she was imprisoned by your grandfather, and so you came into being.' She placed a firm hand on his shoulder, her grip unnaturally strong. 'And so, Perseus of Seriphos, you are our kin, a demi-god whose strength and courage outweighs that of any mortal man.'

A broad grin spread across the young man's face. This explained everything. He had always been physically superior to his peers. He won every foot race, could carry greater loads than any man he knew, and had a pleasing form men and women alike fawned over. Yet it had never been enough. All his life the wealthy landowners had looked down upon Perseus, seeing him as nothing but a poor fisherman whose status would never improve. The king saw him as a minor obstacle to overcome so he could get his hands on Perseus' mother, a woman so desirable the king of gods himself had courted her.

That would all change now. He was the son of Zeus, a brother to gods and goddesses, greater than any of those fools. He had left Seriphos a man, but would return a demi-god.

'I see this news pleases you, brother,' Hermes said, breaking Perseus out of his reverie.

'It does, my brother,' Perseus replied, clasping Hermes' hands in his own. 'Once I return to my homeland with the head of the monster I seek, I believe my life will be transformed due to this news. Thank you,' he turned to Athena, 'thank you both.'

The goddess, who until now had remained impassive, smiled. 'And this monster you seek,' she began, her cool voice gaining an unnerving sharpness, 'is why we are here.'

Eyes wide, Perseus could not hold back his excitement as he spoke. 'You know where she is?'

Athena's eyes became hard iron. 'No, but we can aid you.'

Disappointment rippled through Perseus, but he kept his expression neutral. He would not risk upsetting his newfound brethren. Olympians could be very generous, but they could be equally vengeful, and he did not wish to bring down any wrath upon himself. 'I will accept all aid you are willing to give,' he said carefully, eyeing each god in turn for their reaction.

'Good.' Athena smiled, but there was still ice in her gaze. 'With our assistance, you will not only find her, but you will defeat her.'

Perseus nodded. His prey might be a mortal woman, but she was also a demon, with a deadly gaze and perhaps more powers yet to be revealed. He would take any advantage he could get.

'First,' Hermes interjected, his joviality at odds with the seriousness of his sister, 'we have gifts to aid your journey.' He snapped his fingers, and his legendary winged sandals appeared in his hands. 'Here, to help you reach your destination swiftly.'

Hermes threw the sandals into the air, where they disappeared, reappearing a moment later on Perseus' own feet.

'And this,' he continued, waving a hand. A black hood appeared between his fingers. He flung it to Perseus, who snatched it from the air with a deft hand. 'I took from our uncle, lord of the underworld. Wear it and you will go unseen by mortals and gods alike.'

Perseus marvelled at the material as he held the hood in his hands. It was softer than the finest silk, and yet felt sturdy, like it would take a great deal of force to damage it.

'As for dispatching the monster,' Athena began, eyeing her divine brother with irritation at his performance, 'take this.' She handed over her bronze shield. 'Keep it polished to a fine sheen at all times. You will know when it is needed.'

Perseus took the shield, and marvelled at its craftsmanship. Up close, he could see the finely worked images all over its surface – great battles, unimaginable creatures, and fearsome beasts – and yet it shone like the sun itself. There was a great weight to it, but as he strapped it to his forearm he found he could bear it quite easily.

'Take this, also.' Athena produced a simple-looking leather satchel, which she hung from Perseus' shoulder. 'It may look like nothing, but it can hold far more than would be expected. If you expect to transport the... *gorgon's* head back to Seriphos, you will need to be able to transport it without risk.'

'And finally,' Hermes broke in, eyes sparkling with mischief, 'you will need a suitable weapon.'

'Thank you, brother.' Perseus gestured to the sheathed sword hanging from his belt, given to him by Dictys when he set off on his quest. It was a serviceable, if simple, blade, and must have cost a significant portion of the old man's meagre wealth. 'But I already have a weapon. It is plain and I am sure primitive by your standards, but it should be adequate to kill this creature.'

A burst of laughter erupted from Hermes, which rankled. It was not enough that Perseus was looked down upon in his homeland, but now the gods mocked him too?

'Oh, my dear boy, your innocence is wonderful.' Anger flared in Perseus' chest, but he held his tongue, and waited for the god to continue. 'She may not be alone, and her protectors are powerful creatures. You will want to kill quickly, and cleanly. Here.'

With a flourish, Hermes produced two curved, sickle-like blades, one in each hand.

Handing them over to Perseus, he said, 'these are *harpes,* sharper than any mortal blade. They will cut through flesh and bone swiftly and with ease. One strong swing is all you will need.'

Perseus nodded, and tied the two new weapons to his belt, one on each hip. They were remarkably light, but he could see the edges were razor sharp. Perseus had some experience with a blade – he had insisted on sparring with Dictys growing up so that he would not miss out on the training noble youths his age received – and he was sure he could take down his quarry with no trouble, but he would take every divine advantage he was offered. With these gifts from his godly siblings, Perseus could not fail. Soon, he would be presenting Polydectes with his prize, and Perseus could not wait to see the expression on the king's wretched face.

'Thank you both,' he said, bowing his head to first his brother, and then his sister. 'These gifts are beyond anything I could have dreamed of.' Flattery was received well, he noted as he watched the expressions soften on each of the gods' faces. He stored that fact in the back of his mind; it could be useful later. 'But how do I find this cursed woman?' he continued, 'Neither oracle has been able to provide that knowledge thus far, and you...' He swallowed, and chose his next words carefully. 'Even two as powerful as yourselves do not know her whereabouts.'

Athena's face shifted, a flicker of something between anger and embarrassment passing across her features. 'We do not,' she began, her voice so tight Perseus immediately regretted his choice. 'But we know who does.'

'Who? Tell me.' Perseus said a little too keenly. Heat flushed his cheeks; he had to remember that these were *gods*; he should not make demands of them. 'Please, sister, forgive my eagerness. I want nothing more than to seize the head of this monster.'

Athena's eyes flashed dangerously, and a sinister smile grew on her face. 'That is well, brother, because I desire nothing more than to see her exterminated.'

The goddess' dark gaze sent a shiver down Perseus' spine, but he did not need to respond, as Hermes gleefully offered up the information he desired.

'You should seek out the gorgons' *other* kin.' He laughed, mischief in his eyes. 'Although they may not be as willing to aid you as we were, little brother.'

'Other kin?' Perseus did not like the sound of that. 'There are more of these creatures?'

'Not quite.' Hermes grinned, offering no further explanation.

'You must seek out the Graeae,' Athena interjected, giving her divine brother an irritated glance. When Perseus showed no sign of recognition, she elaborated further. 'Three ancient immortal women, each almost as old as time itself. They dwell in a cave somewhere along the Mysian coast, where they live in solitude, sharing only one eye and one tooth between them.'

Perseus frowned. These... *women*, if they could even be called that, sounded repulsive. 'And they will reveal the location of the woman I seek?'

'Like the gorgon *monstrosities*,' Athena sneered, her face twisted in disgust, 'the Graeae are the children of the sea gods Phorcys and Ceto. They hold little power themselves, but they share a deep connection with their kin. They will know where their sisters are, and you will make them tell you.'

Perseus kneeled before her, and bowed his head. 'Thank you, dear sister. You have done me a great service, and I will be forever in your debt.'

Strong but slender fingers gripped Perseus by the chin, tilting his face upwards. Athena's eyes met his, glittering with cold fury.

'Slay this wretched creature,' she demanded. 'And, once your mission is complete, bring me her head.'

He nodded slowly. 'I swear, it will be done.'

The warm night breeze rustled through the grass, bringing with it the fragrant scent of the herbs growing nearby.

Ismene rolled over, the pleasant aroma doing nothing to help her fall asleep. After a painfully long day, she was grimy, exhausted and aching all over, but her mind would not stop racing.

Even under Belos' protection, it had taken some time to find quarry workers who would engage with her questioning, and even longer to tease out the answers she sought, but it would all be worth it soon.

One old man, Olus, seemed to be given some leeway by those in command, and so had been allowed to converse with Ismene for far longer than the younger workers. While others offered clipped, vague or even hostile responses, Olus was gentle and even eager to share his story.

He had seen them, the two winged women. And what's more, he had seen them more than once. Not only had they flown over the quarry as they absconded with Medusa – which several of the men could attest to, even if they were less than willing to divulge the details, apparently afraid of what retaliation might be in store – but he had seen them from a distance several times before. He could not be certain, but he believed they must have been visiting the fields of herbs that flanked the quarry and nearby farmland.

It wasn't much, but it was the greatest lead Ismene had found since leaving Miletus, and she practically buzzed with excitement when she left the quarry for what was hopefully the final destination in her hunt for the woman she loved.

Ismene rolled onto her back and stared up at the starry night sky. Lying on a thin mat with no other shelter to speak of, she was grateful for the balmy Kretan climate. She could have stayed at the workers' camp by the quarry, and would have been grateful for the modicum of comfort it offered, but Olus had warned her off. A lone, vulnerable woman surrounded by a large number of unsupervised men would not be safe.

Ismene shuddered at the memory of Timon and Nikandros, and what might have happened had Belos not been there to help her. She hadn't been safe at home with her father, she wasn't safe travelling alone... The only place she had ever felt safe was with Medusa, and until she found her again, she wasn't sure she would ever feel safe again.

A great gust of wind blew over the field, and every bird that had been resting in the trees took to the air and scattered. Ismene sat upright, anxiety roiling through her insides. She willed her heart to beat slower, for the pounding in her ears to abate so she could hear what was approaching.

Another gust swept over her, and then another, and another, and Ismene finally recognised them for what they were: wingbeats.

The monsters were here.

Ismene crouched amongst the long grasses and held her breath. Excitement mingled with terror in her gut as the wind continued to whip at her, pushing back her headscarf and freeing her mass of curls. Moments later, the creatures themselves appeared, their massive feathered wings beating the air as they lowered themselves to the ground and landed with more grace than Ismene could have imagined possible from their great size.

In other circumstances, Ismene would have found the two women fascinating. Despite the frightful nest of serpents atop each of their heads and the curled talons that served as their feet, they were quite striking. They stood tall and statuesque, the moonlight glinting off their dark eyes as they spoke to each other in hushed voices.

For a short while, Ismene simply watched as the two serpent-haired women collected herbs. They worked in near-silence, only picking certain plants out of the many varieties growing around them and carefully packing them away in small bags. She had expected them to be clumsy, hostile creatures, but they were nothing of the sort. They moved gracefully, helping each other find what they needed with tender touches and quiet words.

Ismene continued to observe the two creatures, entranced, until they ceased picking herbs, stood upright, and unfurled their wings once more. Panic erupted in her chest; she had been so focused on the women she hadn't moved once, and now they were about to leave before she had found out anything more about them.

One of the women beat her wings, sending gusts of herb-scented wind rolling towards Ismene, blowing her hair back over her shoulders. Without thinking, Ismene jumped up from her hiding place and stepped forwards. The winged woman turned and took off into the sky, but her companion didn't move. Her head shifted, and even in the gloom, Ismene felt her dark gaze land on her. She froze in place, heart crawling up her throat.

The woman walked towards Ismene, the hissing of the snakes atop her head growing louder with each step. The moonlight shimmered off their writhing golden bodies, and fear stirred in Ismene's chest. She stumbled back, desperate to escape the stare of this strange creature and her spitting serpents, but it was no good; the woman's strides outmatched Ismene's staggering steps, and she reached her easily.

'I... I...' Ismene stuttered, her voice dying in her throat under the winged woman's gaze.

The woman frowned and tilted her head as she looked down at Ismene, as if observing the strange behaviour of an unusual animal. Long fingers reached out and a gentle claw brushed Ismene's cheek.

A scream burst from Ismene's throat and she ran.

She sprinted blindly forwards, tears blurring her vision. Thorns and branches ripped at her chiton as she barrelled through trees and bushes, her lungs burning. Her foot struck something hard and she tumbled over, landing in the grass on her knees. She rolled over and hugged her legs to her chest, wide eyes staring in each direction for any signs of pursuit.

Ismene could hear nothing but her own ragged breathing. She covered her mouth and nose with her hands to stifle the sound, fear pulsing through her veins. A twig snapped somewhere behind her, and a fresh wave of terror shot up Ismene's spine.

The woman had followed her.

Ismene crouched as low as she could and prayed the long grass and shrubbery hid her from view.

*Oh gods, oh gods, oh gods.*

Sweeping footsteps sounded as the woman waded through the brush, getting closer.

Ismene held her breath. The steps slowed and her heart hammered in her chest. She braced for an attack, for the woman to leap on her and slash open her flesh or rip her throat out, but it never came. Instead, Ismene was buffeted with a sudden blast of air as the woman took to the sky. She watched as great wings lifted her into the night, carrying her southwards until she disappeared from view, lost between the stars.

A potent mix of relief and shame flooded Ismene, and she sagged forwards, her head in her hands. Fat, hot tears flowed down her cheeks. She had come face to face with one of the monsters she had been so desperately searching for, and instead of seizing the opportunity, she had fled.

Great, heaving sobs wracked Ismene's body. Waves of anger and despair tore through her. After all she had been through, despite how hard she had fought to escape her father, and how determined she had been to track down the woman she loved, she had crumbled in the end, and succumbed to fear once again.

*I failed.*

Ismene dug the heels of her hands into her eyes in a futile attempt to stem the flow of tears.

*I failed you, Medusa, and I will never forgive myself.*

Leaves crunched underfoot as Medusa wandered between the trees. She brushed her fingers along trunks and branches as she walked, savouring the feel of nature. So simple, so easy. There, with nothing else but the fresh, woody scent of the fig and pomegranate trees around her, she could forget everything else, and ignore the messy and complex whorl of emotions that plagued her day and night since she learned she was carrying Poseidon's child.

Autumn was almost over, and very few fruit hung from the trees, but that did not matter. Picking what remained of the year's harvest had in truth been a flimsy excuse to escape the watchful eyes of her sisters for a short time, and Medusa was almost certain they knew it. She appreciated their care and close attention, but since learning of her pregnancy it had increased ten-fold, and Medusa was beginning to feel suffocated.

Her hands wandered to her abdomen, and Medusa shuddered. Poseidon's child. The thought filled Medusa with horror and wonder in equal measure. The child of a *god*, growing inside her... It was almost unbelievable. But she knew it had to be true. Not only did Medusa have faith in her sisters' divine abilities, but as soon as they had uttered those words, every strange sensation afflicting her body suddenly made sense. The mere knowledge of her unborn child seemed to shift her bodily response, welcoming the divine intrusion rather than fighting against it.

Tentative fingers cradled her stomach, and a strange warmth bloomed under her touch. Despite the manner in which the child came into being, despite the horror that had followed its conception, despite the deep, conflicting emotions it elicited, Medusa already loved it. If this one good thing could come from all that had happened, she would cherish and protect it at all costs.

Cold drops of water hit Medusa's cheeks, pulling her back to reality. She looked up. Rain clouds had gathered while she was lost in thought and, judging by the dark grey shadows rippling through them, a storm was on its way. She looked down at the basket hanging from the crook of her arm – it held barely a handful of fruits. The rain was still light; she had time to gather more before the deluge.

No sooner had Medusa plucked a dangling fig from a low-hanging branch than the voices of her sisters rang out from across the grove.

'Medusa!' Euryale called, her voice muted by the branches rustling in the wind. It was tempting to ignore her sister, to pretend she heard nothing and savour being alone for just a little while longer.

'Medusa!' Stheno's commanding tone tore through the trees, and any hope of pretence evaporated.

'Here, sisters,' Medusa called back, dropping the freshly picked fig into her basket.

Euryale appeared between the trees, her golden head of serpents hissing softly. 'There you are,' she sighed, walking to Medusa and taking her gently by the elbow. 'It is raining, little sister. You should come inside before you catch a chill.'

'I'm fine,' Medusa insisted, but she allowed Euryale to lead her towards their home. 'The temperature is still mild, and I wanted to help with the final harvest.'

'Do not worry about that,' Euryale cooed, steering Medusa away from the fruit trees. 'We can easily provide for you, and the babe.'

Medusa frowned and unconsciously stroked her abdomen with her free hand. 'I value your protection, sister, but the babe is mine, and I cannot care for them sufficiently if I need constant care myself. I hope you do not think me ungrateful. I...' She took in a breath, unable to keep the quiver out of her voice as she spoke her next words. 'In the temple, I was the one who took care of the others. I drew up the schedules, I schooled the newer acolytes, I advised on rituals and ceremonies. I just... I need to feel useful again. For the sake of the babe, and for the sake of my own sanity. Do you understand?'

A small smile touched Euryale's lips. She halted, drawing Medusa to a stop with her, and took Medusa's hands. 'Of course I understand, little sister. You yearn for who you used to be – anyone could understand that. We coddle you because we are so deeply afraid of losing you, but that should not come at your expense. We will help you prepare for motherhood in whichever way you would prefer. However...' She glanced to her right, towards their temple home. 'You will need to be patient with Stheno. She waits for us a little way ahead, and while her heart is great, her temper is short, and you know how she likes to fuss.'

Euryale laughed, and Medusa could not help but join in. She loved Stheno dearly, but their other sister's stern demeanour never faltered, and Euryale's gentle teasing of her was a great source of amusement for herself and Medusa both.

As if sensing their mirth, Stheno called out from somewhere a short distance ahead, 'Sisters! The rain grows heavier – move quickly!'

Euryale did an exaggerated roll of her eyes before pulling a giggling Medusa forward. A moment of mirth was very welcome, but Medusa's mind did not stray far from the life growing inside her. As strong as her sisters were, they could not protect her child from the greatest danger it would face on this island: Medusa herself.

Until she mastered her gaze, Medusa could not hope to be a mother. Before, she had been testing herself because her sisters demanded it, but now there was a much more significant motivating force. If it guaranteed her unborn child's safety, she would practice each day and night until its birth.

She had a great deal of work to do.

Medusa's heart clenched as she placed the stone rabbit on the small shelf, nestled between a shrew and a small nightjar, similarly petrified. Each brought its own heartbreak, but as the child in her belly grew, so did the dread writhing through her gut.

'If I cannot control myself properly, the baby must be taken away from me.'

'Do not say that!' Euryale said from behind Medusa. Her gentle hands found Medusa's waist, and she drew her sister into her body, resting her face on her shoulder. 'Someone as loving and caring as you will make a wonderful mother.'

'Impossible.' Medusa closed her eyes and leaned her head back so it rested on Euryale's chest. The rhythmic thud of her sister's heartbeat soothed her somewhat, but it did not still the unease fluttering through her insides. 'A mother should not put their child in mortal danger. I am unfit.'

'Darling sister.' Euryale spun Medusa around and tilted her chin so their gazes met. 'You are not alone in this. You have two sisters who will help you raise this babe, and help protect them as if they were our own. No harm will come to them while they are with us.'

Medusa smiled, but her sister's words brought little comfort. Euryale and Stheno were powerful, but they could control Medusa's affliction no more than she could.

'Come,' Euryale continued, pulling away from Medusa and taking her by the hand. 'Stheno is brewing tea. It will calm you.'

With a solemn nod, Medusa followed her sister out of her chambers to their shared living quarters, where Stheno stood stirring a pot of tea which hung over the fire in the hearth. A strange but warming scent wafted through the space: floral yet savoury, with a slight bitterness underneath.

'What is that, sister?' Medusa asked as she lowered herself into a chair, a hand cradling her already-protruding belly. Her divine child was growing quickly. It was difficult to follow the passage of time in their isolated home, but it seemed months of growth had occurred in mere weeks.

'Erontas,' Stheno murmured, staring into the bubbling liquid as she stirred. 'A powerful herb from the island of Krete that will stave off sickness and strengthen both you and the child.' She closed her eyes and inhaled the vapour rising from the pot, and nodded. 'It is ready.'

Euryale helped Stheno ladle the steaming amber liquid into a small cup and handed it to Medusa. Tendrils of the complex aroma wrapped around Medusa, as if greeting her with a warm embrace.

'Let it soothe you,' Stheno said as she lowered herself onto the bench across from Medusa. Her gaze flitted between Medusa and Euryale, an uncharacteristic sense of uncertainty radiating from her.

Medusa frowned. 'What is it?' She lifted her cup, yet to take a sip of the fragrant tea. 'Is it this? Is it dangerous?'

A melodic laugh fell from Euryale's lips as she strolled past Medusa to sit by Stheno. 'Not at all, little sister. Stheno is right, it is good for you *and* the babe, and, we hope...'

Her eyes met Stheno's, who sighed and finished the thought on Euryale's behalf. 'We hope it will remove whatever it is that prevents you from controlling your gaze.'

A spark of anxiety shot up Medusa's spine. Her sisters could not know what troubled her deep down, what – despite their love and care, despite her own love for her sisters and her unborn child – kept her up at night. She forced out a response, her throat suddenly tight. 'How?'

'Sister,' Stheno began, taking the lead where Euryale could not, 'you have been through a great deal, and suffered much emotional stress. Your mind cannot be stilled, and so you cannot control your power. This tea will not only aid you physically, it will purge your mind of those memories that continue to haunt you.'

'No!'

Stheno and Euryale stared wide-eyed at Medusa. She had jumped out of her seat without realising, and the shattered remains of her cup lay strewn about the floor before her feet. Her chest heaved as she stared back at her sisters, her pulse throbbing in her ears.

'I... I apologise,' she breathed, struggling to bend over to collect the broken shards.

'Leave it.' Stheno's voice was firm, but not unkind. She rose from her seat and motioned for Medusa to sit. 'Do not strain yourself, little sister. Be seated, and I will bring you another cup.'

'I do not know that I want one,' Medusa replied slowly, her stomach fluttering. Images of Ismene's face floated before her eyes. 'There are memories that, while painful, I could not bear to lose.'

Stheno frowned at Medusa, clearly confused. 'You do not need to prove yourself to us, Sister. We know you have great strengths, but you need to let us help you. It does you no benefit to cling to past suffering.'

'It isn't that.' Medusa almost scoffed, but she knew her sister's words were in good faith. It was possible Stheno had never known love beyond the familial, and Medusa had never hinted at a romantic past. She could not bear to reopen wounds that, once brought to the surface once more, might never close again.

Euryale's dark eyes shone with sympathy. She motioned for both sisters to return to their seats before fixing her soft gaze back on Medusa. 'Tell us, little sister.'

Medusa swallowed down the lump forming in her throat, her mouth uncomfortably dry. 'I... I am not sure I can.'

'Please,' Euryale implored, 'until you share what is burdening you, your heart will never find peace, and you will never gain control of your gaze.'

'You can tell us, little sister,' Stheno added. 'We will not pass judgement. Nothing you say will diminish our fondness for you.'

Medusa's heart warmed at her sisters' concern, but it did not ease the tension in her chest. The time she had shared with Ismene was kept carefully locked away inside, to be treasured but never opened. Medusa was not sure she could bear the pain of reliving their love affair when she knew she would never see Ismene again.

'You have lost a lover.'

Medusa gaped at Euryale. Her sister's face was a picture of understanding: a small, sad smile on her full lips and her large, dark eyes glistening with sympathetic certainty.

'How did you know?' Medusa whispered, the sting of tears already pricking the backs of her eyes.

The golden serpents atop Euryale's head writhed and hissed. 'We were not always sheltered as we are now, little sister,' she said softly, a tinge of sorrow in her voice. 'I know the pain of a lost love, and I see it written all over your face.' Euryale reached out and offered a hand to Medusa, bridging the gap between them. Medusa leaned forward and took it gladly, and Euryale gave her a gentle squeeze before she continued. 'Why not start by telling us their name? If it is too painful to continue after that, we will ask no more.'

Taking a deep shuddering breath, Medusa nodded. A name. She could do that. Perhaps sharing something so small would ease her torment without opening the floodgate of painful memories she had been so afraid of releasing and drowning in.

'Her name is... Ismene.'

Before she could stop herself, Medusa was telling her sisters everything. How she had first stumbled upon Ismene at the temple, how she had convinced Thaddeus to let her apprentice with Medusa, how they had found themselves drawn to each other ever since, and their final plans to run away together before it was all snatched away. By the time she had finished speaking, her cheeks were raw with tears, her chest was heaving, and her sisters remained sat in stunned silence.

Finally, Euryale spoke. 'Thank you for sharing this, Sister. That is a very moving story, and I am truly sorry for the way that it ended.' There was deep sympathy in her voice, yet her eyes were like two dark saucers

– wide as if with great alarm. 'But, please, can you describe this Ismene to us again?'

That was not the question Medusa had expected after all she had said, but she complied, telling Euryale of Ismene's honey-coloured eyes, her soft chestnut curls, and the unusual scar that stretched across her cheek, which did not detract from her great beauty, but instead told the story of the strife she had overcome.

Her sisters listened with great interest, Euryale especially so, and once Medusa had finished she rose from her seat on the bench she shared with Stheno.

'You have done a tremendous thing tonight,' she said, bending to lay a gentle kiss on Medusa's forehead. When she drew back, something akin to determination shone in her features. 'I am sure you will gain control over your power very soon.' She straightened, her expression serious. 'Now, please return to your chambers and rest. This conversation has clearly taken a toll on you, and you must allow yourself to recover.'

Medusa opened her mouth to protest, but Euryale silenced her with a raised hand.

'I am afraid I insist,' Euryale replied firmly, gesturing for Medusa to vacate the room. 'Besides,' she continued, turning to Stheno, whose eyes were narrowed at her divine sister, 'I have something I would like to speak to Stheno about in private.'

An indiscernible look passed between the two, and Stheno nodded. 'She is right, little sister,' Stheno said, rising from her seat to stand by Euryale. 'You must rest now. For the sake of yourself, and the babe.'

Medusa heaved herself to her feet, strode to the doorway, and looked back at her two sisters. Two tall, black-eyed, snake-haired women, radiating a power Medusa could never fully understand and sharing a bond she could never quite match. Of course they had things to discuss that didn't concern her – she was a mere human, after all. They knew of things she could not even imagine, and had memories that stretched long before her existence. For the first time since she arrived Medusa felt like an outsider, an imposter. She had been naive to presume to be their peer, and as the thought struck her, a great embarrassment settled over her, warming her cheeks.

They watched her in silence, and Medusa knew they were waiting for her to leave before commencing their discussion. She would leave, and they would whisper secrets she did not deserve to be privy to.

'Goodnight, Medusa.' Euryale offered her a smile, but Medusa knew it to be an instruction to depart.

'Goodnight, sisters,' Medusa muttered before scurrying back to her quarters and dropping onto her bed. She slumped forward and buried her face in her hands.

How could she ever have considered herself equal to these divine beings? They called her sister, and yet she would always be different.

Small. Weak. Inept.

A nuisance requiring careful supervision, like a stubborn adolescent who was not ready to join the adult world.

She could barely stand it. Her only hope was that reliving her time with Ismene brought about the improvements they sought, or else she would become an even greater burden once her child was born.

Medusa rolled onto her side and faced the wall, cradling her growing stomach as fresh tears threatened to burst free. Recollections of Ismene swirled through her mind, each intimate moment laid bare before her eyes as if it had happened only yesterday. Loneliness enveloped her, and it was many hours before sleep relieved her of her pain.

# I

Scuffing the dry dirt with her sandal, Ismene trudged along the dusty road. Despondency enveloped her like a shroud, but she pressed forward. The road back to Knossos was long and difficult without any transportation, but it was her only hope after her recent failure.

Images of the winged woman flashed in Ismene's mind, and a great shame pooled in her stomach. All of her efforts wasted in a single moment of cowardice. It was pathetic, and Ismene hated herself for it. Medusa had always shown courage. She had faced Thaddeus' criticism with her head held high every single time, despite the danger she knew he presented, and could stand up in front of a crowd of acolytes and give lessons without a hint of nerves. Ismene could not even face one beastly woman to save the person she loved more than anything. She was not sure the shame would ever lift.

As weak and miserable as she felt, Ismene was determined to start her search again. It gave her purpose, a reason to keep going. A life without Medusa was not a life worth living, and she would continue to seek out her lover's captors, even if it destroyed her.

The city of Knossos would once more be her best chance of success. After being spotted by Ismene, the winged women might never return to the field of herbs again, might never return to Krete, even. Such creatures were supposed to value secrecy and anonymity, and for all the creature knew, Ismene might bring back a mob of soldiers, armed and ready to capture her. Staying in the field was not an option. Supplies were already low, and Ismene could not help Medusa in any way if she ended up stranded in rural Krete with no food or water. She would return to Knossos, replenish her supplies with what little currency she had left, and try again. There would be other areas of interest, other fields where a monster might seek out valuable crops, or even prey on livestock. Ismene would search and surveil every one of them if she had to.

The sun sank lower in the sky, and Ismene's legs began to ache. Travel was beginning to take its toll on her body; her feet were blistered, her clothes were ragged and stained, and she ached from head to toe. Her steps were already beginning to slow, her stride becoming a staggering shuffle.

Ismene glanced over her shoulder, and couldn't contain a groan as she saw how little progress she had made towards the city. The field of herbs where she had previously camped could still be seen on the horizon, a green blur of shrubs and grasses she would rather forget. She was about to turn back to the road to continue her trek when she noticed movement in the corner of eye. Ismene stood, mouth agape, as a familiar shape formed on the skyline.

Wings! The winged woman – she was back!

Elation flooded Ismene's body, but it quickly turned to alarm when she realised the woman was returning to the same field – the one Ismene had spent the day journeying away from.

Panic took over, and Ismene burst into a sprint. The aches and pains fell away and she charged down the road, eyes locked on the figure descending ahead of her. There was still a great distance between them, and the small amount of progress she was making was excruciating.

The winged woman landed, disappearing from view amongst the vegetation. Fear shot up Ismene's spine and she surged forwards. Blisters burst underfoot and her chafing thighs were slick with sweat, but Ismene didn't slow. This was it: her chance for redemption.

Lungs burning, the field of herbs inched closer, and Ismene could see the woman she sought once more. Relief soon gave way to panic once more as the woman spread her wings wide, and sent great gusts of wind blowing in her direction.

'Wait!' Ismene shrieked, waving her arms as searing cramps wracked her legs and feet. 'Wait, please!'

Hot tears welled in her eyes. She was going to miss her. A day of pain and sorrow spent, just to fail again.

'Wait!' she called once more, her throat raw. 'Medusa!' she screamed into the wind, hoping beyond hope any of her words would make it to the ears of the creature before her. 'I need to find Medusa!'

The wind stopped, the only sound Ismene's ragged breaths as the winged woman turned and met her gaze.

'Take a deep breath, little sister, and tell me how you feel.'

Medusa followed Stheno's instruction, but no amount of deep breathing could quell the anxiety roiling in her stomach. 'It is no good,' she sighed, 'my nerves will not settle.'

Stheno's brow furrowed. 'Our conversation yesterday did not help, then?' She would not tell Medusa she was disappointed, but it was clear on her face. The two of them had been outside in their usual practice clearing for most of the morning, Stheno attempting to help Medusa reach a level of calm which would allow her to control her gaze while Medusa's anxiety grew with each exercise.

'I do not think we can force it, sister,' Medusa responded with as much grace as she could muster. Stheno was wonderful, and cared for her sisters with a fiery passion, but patience was not a virtue she possessed, and they were both growing frustrated. 'It has been one night, and truthfully I did not sleep well, so perhaps we should stop for today and head ba—'

'No!' Stheno's black eyes flashed dangerously and Medusa recoiled.

The serpents atop Stheno's head rose as if threatened, hissing and spitting.

Stheno blinked, and her expression softened. The green vipers settled into stillness and became quiet. 'Apologies, sister, I do not mean to be short with you. My sleep was also disturbed, but that is not your fault.' Stheno smiled, but it did not quite reach her eyes. 'Now, let us try something else.'

Grasping Medusa by the shoulders, Stheno bent so their eyes met and took a deep breath. When she spoke again, her voice was soft. 'Look into my eyes, and clear your mind.'

Medusa pursed her lips, but she complied. She had to keep trying, no matter how frustrated she became. She peered into Stheno's dark eyes, two shining, bottomless pools that drew her in completely. The surrounding trees blurred into nothingness and the sun shrank into a pin-prick, leaving nothing but her sister's mesmerising gaze.

'Focus on nothing but my eyes and the sound of my voice,' Stheno continued. The words became faded and distant, and Medusa struggled to cling on to Stheno's presence as she drowned in her gaze.

'Relax your mind and body.'

The words were eerily thick, like they were travelling through honey.

'It is just you and me, little sister. You can let everything else go, and trust me completely.'

A cool serenity washed over Medusa then. She felt as though she was floating, with nothing but the air beneath her feet. No thoughts entered her mind, no worries penetrated the eerie calmness that embraced her.

A *crack* sounded out from somewhere nearby, but Medusa could not place its source. It could have been right behind her, or it could have been a hundred paces away. Another crack, and the bubble Stheno had built around them wavered.

'Remain calm,' Stheno murmured, her words still quiet and garbled. Her eyes shifted to something in the distance. 'Stay here, and continue the exercise. I will be one moment.'

Medusa tried to maintain the stillness in her mind as her sister strode behind her. But try as she might to retain her focus, it was impossible to ignore the whispered conversation happening nearby. The words themselves she could not decipher, but there was clearly an animated discussion taking place.

'Euryale?' Medusa asked, the final remnants of her trance dissolving. She began to turn around. 'When did you—'

'Sister, wait!' Euryale appeared by Medusa's side, and held her in place by the shoulders. 'Before you do anything, I want you to be fully aware of what you are about to face.'

An uncomfortable sense of unease writhed through Medusa's insides. Her sister emanated a strange energy, a nervous excitement she had never shown before.

'What do you mean?' Medusa asked. 'Another animal? Is it dangerous?'

Stheno appeared by Euryale's side, concern creasing her features. 'Please relax, little sister. You must remain calm if this is to be successful.'

Euryale cupped Medusa's cheek delicately, a gentle smile on her lips. 'You do trust us, Medusa?'

Pulse quickening, Medusa nodded. These two women had saved her life when they owed her nothing, and they had taken care of her as if they had known her since birth ever since. She could do nothing but trust them.

Medusa tried to swallow down her nerves as Euryale gestured to someone over Medusa's shoulder. 'Come closer, please.'

Footsteps approached. Not the heavy, clawed scrapings of her sisters, but the light, uncertain footsteps of someone else. Medusa's stomach dropped as realisation struck, and bile burned the back of her throat. They were going to make her practice her gaze on a human.

'Wait!' Medusa spluttered, her heart racing. 'You cannot wish to risk someone's life?'

'Medusa,' Euryale soothed, 'you need to trust us.'

'I do, but I... I cannot do this. I... I...'

'Medusa?'

Her breath caught.

That voice.

It was impossible. A trick of the mind, or an unbidden memory. It had to be. Medusa shook her head, unwilling to let herself believe, to open her heart to even the slightest possibility.

'Medusa, it's me. I'm here.'

Tears sprang to her eyes. Tears of overwhelming joy, and of absolute terror. She was here. Medusa had no idea how, but Ismene was here.

Hurried footsteps approached, and a dreadful fear overcame her. Clamping her eyes shut, she waved an arm to bar any approach. 'No! Stay away from me, please! I... I...' She buried her face in trembling hands. 'I'm dangerous. A monster.'

Ismene would not meet the same fate as those poor creatures. Medusa would die before she let that happen.

'Medusa...'

Gentle hands pulled Medusa's fingers away from her face. Familiar hands. Hands that had explored parts of Medusa's body which had until then been untouched. That had held her with a desperate passion that left her breathless every time. She had unravelled as they cradled her cheeks before each stolen kiss, and she had reached heights of pleasure she could never imagine as they found her most intimate areas. She would know them anywhere.

'You're no monster.' Ismene's voice was like something from a dream. Heavenly and utterly unbelievable. 'You're my sweet, wonderful Medusa, and I know you would never do me harm.'

'I would never choose to,' Medusa insisted, eyes still tightly closed and tears flowing freely down her cheeks now. 'Never! But I can't control it, no matter how hard I try. Tell her, sisters! Tell her, please!'

'Shhh.' Ismene's fingers cradled Medusa's cheek, and a sob rose unbidden from her chest. 'They've told me, and I understand why you're scared, but I have absolute faith in you, Medusa. You would never hurt me.'

Medusa could only shake her head, the fear of destroying the person she cared about more than anything else in the world too overwhelming. Her heart was in her throat, her stomach roiled with dread, but underneath it all there was a spark of joy that she almost did not dare acknowledge in case it was snatched away from her. She could not lose Ismene again; it would kill her.

'Medusa.'

Ismene wrapped her arms around Medusa and pulled her into a tight embrace. Medusa's very soul lit up as she held the other woman in her arms. She buried her face in Ismene's soft curls, her familiar earthy scent filling Medusa's nostrils and bringing her a peace she had lost all hope of ever feeling again.

'Medusa,' Ismene whispered into her ear, sending goosebumps fluttering over Medusa's skin. 'The only times in my life that I've genuinely felt safe have been when I've been looking into your eyes. I trust you. Let me see them again. Please.'

'I love you,' Medusa breathed, pulling Ismene even closer. Hot tears continued to fall as she felt Ismene's heart pounding against hers, her warm breath on the side of her neck. She felt whole again, the aching void that had plagued her since she left everything she knew behind finally dissipating. It allowed her to hope. 'Whatever happens, please know that.'

'I love you too.' Ismene moved back, her hands tracing down Medusa's arms until their fingers intertwined. 'Please look at me.'

Focusing on the feeling of Ismene's hands in hers and the warm comfort they brought, Medusa took a slow, deep breath and opened her eyes.

Time seemed to slow as Medusa's eyes fluttered open, and the two women beheld each other for the first time since their worlds fell apart.

Medusa blinked at Ismene, her eyes wide, and Ismene's heart fluttered. They were darker than she remembered – the irises almost black – but still utterly beautiful.

'You... you...' Medusa stammered, her perfectly plump lips parted in shock. 'You are all right?'

Ismene's heart was in her throat. 'I am... now I'm with you again.'

Medusa's lips crashed into hers, desperate and urgent. The taste of sweet fig mingled with the salt of their tears as they came together into a deep kiss. The time they'd spent apart faded away, the longing and heartbreak forgotten for one long, perfect moment.

They broke apart, their foreheads pressed together and their chests heaving. Ismene squeezed Medusa's fingers, barely able to believe what was happening.

*She's here! She's really here!*

'I can't believe I finally found you,' she murmured. 'I can't believe you're here, standing in front of me.'

Movement to her right caught her attention, and Ismene remembered that they were not alone. She stepped back, keeping one of Medusa's hands held firmly in hers – she couldn't let go already when they had only just been reunited – and regarded the two strange women who had been watching them.

They towered over Medusa and her, writhing snakes atop their heads and vicious talons for feet. As their piercing black eyes met hers, a deep fear stirred inside Ismene's stomach, but Medusa had called them sisters, and if she trusted them, so could Ismene.

The one with green vipers for hair regarded Ismene with narrowed eyes and a stern expression, but the other one – Euryale, she had called herself – beamed.

'Oh, little sister, I am so proud of you,' she declared, grasping Medusa by the shoulders and pulling her into her arms. A twinge of sadness pulled at Ismene when Medusa's fingers were tugged from her grasp, but she hid her disappointment behind a polite smile.

'You have done well,' the green-haired sister added, placing a hand on Medusa's shoulder as her embrace with Euryale continued. While there was very little emotion in her low voice, genuine affection shone on her face.

The three women looked like a little family, the bonds between them clear to see as they murmured terms of endearment and shared easy physical contact. While Ismene had been travelling from place to place, never lingering anywhere long enough to forge even the most superficial of friendships, Medusa had built a life here. A sisterhood. Ismene, despite the rush of joy at her reunion with Medusa still pulsing through her, couldn't help but feel left out.

Finally, the sisters pulled apart, and Medusa's eyes fell on Ismene again. Her cheeks were flushed with excitement; she looked radiant. 'How?' she asked, an unbelieving laugh tumbling from her lips. 'How did you find me?'

'Your... Your sister.' Ismene gestured to Euryale, whose smile never faltered; she seemed truly overjoyed by the turn of events. 'She carried me over from Krete.'

The journey had been truly bizarre. When she had seen the winged woman return to the field of herbs after their encounter just one day prior, Ismene had been worried that she meant to kill her. Ismene had seen her up close, and she could have been there to ensure her silence. But when she had revealed to Ismene that she was there to discuss Medusa, to *help* her, Ismene could hardly believe it. After her prior failure, she had no choice but to take the risk, and so she had willingly offered herself to Euryale, who had held her close while she took flight and brought them south to this small, inconspicuous island.

'Krete?' Medusa's eyebrows rose in surprise. 'You journeyed that far?'

Heat filled Ismene's cheeks. Her part in all this felt very insignificant now. 'Yes... I had to find you, so I followed your trail as far as Krete, and that's where Euryale found me.'

Medusa approached and planted a soft kiss on Ismene's cheek. 'You continue to astound me, my love.' Worry flickered over Medusa's features and she held Ismene by the shoulders, looking her over from head to toe. 'You are not hurt, are you? Have you been eating?'

Ismene couldn't help but chuckle. 'Medusa, I came here to save *you*, not the other way around. You haven't changed at all – still protecting me at every opportunity.'

Medusa laughed in return, but something about it sounded off. Forced. 'That is true,' she said, dropping her eyes as if taken by a sudden shyness. 'Though I am sure you were not expecting this.'

Medusa gestured to her head, where a tangle of black snakes quietly nested. Ismene blinked, now taking the time to fully take in Medusa's appearance. In truth, she had been so absorbed in their reunion she had barely noticed Medusa's physical changes. Even her clothing was different. Where before she had worn a finely beaded chiton that showed off her shapely figure, Medusa wore a simple linen dress which hung loosely from where it was pinned at her shoulders. Ismene was just so thrilled to see her again that everything else faded into the background.

'I'll admit, I wasn't,' she said carefully, 'but it makes no difference to me.' She cupped Medusa's cheek and gently tilted her face so their gazes met. 'No matter what curse has afflicted you, under those serpents you're still the most beautiful woman I've ever seen.'

A small smile pulled at Medusa's lips, but it didn't reach her eyes. Ismene knew she didn't believe her, but she would.

In that moment, Ismene made a silent promise to herself, and to Medusa. No matter how long it took, she would make Medusa feel beautiful again.

The day passed in a euphoric blur. Medusa could not take her eyes off Ismene, could not believe that her love had travelled across the Grecian world to seek her out. Ismene, the woman who when they met had been forbidden from straying beyond her family home without an escort, had not only left the city of her birth, she had sailed across the sea and into the unknown with nothing more than a rumour to guide the way.

Medusa did not deserve her.

Euryale and Stheno welcomed Ismene into their home, but Medusa noticed very different demeanors from each of her sisters. Euryale was practically giddy with excitement, hurrying the women back to the temple to prepare tea and set up a place for Ismene to sleep in Medusa's quarters. Stheno, on the other hand, was decidedly cool. She said very little – although the few words she said were polite enough – and watched Ismene through sharp, narrow eyes, as if she expected the new arrival to morph into a dangerous creature at any moment.

Ismene was equally quiet, but that was to be expected. When Medusa had first arrived at the island, the shock of her situation had stunned her into several days of silence. It would be an adjustment, but Medusa would be there to ease her through it. Whatever Ismene needed, Medusa would provide it for her.

When the sun dipped below the horizon, they could finally retire to their private chamber, and Medusa and Ismene found themselves alone together for the first time in months.

The two women stood staring at each other, the air thick and charged with an energy that sent goosebumps rippling over Medusa's flesh.

'You're here,' she whispered, still reeling from that simple truth. The words had barely left her lips before Ismene was there, pulling Medusa into her arms and holding her so tight it took her breath away.

'I'm so glad you're safe.' Ismene held her as if she was scared Medusa would drift away or dissolve into nothing if she let go. 'I was so worried.'

Medusa melted into Ismene's body. 'I am so sorry,' she said quietly, burying her face into the comforting embrace of Ismene's curls. 'I thought I was doing the right thing by leaving you behind, where you would be safe.' She swallowed down the rising tears. 'Safe from me.'

'Don't talk like that.' Ismene pulled back just enough for Medusa to see her beautiful golden eyes, shining in the flickering candlelight. 'You did what you thought you had to, and I'll never blame you for that. When you're ready, you can tell me everything that happened, but for tonight, I'm just overjoyed to be in your arms again.'

Warmth blossomed in Medusa's chest. 'And I'm overjoyed to be in yours.'

Ismene's lips found hers again, but where before her kiss had been bold and desperate, it was now slow, and deep. Everything Medusa had been through in recent months fell away as Ismene's hands moved down her back and rested on her hips. Longing pulsed through

Medusa's body as each firm fingertip pressed against her flesh, a flicker of heat burning between her legs.

Somewhere in the back of her mind, Medusa knew she should stop this; Ismene did not know she was with child, could not see her swollen stomach beneath her loose clothing. There were so many things they needed to discuss, but every fibre of Medusa's being begged for Ismene's touch. She wanted – she *needed* – to lose herself in Ismene's kisses, to drink her in and forget that anything had changed since they were last in each other's arms.

Everything else could wait for the morning. Until then, she would give herself to Ismene, body and soul.

'Ismene...' she breathed, stepping back and moving Ismene's body with hers as if they were one towards the cot that lay beside the wall. 'Come to me.'

'I've waited too long to hear you say my name again,' Ismene whispered into Medusa's ear as she moved with her, pressing herself against Medusa so hard she could feel every curve of Ismene's supple body. 'I want to hear it again, and again, and again.'

They sank to the bed together. Medusa lay back on the soft linens and pulled Ismene down beside her, entwining their legs together. This was no city temple; there were no acolytes that could walk in on them at any moment, no need to hide their kisses in dark corners or dusty storerooms. They could be with each other fully, and without restraint.

'I love you,' Ismene murmured, planting a trail of slow kisses down Medusa's neck to her collarbone.

A soft moan escaped Medusa as Ismene moved lower. Each kiss was a joy, the feel of Ismene's delicate lips on her skin pure bliss. Ismene drew back, her honey-coloured eyes blazing with lust as she reached up and unpinned the shoulder of Medusa's dress, pulling back the linen to reveal her breasts. The cool evening air drifted over Medusa's bare skin, and a shiver of anticipation rippled through her.

Ismene's lips peppered kisses down Medusa's chest until she found her nipple and took it into her mouth. Medusa gasped as Ismene's tongue explored, each movement growing the pulsating heat between her legs.

'Ismene...' she sighed, running her fingers up her lover's back and neck and grasping a handful of thick curls. She could feel every movement of Ismene's head beneath her fingers as her tongue swirled and stroked, doubling each shuddering thrill. Medusa's back arched as Ismene's fingertips traced over her other breast to the nipple, her kisses never slowing as she gently caressed, the dual sensations drowning Medusa in waves of pleasure.

'Oh... Oh, gods...'

Ismene lifted her head, her hand still moving, the heat inside Medusa still building. 'More?' she asked, her voice low, and eager.

'Yes,' Medusa breathed, her heart pounding harder and harder as Ismene brought her kisses slowly back up the side of her neck. 'I want... I need...'

Ismene's lips found Medusa's mouth again, hungry and urgent. Medusa responded in kind, kissing her back deeply, drinking her in. She pulled Ismene on top of her, revelling in the feel of her firm body writhing against her own. Ismene panted into Medusa's mouth as they devoured each other, their bodies pressed together so tightly it felt as though they could melt into each other and become one.

Strong fingers gripped the flesh of Medusa's inner thigh and she gasped into Ismene's open mouth. Medusa grasped the back of Ismene's head, grabbing another handful of curls and pressing into her, her tongue delving even deeper.

Ismene's hand moved upwards, inching tantalisingly close to the fire blazing between Medusa's legs. She ached for Ismene to touch her there, to feel the rapture of her fingertips, and bucked her hips, her body desperate to close the distance.

'Say my name again,' Ismene whispered, her breath hot in Medusa's mouth, her fingers hovering painfully close to where Medusa craved them.

'Ismene,' Medusa moaned, thrusting upwards, the anticipation almost too much to bear. 'Touch me. Please.'

Ismene's fingers found her, and Medusa was undone.

Medusa woke first, slipping from under Ismene's arm as the dawn sunlight began to filter into the ruined temple. She left Ismene sleeping soundly and stood by the narrow window of her chamber. Beyond the surrounding copse of trees the sky was streaked with amber and violet; a new day had begun.

The previous night had been incredible. To be reunited with the woman she loved and able to celebrate each other in such an unrestrained and intimate way... It was nothing short of bliss. But as the sun peeked over the tree line, Medusa was reminded of the stark reality the pair of them now had to face together.

Medusa was no longer the woman Ismene fell in love with. She was forever changed, transformed into something inhuman.

And she was carrying the unborn child of a god.

Was it unfair to ask Ismene to stay by her side? To chain herself to a monster and the burden of its bastard child? It felt like a monumental sacrifice to expect of someone you loved. And yet, now Ismene was back in her life, Medusa could not bear the thought of ever being without her again.

'Good morning.'

Medusa jumped as an arm slipped around her waist from behind. She had been so absorbed in her thoughts she had not heard Ismene approach.

'Sorry, I didn't mean to startle you.'

Medusa laced her fingers through Ismene's. 'No need to apologise, my love,' she said softly, welcoming the warmth of Ismene's body against her back as the other woman rested a head on her shoulder. 'I was merely lost in thought.'

'What are you thinking about?'

Medusa took a deep breath. How could she explain her anxieties without seeming unsatisfied by Ismene's return? She was overjoyed to be with her again, she felt whole for the first time since that awful day in the naos, but that did not assuage her rising guilt.

'Just...' she said slowly, choosing her next words carefully. 'Just of how different everything is. Different to what we had planned, to anything we could have expected.'

'It's not so different, when you think about it. We got away; we're finally together like we always hoped we would be.'

Medusa turned to face Ismene, incredulous. 'How can you say that?' She gestured to her head, to the nest of snakes she could never be rid of. 'Look at me, at what I have become.'

Sympathy shone in Ismene's eyes, but instead of shying away from the hissing serpents, she reached towards them.

'No, don't—!'

But it was too late. A single snake rose from the rest, its gaze fixed on Ismene's fingers. She did not flinch, but turned over her hand to offer an open palm. The serpent hesitated for a moment before tentatively sliding on to Ismene's hand. She smiled as she cradled its head in her palm, the creature entirely passive and almost seeming to relish her touch.

'They're quite gentle.' Ismene smiled as she watched the serpent slowly advance across her palm, tasting the air with its pointed tongue. 'I don't fear them.'

'It is what they represent that terrifies me,' Medusa murmured, frowning at the creature undulating in her lover's hand. 'The way I have changed. The monster I have become.'

Ismene pulled her hand back from the serpent, then, and shifted her gaze to stare into Medusa's eyes.

'You're not a monster, Medusa.' She cupped Medusa's face with her hand, running a gentle thumb over her cheek. 'You taught me that I was beautiful despite my flaws,' she continued, fighting the urge to touch her own cheek, to run her fingers over the scar that had almost destroyed her life. 'That being broken didn't make me any less worthy of love. And the same applies to you. You were always magnificent, Medusa, and you still are.'

Medusa closed her eyes, wishing more than anything that she could believe Ismene's words, that she was still as worthy of this incredible woman's love as she once had been. 'Those are sweet words,' she sighed, 'but I am not sure you would say them if you knew what I had done.'

'I know.'

Medusa's eyes opened, and she saw her pain reflected in Ismene's gaze. 'You know?'

'I saw them, Medusa.' Ismene swallowed, all prior levity vanished. 'I saw Kephissa.'

Images flashed through Medusa's mind, images she had been fighting day and night to forget. Horrified faces struck with terror and disgust. Piercing screams, cut short and frozen forever in stone.

Kephissa.

Sweet, kind, faithful Kephissa. She had rushed to her priestess' aid, and was rewarded with the hell of a living death.

'I didn't mean to do it.' Tears sprang to Medusa's eyes as the memories swam across her vision. People running. Men, women and children shouting and crying until their voices were cut off forever. 'I swear I didn't.'

The silence hung between them. It only lasted a moment, but it felt like a lifetime as Medusa waited for Ismene's response.

'I believe you.' A sad smile pulled at her lips and she leaned forward to place a gentle kiss on Medusa's cheek. 'Of course I believe you.'

Relief flooded Medusa's chest, but it was tainted with a twinge of doubt. 'How can you be so sure? Is there no uncertainty in your heart? Some small doubt that makes you afraid?'

Medusa was rambling, she knew that, but she could not stop herself. She needed Ismene's reassurances, needed to hear the words spoken out loud or she would drive herself insane wondering.

Ismene sighed, and Medusa's chest tightened. 'Medusa, you are the only one who thinks you monstrous.' She pulled Medusa away from the window and sat her down on the bed, the tangle of linens still disheveled from their incredible night together. 'Your sisters love you. They see you as a true sibling, as an equal. And I...' She glanced away, trying to find the right words, and butterflies erupted in Medusa's stomach as she waited for her to continue. 'I simply see you – Medusa, the woman who brought me into her life when I did nothing to deserve it, who cared for me and all those under her protection, who taught me I could be more than I ever dreamed of. The Medusa I knew would never have harmed those people willingly, and that same woman is sitting before me now. I don't need to have been there and witnessed it myself to know that to be true.'

'You mean that?' Medusa asked, emotion swelling in her chest. 'Truly?'

Ismene nodded, and smiled. 'Truly.' She wiped away the fresh tears forming in Medusa's eyes. 'And I don't want to hear such nonsense again.'

Medusa laughed. A real, unforced laugh that lifted her spirits in a way she had not experienced in many months. The lightness Ismene could bring to Medusa's heart was nothing short of miraculous. 'Gods, I have missed you,' she said, clasping Ismene's hands in hers. 'Don't ever leave me again.'

Ismene's eyes sparkled, flawless drops of shimmering amber that Medusa could lose herself in forever. 'I don't plan to.'

There was still so much more to be said, but Medusa could not bring herself to disrupt this perfect moment. There would be time to share her full story with Ismene, but for now, they were at peace with one another.

'Tea?'

Ismene nodded and accepted the steaming cup from Euryale's hands. The soothing aroma of oregano, sage and lemon balm filled her nostrils. 'This smells wonderful, thank you. You have quite the skill with herbs.'

Euryale beamed as she continued filling cups and handed them to her sisters. 'When you are as isolated from others as we are, you must learn to be self-sufficient, and over the years Stheno and I have perfected a variety of blends that complement our magic. I brewed this mainly for Medusa's benefit, but you will find it has a pleasant taste, and I am sure it will enhance the recovery from your travels.'

Ismene took a sip, and marvelled as the hot, revitalising liquid slipped down her throat. It was delicious, and she already felt some of the fatigue from her journey lift off her shoulders. 'Do you two...' She glanced between Euryale and Stheno, seated across from her in the shared living area. 'Do you need medicinal brews like this?'

'Sometimes,' Euryale answered. Stheno shot a warning look in her sister's direction, but Euryale waved it off and continued, 'As the children of gods, we cannot die, but we can experience illness, exhaustion, and pain, just like any mortal. We would rather not suffer if it can be prevented.'

'Of course.' A thought occurred to Ismene, and a spark of nervous excitement shot through her. 'Wait, Medusa... does this mean you're also immortal now, like your sisters?'

An awkward silence fell between the three snake-haired women, until finally, Euryale spoke again. 'In truth... we do not know. Unlike us, Medusa was not born as she is, but was transformed later in her life. While she possesses some of our gifts, we do not know how far that extends.'

Stheno met Ismene's gaze, then, and her jet-black eyes flashed with warning. 'It is why we are so protective of her.'

Ismene nodded, squirming a little under Stheno's stare. Unlike Euryale, who had welcomed Ismene with open arms from the moment they met, Stheno had remained cold and distant. The green-haired sister had not been hostile since Ismene joined them on the island, but she had regarded her with thinly-veiled suspicion throughout their time together.

'I'm not surprised,' Ismene said lightly, smiling at Stheno to try to diffuse the tension somewhat. 'She's a very special person.'

Medusa, sitting beside Ismene on the marble bench by the hearth, reached over and squeezed Ismene's hand. 'Not as special as you, my love.'

Ismene's heart soared, but even as she drank in the warm smile of her lover she felt Stheno's glare burning into her.

Euryale rose to her feet, either unaware of the animosity radiating from her sister or choosing to ignore it. 'The grape vines on the east side of the island should be ready to harvest today. Medusa, Ismene, would you like to join me so I can show you how it is done?'

Nodding eagerly, Ismene rose to her feet. She hadn't tasted the sweetness of grapes since the Temple of Athena, and her mouth watered at the thought.

'Is it far?' Medusa asked as Euryale helped her up from the bench.

'Not at all, little sister. We will walk slowly so you do not tire.'

Ismene frowned at their strange exchange.

*Is Medusa ill?*

But before she could ask any questions, Euryale was ushering Medusa through the doorway. Ismene moved to follow, but was stopped short by a strong hand grasping her wrist.

'Wait.'

She turned and came face to face with Stheno, whose long fingers held Ismene in place with an iron grip.

'What...' she stuttered under Stheno's stern gaze. 'What's wrong?'

'Medusa is very precious to me,' Stheno said, her voice low and laced with warning. 'Do not hurt her.'

Ismene drew herself up to her full height and squared her shoulders. She was still considerably shorter than Stheno, but she would not cower before someone who thought she would ever hurt Medusa. 'I would never. I love her more than anything.'

Stheno raised an eyebrow. 'I hope for your sake that you are right.' She leaned closer so the two women were face to face. 'If you cause any harm to come to Medusa or the child, I will make you wish you had never set foot on this island.'

Ismene blinked.

*Child?*

'What do you m—'

'Go,' Stheno snapped, releasing Ismene from her grip and pushing her towards the door. 'You need to earn your keep, and my sisters are waiting.'

Confused, Ismene stumbled through the doorway into the cool morning air where Euryale and Medusa were waiting expectantly.

'Are you all right?' Medusa asked, concern creasing her brow.

'Yes…' Ismene muttered. She shook her head, trying to rid herself of the unpleasant interaction with Stheno and the questions it generated. 'Yes, of course. Let's go.'

Ismene followed Medusa and her sister towards the grapevines in a haze, deaf to their polite chatter. Stheno's words echoed around her mind with every step.

*If you cause any harm to come to Medusa or the child.*
*The child.*

Anxiety twisted Ismene's gut. How had she not seen it? Medusa had hidden herself under loose clothing, true, but her sisters also wore dresses unlike the chitons and himations typical of Ionian fashion. Besides, she had changed in such other, more marked ways, all of which had faded into the background when Ismene saw her face again. She had been so overcome with excitement at being reunited with Medusa she'd been blind to how her body had changed, even when she was exploring it in the most intimate of ways.

In ways a man must have explored it, and in doing so, impregnated Medusa with his child.

Ismene's stomach churned as unwelcome images flashed in front of her eyes. A man, lying with Medusa. Touching her. Kissing her.

It made her feel sick.

'Ismene?'

Euryale's voice broke Ismene out of her spiralling thoughts. She looked around; they had reached the vines and she hadn't even realised. The trees surrounding the old temple had given way to a more open, sloped shrubland filled with several clusters of flourishing green grapevines. This was no well-ordered vineyard, but instead a cacophony of free-growing plant life, where nature arranged itself for maximum abundance.

'Sorry,' Ismene said hurriedly. Heat filled her cheeks as the other two women watched her, no doubt wondering why she had been ignoring them. 'I was lost in thought. What were you saying, again?'

Euryale gestured to the bunches of grapes hanging from the lush vines, and restarted her instructions on identifying the ripest fruit. The words were lost to Ismene. They washed over her as she watched Medusa, perched on a nearby boulder and listening to her sister with rapt attention.

She was beautiful even now, her big, bright eyes narrowed in concentration as she took in every word. Ismene knew Medusa would want to know everything, to soak up as much knowledge as possible so she could support her sisters. It was one of the things she loved about her, but when Medusa's hand drifted subconsciously to her stomach, Ismene's chest tightened.

*Oh, Medusa, what did you do?*

The sun was high in the sky when Euryale finished her instruction and let them get on with picking the grapes. It was clear the golden-haired woman considered the vines precious, and the care she demonstrated when inspecting the fruit and explaining how to test for ripeness was very endearing.

Her sister helped Medusa up from the boulder she had chosen as a seat during her lesson, and handed her a small woven basket. 'We will only pick for a short while, little sister. Rest if you need to, and Ismene and I will keep going.'

'I will be fine, but thank you.' Medusa took the basket and stood by Ismene, facing a vine that was bursting with dark purple fruit. 'Shall we?'

Ismene nodded, but her eyes remained fixed straight ahead. Medusa watched as she slowly picked grapes, assessing each bunch and dropping it into her basket as if in a trance. Her movements were stiff, and she performed the actions automatically like a puppet on invisible strings.

'Are you all right?' Medusa asked quietly. Ismene nodded again, her picking not slowing, her gaze never shifting from her task. Something wasn't right. 'Ismene, look at me. Please.'

Ismene turned to face Medusa, her eyes ringed with red.

'Have you... have you been crying?'

'No,' Ismene mumbled, scrubbing her eyes with the back of one hand. 'I think I'm just tired, that's all.'

'Please don't lie to me.'

Medusa's words seem to strike Ismene, and her face crumpled. 'I just need a moment.'

Before Medusa could react, Ismene turned and fled. She skirted around the vines and into the underbrush, disappearing as she reached the tree line. Medusa followed, ignoring Euryale's shouts and questions.

'Ismene!' she called. 'Ismene, wait!'

She stepped under the canopy of trees and shivered as the temperature dropped. Thick trunks of juniper and laurel surrounded her, pressing in on all sides, and it was impossible to decipher where Ismene had run off to.

'Ismene!' she tried again, but the thick foliage dampened her calls, the leafy branches absorbing her voice and rendering it utterly ineffective. 'Where are you?'

Medusa stepped forward and felt something burst beneath her sandals. She looked down and saw a handful of crushed juniper berries under her foot, their bitter, floral scent already reaching her nostrils. The ground was littered with the strange, dark fruit, and Medusa's heart leapt as she spotted a trail of broken berries leading off to the right. Whether she had meant to or not, Ismene had provided directions for Medusa to follow.

'Ismene?' she called again, bending to duck under a low-hanging branch as she ventured deeper into the wood. 'Are you there?'

Medusa listened, and beyond the rustling of the leaves in the low breeze and the chirping of birds high in the branches, there was another sound, barely perceptible through the brush. A sound that broke Medusa's heart. It was the soft sound of crying.

She hurried towards it, ignoring the thorny undergrowth tugging at her dress and scraping her ankles. A small clearing opened up before her, and there, sitting on a fallen log with her head in her hands, was Ismene.

For a moment Medusa remained still, paralysed by the sorrowful sight of her lover so broken. Perhaps it had been too much to expect Ismene to be content with living here, in solitude, with three strange creatures that were only half-human. Medusa had hoped with all her heart that she could make Ismene happy, that being together again might be enough, but looking at how she sobbed into her hands as if the world itself was ending, Medusa realised that was unfair.

She walked slowly to the log and lowered herself down next to Ismene. They sat in near-silence, the only sign of recognition from Ismene her transition from openly weeping to sniffing and wiping her eyes. Initially, Medusa did not speak. She simply slid her hand over to Ismene's lap, and was relieved to feel warm fingers intertwine with hers.

When she could not hold her words back any longer, Medusa spoke. 'I am sorry you are not happy here.'

Ismene's head shot up, and she stared at Medusa with red, swollen eyes, incredulous. 'Not happy here?' Her voice was shrill, almost hysterical. 'I am overjoyed to be here, Medusa. To be with you again. I've never wanted anything more in my life.'

'Then why...' Medusa swallowed, her throat suddenly tight. 'Why are you upset? Has something happened?'

'What has happened,' Ismene began, taking a breath to steady herself, 'is that you are pregnant.'

Medusa's stomach dropped. A creeping dread slithered up her spine. Her heart pounded, and she could not breathe. Could not think. The moment she had known must come but had been too cowardly to create had been thrust upon her, and now it was here, she was frozen with fear.

'What happened, Medusa?' Ismene asked, the pain in her voice tearing Medusa's heart in two. 'Why did you lie with a man?'

Betrayal laced each word, and the crushing realisation choked Medusa. Ismene thought Medusa had been unfaithful, that she had sought out the arms of a man while they were separated – perhaps even back in Miletus, so advanced was her pregnancy. Medusa's mouth turned dry as she stared into Ismene's eyes, those perfect golden pools shining with tears that she herself had caused. She should have told Ismene right away. Better that than to let her think for even one second that Medusa would choose to lie with anyone but her.

Medusa looked up at the trees, unable to meet her lover's gaze any longer. Tears pricked the back of her eyes now as she held her stomach, the love she bore for her growing child warring with the agonising memory of its conception. But she had to tell Ismene; Medusa could not let her believe she had betrayed her.

'I did not do it willingly.'

A quiet gasp sounded beside her. When Ismene spoke, her words were barely a whisper. 'You don't mean...?'

Medusa nodded, unable to voice the truth. She knew she must, but how could she inflict that terrible knowledge on Ismene, who had already gone through so much?

'Oh, Medusa.' Ismene threw her arms around Medusa and squeezed her tight. Her strong but gentle fingers rubbed circles on her back, and relief swelled in Medusa's chest. 'I am so, so sorry,' Ismene murmured softly, and Medusa's throat tightened on hearing the grief in her voice.

'No, I'm sorry,' she said into Ismene's curls, inhaling her earthy scent. 'I should have told you right away. I wanted to, I promise. I just...' Fresh tears spilled down her cheeks. 'I could not bring myself to say the words.'

'I understand.' Ismene clung to Medusa as if she was scared she might crumble into pieces if she let her go. 'Gods, you must have been so frightened.' She pulled back, still grasping Medusa by the upper arms. Her eyes shone fiercely. 'Is this how... how it happened? How you were... changed?'

Medusa took a deep, shuddering breath. 'Yes.' Her stomach soured as she remembered her goddess' miraculous appearance, remembered the soul-destroying moment Medusa realised she was there to harm, not to save. 'It was my punishment.'

'Punishment?' Ismene's eyes darkened, and a cold rage laced her voice. 'Tell me. Tell me who did this to you.'

'I... I can't.' It was still too fresh, too raw. Medusa was not sure she could live through the pain again.

Ismene's expression softened, sympathy painted across her features. 'I understand, I do. And I won't force you, but...' Ismene ran her hands down Medusa's arms and entwined their fingers together. 'Perhaps if you finally let it out, you will start to find peace. Peace for you, and for the baby.'

Medusa inhaled slowly, and considered Ismene's words. She was right – of course she was right – but that did not make it easy. The memories of that day had been locked away in the back of Medusa's mind ever since her sisters rescued her, never to be touched in case it broke her beyond recovery. But she was not the only one who mattered. She bore Poseidon's child, and no denial of its conception would erase that fact. If she did not come to peace with it, would she even be able to fully devote herself to her child, to love it as it deserved to be loved? Or would she find herself paralysed with horror at the thought of its parentage every time she beheld it?

Somehow, with Ismene's love and support, she had to find a way to face it.

'I am not sure you will believe me...' she began, already feeling razor-winged butterflies erupt in her stomach.

'I've seen your sisters, Medusa. I will believe whatever you tell me.'

Medusa took a deep breath, and forced the name out through her clenched teeth.

'Poseidon.'

Ismene blanched. 'W-what?'

Before she could stop herself, Medusa told Ismene everything. Each painful detail spilled out of her, each moment of horror was relived until Medusa was left drained and hollow. When it was over, she sagged against Ismene, numb to everything except the warmth of her body and the softness of her touch.

'You didn't deserve this,' Ismene murmured as she pulled Medusa close and held her tightly in her arms. 'Any of it.'

Medusa buried face in Ismene's shoulder, too depleted to even speak. Images of Poseidon flashed in her mind. She could still feel the weight of his body pinning her to the cold ground, could smell the tang of salt on his skin. It turned Medusa's blood cold.

'When I was young,' Ismene said softly, rubbing Medusa's back, 'before… before the accident.' Her voice was light, but a tinge of bitterness touched it as she mentioned the injury that would mar her life forever. 'There was a song my mother used to sing to me when I was upset. Father would have been shouting at me for getting in his way, or he'd hit me for not helping Mother quickly enough, or some other nonsense, and I would hide from him in the gynaeceum. And my mother – this was before she became utterly docile – would hold me and rub my back, like this.' She continued to run a hand up and down Medusa's back, the gentle rhythm pleasant and soothing. 'And she would sing. I don't remember the words – maybe there weren't any – but I still remember the tune.'

Ismene began to hum. It was stilted at first, as if she had to remind herself of the melody after so many years, but once she found it, each note was perfect. The song was nothing like the solemn hymns they had performed together in the Temple of Athena. Rather than a somber processional or a repetitive chant, it was lively and bright, almost playful. It evoked images of dancing, of children playing, of fantastical creatures frolicking with nymphs and dryads in a summer meadow.

Medusa closed her eyes and listened. Warmth spread from Ismene's fingertips as they stroked up and down while she hummed, and some of the tightness eased in Medusa's chest. The pain was still there, the vile, bitter memories that would never disappear, but they were somehow different, lighter. Only a fraction, but it was enough. Enough to convince Medusa that a happy future might be possible.

'Oh, look!'

Medusa drew back, confused by the delight in Ismene's voice. 'What?'

Ismene reached a hand up to Medusa's head and when she brought it down to eye level, a serpent rested in her palm. It was changing colour.

'What's happening?' she breathed. Inky black scales lightened before their eyes, growing paler and paler until they were almost white. As Ismene rotated her hand, the snake's skin shimmered, the dappled sunlight highlighting rose-coloured markings along the length of its spine.

'It's beautiful,' Ismene murmured, captivated by the reptile softly hissing in her hand. 'They're all changing.'

Medusa raised a tentative hand up to her head. She had not handled the serpents since they burst into existence, had instead preferred to pretend they did not exist, but as she let one of them slither onto her palm, she felt a strange new feeling stir in her chest. A kinship. These creatures were part of her, and she had been shutting them out, denying an aspect of her body and soul that she could not change. Perhaps it was time to let them in.

'They *are* beautiful,' she agreed, letting the serpent pass across her hand and enjoying the pleasant sensation of its smooth scales on her skin. 'I wonder why they changed.'

'Perhaps because you let out some of your pain,' Ismene mused, releasing the snake in her hand so it coiled back into its nest with its kin. 'Perhaps you've moved towards being at peace, and they've responded.'

'Perhaps it is you.' Medusa smiled as Ismene's surprised eyes met hers. 'I think they like you better than me.'

A giggle burst from Ismene's lips. It was a simple, joyous sound, and before she knew it, Medusa was giggling along with her. It was a perfect moment of levity, all their pain and misadventures briefly forgotten as they laughed together.

Medusa leaned back on the log, and cradled her stomach with one hand. 'I wonder if the child will have serpents of their own.'

'Between your beauty and the magic inside them, I bet they'll be astounding.'

'I hope so.' Medusa sighed, trying to remain positive, to match Ismene's optimism, but a niggle of doubt tugged at the back of mind. 'I hope they are not monstrous.'

'Medusa.' Ismene leaned closer and placed a hand over where Medusa's rested on her abdomen. 'The baby is yours – it's going to be magnificent. And besides,' she continued, 'they will be loved regardless of what they look like. Between you, me, and your sisters, they will have all the love they could ever need.'

Medusa's heart swelled. 'You will love them? Truly?'

Rolling her eyes, Ismene laid a playful kiss on Medusa's cheek. 'Of course I will, you foolish woman. I'll love them as if they're my own. No matter how they were conceived, this child is yours, and I will love and care for them until the end of my days.'

A surge of emotion overwhelmed Medusa, and she threw her arms around Ismene, drawing her close. 'How fortunate I was that I stumbled upon you in the temple that night,' she said. 'You are more than I ever deserved.'

Ismene pulled back, her golden eyes sparkling with mischief. 'I was enchanted by you the moment I saw you. I would have found a way to bring you into my life one way or another, I promise.'

Medusa chuckled and planted a soft kiss on Ismene's forehead. 'I believe you.'

They sat in comfortable silence for a short while, Ismene resting her head on Medusa's chest as she held her in her arms. Eventually, they heard Euryale call their names, and reluctantly returned to the vines, hand in hand.

As Medusa walked, she felt a great weight lift from her shoulders. She had the woman she loved more than anything in the world by her side, she finally had a family who truly cared for her, and her child would be raised in an environment full of love.

For the first time in many months, Medusa felt truly happy.

Droplets of seawater spat up at Perseus as he neared the coastline, skirting the Sea of Propontis and flying so close to the rolling waves he could taste the salt in the air.

It had taken him some time to get used to the sandals Hermes had offered to aid his quest, but after surveying most of the Mysian coast, he was fully proficient and moving at significant speed. Perseus relished the feeling as he rushed over the water, the wind whipping at his hair; he felt powerful. He had always known there was something special about him, and now he knew why; he was the son of Zeus himself. He deserved this rush of power, this chance for glory and elevation above those who had considered themselves his betters. It was his birthright.

Perseus slowed as he spotted something dark at the foot of the cliffs. He drew to a halt, hovering in place, the undulating waves showering his feet and legs with salt and spray. Ahead, the mouth of a small cave yawned up out of the water, swallowing the rippling tide into blackness. At first glance, it looked much like every other cave he had identified in his search, but as he approached, he was struck with a strange energy radiating from the entrance.

There was power within this cave. It felt ancient, like something older than time itself.

A grin spread across Perseus' face. Finally, he had found it. The home of the Graeae.

Soon he would know the location of the monster he sought.

Watching Medusa blossom was a joy to behold.

Day by day, as her belly grew bigger, her old self shone through more. She relished showing Ismene around their new home and instructing her on each chore required to keep them sustained, falling back into the teacher role she so excelled at. Ismene tried to learn quickly so she could take the burden away from Medusa and her sisters, who had already relieved Medusa of most of her physical duties. She took over collecting water from the nearby stream, finding the firewood needed to keep the hearth burning, and enjoyed learning how to tend to the fruit and vegetables the sister cultivated around the temple.

Stheno, slowly warming to Ismene as she saw the effect she had on Medusa, even offered to teach her to hunt and prepare animals, but after seeing the winged woman swoop down and kill a hare and then gut it in front of her, Ismene realised she didn't have the stomach for it.

Medusa took up the more sedentary activities, repairing damaged clothing and even weaving basic linens herself, demonstrating a level of skill Ismene had never seen before.

'What is it?' Medusa asked one morning as Ismene watched her weave on the loom Stheno and Euryale had retrieved from an abandoned home on a nearby island. 'Why are you staring?'

'I can't believe how good you are,' she replied, marvelling at how little effort Medusa seemed to use to generate flawless woven fabric. 'Mother used to make me weave and I was so clumsy; it always came out terrible.'

Medusa laughed, but there was an air of sadness to it. 'I was raised to be a perfect wife.' She sighed. 'My parents made sure I was skilled at everything a good housewife needed, which included weaving. Once I was married off to some wealthy, influential middle-aged politician I could impress his associates' wives with my embroidery upstairs while they did their important business downstairs.'

Ismene stepped behind Medusa and placed a soft kiss on her temple. 'I'm very grateful that's not the future the Fates had in store for you.'

Medusa shrugged, and the lightness returned to her voice. 'I don't think the Fates had this planned for me either.'

'Maybe not,' Ismene mused, wrapping her arms around Medusa from behind and resting her chin on her shoulder. 'But, despite how we got here, I'm happy, and I'd be content to stay here with you forever.'

'So would I,' Medusa replied, leaning her head against Ismene's and letting out a contented sigh. 'Although, once the baby arrives and they spend each night screaming and crying, you might have a change of heart!'

'Nonsense!' Ismene pulled Medusa's stool back from the loom and knelt in front of her, placing a hand on her swollen stomach. 'I already love this little one with all my heart, and no amount of crying, or whining, or kicking, or screaming will change tha—oh!'

Something pushed up against Ismene's hand, and she jumped.

'Ah!' Ismene yelped, delighted. 'They kicked me!' She looked up at Medusa, beaming. Medusa had her eyebrows raised at Ismene's exclamations, but there was a fond smile pulling at her full lips. 'When do you think they will come?'

'Soon, or so my sisters think.' Medusa frowned, unconsciously rubbing the side of the bump protruding under her loose dress. 'Although that does not seem quite right to me.'

'Why not?' Ismene asked, still marvelling at the feel of the unborn child moving under her fingers.

'Too fast. I am no expert, but does it not take longer?'

'This is a divine infant, Medusa. Maybe it grows quicker than us mere mortals?'

Medusa laughed, but Ismene wasn't sure her heart was in it. She worried about the baby, that much was clear, but between Ismene, Stheno and Euryale, it would be very well cared for.

'You should take a break,' Ismene continued, rising to her feet. 'Why don't we see what tea Euryale has brewing?'

Nodding, Medusa attempted to lift herself to her feet. Ismene saw her struggling and rushed to her back to help her. 'Gods...' Medusa huffed as she managed to stand upright. 'Perhaps my sisters are right, and the child is due soon. I will be as round as I am tall before long.'

'Maybe,' Ismene replied, taking Medusa's hand and leading her out of their shared chambers, 'but you will be no less beautiful for it. Now, come on. Some tea, figs and honey will have you feeling as sprightly as ever.'

Medusa raised a sceptical eyebrow, but smiled and let Ismene drag her into the shared quarters. There, Euryale stood stirring a pot above the hearth. The scent of something savoury drifted over to the two women.

'Apologies, sisters,' Euryale called out when she noticed them enter, waving them over. 'I have no tea for you. Stheno has left me in charge of her stew, and she will be furious if I burn the fruits of her labour.'

'Where is she?' Medusa asked as she eased herself down into a chair. 'It is unlike Stheno to be late for dinner.'

'The beach, scavenging,' Euryale replied, not taking her eyes off the pot as she stirred. 'But I expected her back before now. She does not usually tarry when out on her own. You know how she prefers to be here, watching over us.'

Ismene glanced between the other two women. Euryale's movements were stiffer than usual and concern was plastered across Medusa's features.

'Are you worried?' she asked, watching their reactions carefully.

'Of course not,' Euryale answered quickly, taking the pot off the fire and lowering it to the ground. 'Stheno is more than capable of looking after herself. Besides, the island is well-hidden, and I would know if anyone trespassed. She is in no danger.'

'Even so,' Ismene replied, noting Medusa's demeanour remained unchanged, 'perhaps I should go and fetch her. Like you said, she'll be angry with herself if she ruins dinner for us all.'

Euryale shrugged and began taking down bowls from a shelf built into the wall of the temple, but as Ismene's gaze settled on Medusa, she saw gratitude in her smile.

'I'm sure she's fine,' Ismene murmured as she bent down to kiss Medusa's cheek. 'Be back soon.'

The sun was low in the sky as Ismene picked her way down the rough path towards the small beach to the south of the temple. In truth, she hadn't spent any time there since her arrival on the island, though Medusa and Euryale had pointed it out to her when they gave her a brief tour of her new home. The way was easy to find, however, and as she descended the gentle hill to the beach, the sight of the sea, streaked with a band of amber from the dropping sun, was enough to take her breath away.

When she reached the sand, Ismene removed her sandals and stepped onto the beach barefoot. The sand, warm from a day bathed in sunshine, felt pleasant between her toes. Even before the accident, Thaddeus had never let Ismene play on the beach. He thought any frivolity a waste of time – time that she could spend assisting him in his workshop, or her mother with her chores. Ismene couldn't wait to bring Medusa's child to the sea and let them play on the beach for as long as they wanted.

It took a moment for her to spot Stheno a short distance away, but she was not scavenging. Stheno knelt in the surf, her torso bare and her hands either side of her in the water.

Ismene watched, uncomfortable about intruding on what appeared to be a private moment, but not knowing what else to do. Stheno had her eyes closed, and when Ismene focused, she thought she could see her lips moving, almost as if she was in prayer. Ismene lowered herself to sit on the sand, curling her knees to her chest and staring out at the sea itself to give Stheno some degree of privacy.

The lapping tide was mesmerising, the water caressing the soft sand in a slow and soothing rhythm. Before long Ismene found herself lulled into a daze, deaf to the footsteps that quietly approached.

'Ismene?'

She jumped, and looked up. Stheno was standing over her, dressed again, though her skin still glistened with seawater.

'What are you doing here?'

Ismene rose to her feet, a little flustered. 'I'm sorry,' she said quickly, her cheeks flushing. 'I came to let you know dinner is ready, but I didn't want to intrude on your... ah...'

'My prayers?' Stheno finished for her, her brow furrowed but the hint of a smile curling her lips. She was amused by Ismene's embarrassment. 'I am not ashamed of divine communion. The human race may have disowned us long ago, but our family still answers us when they deem it necessary.'

'And did they answer?' Ismene asked as they began walking side by side back to the ruined temple they called home.

Stheno nodded, a proud gleam in her black eyes. 'Father heard my call, and he answered. Phorcys may not carry the authority of the Olympians, but he is an old god, and his power reaches all his children.'

'What did you ask for?' Ismene's cheeks warmed; she was letting her curiosity get the better of her again. 'If you don't mind me asking, of course.'

Stheno barked a short, sharp laugh. 'You share Medusa's love of asking questions.' She laughed again and shook her head. 'But no, I do not mind. I sought Father's protection over the child. I asked that he ensure a safe delivery, and that they are born healthy and strong.' Stheno held her head high, a small, satisfied smile on her lips. 'He assured me it would be done.'

Ismene's heart fluttered. 'That's incredible!' She stared at Stheno as they walked, reminded once more that she found herself sharing a home with divine beings, with demi-gods who had access to power she couldn't even imagine. 'You're amazing,' she muttered, partly to herself. 'Both of you are amazing.'

Stheno shrugged. 'In this manner, perhaps. But each person is special in their own way. You bring Medusa a sense of love and peace we could not, no matter how hard we tried. Some might call that amazing.'

Cheeks warming again, Ismene said, 'I've never felt particularly amazing.'

Stheno stopped, then, and looked down at the shorter woman, brow furrowed. 'You must not say that. Medusa was lost until you were returned to her. You did not see her when she first arrived here. There was something missing, clearly, and it was not until you arrived that we knew it was you.' She placed a hand on Ismene's shoulder, firm yet warm. 'I know I was not welcoming to you at first, and for that I apologise. I let my concern for Medusa cloud my judgement, but I see now that you are everything she needed, and I am glad to call you my family, and to share my love with you.'

Tears pricked Ismene's eyes. In all her life, she could not remember a time when either her mother or father told her they loved her. The people she had met during her journey to find Medusa had described Stheno and Euryale as frightening monsters, inhuman creatures that were too terrifying to approach, and yet these two snake-haired women had shown her more love and compassion than any of her own kind ever had.

'Thank you,' she whispered, blinking back the tears that were now threatening to burst free. 'That means a lot, truly.'

'I am glad.' Stheno squeezed Ismene's shoulder and looked forward, where the temple was just visible in the distance. 'Now, let us see if Euryale has ruined my stew.'

They walked the rest of the way in comfortable silence. As they neared the entrance to the old temple, the aroma of herbs and slow-cooked meat washed over them, and Ismene's stomach growled.

'It smells like Euryale didn't ruin your— Stheno?'

Besides her, Stheno was bent over, hands on her temples and her face contorted with pain.

'Stheno, are you—?'

Stheno held her hand out to silence her. 'Wait.'

Dread crept down Ismene's spine as Stheno's eyes clouded over and turned white. The snake-haired woman's face went slack, and she stood straight again, staring into the middle-distance with that unnerving milky gaze.

For what felt like an eternity, Stheno stared in silence. Ismene watched, helpless and afraid, unease building in her stomach and chest until she could feel bile crawling up the back of her throat.

Finally, Stheno blinked and her gaze cleared, returning to the sharp onyx Ismene was used to. She turned to face Ismene fully, and a shock of worry shook the smaller woman as she took in the panic colouring Stheno's usually stoic features.

'W-what happened?' Ismene stammered. 'What's wrong?'

Stheno grasped Ismene's arm so hard it hurt, and pulled her towards the temple.

'I need to speak with Euryale. Now.'

Stheno burst into the living quarters while Medusa was still hunched over Euryale, where she lay on the tiled floor, eyelids fluttering and barely conscious.

'She collapsed,' she called to Stheno, startled by the panic already evident on her sister's face. 'What is happening?'

'A message,' Stheno stated, as if that answered everything, and knelt at the other side of Euryale. She cupped Euryale's cheek in her hand. 'Sister, wake up. Come back to yourself.'

Ismene entered the room then, visibly perspiring and out of breath. 'Is she... is she all right?' she panted, clutching her side.

Medusa looked down at Euryale, who was now being helped to her feet by Stheno. Physically, she looked to be fine, but her frightened expression sent Medusa's stomach churning.

'What happened?' she asked both sisters, struggling to stand herself and welcoming Ismene's hand as she pulled her up to her feet. 'Are you both ill?'

Stheno hesitated for a moment. 'I need to speak to Euryale. Alone.'

'No.' The three other women stared at her, but Medusa did not care. She was not a child to be sheltered from the truth, and she could not stand being shut out anymore. 'We are all family here,' she asserted, her tone firm. 'There should be no secrets between sisters. Whatever is happening, you can discuss it in front of us.'

Gentle fingers curled around hers and squeezed. Medusa did not need to look at Ismene to understand this was a show of her support, and warmth blossomed in her chest.

Stheno's gaze met Euryale's, and the two winged women seemed to hold an unspoken conversation between themselves through their eyes alone. Their faces gave away nothing as they held each other's stare. Finally, Euryale nodded, and Stheno faced Ismene and Medusa again.

'We both received a message, from our distant kin.' Stheno took a breath; this was not news she wanted to deliver. 'It was a distress call. We must go to them. Now.'

A shiver ran unbidden down Medusa's spine. 'Kin?' she asked, unsure why the word caused a knot to form in her stomach. 'Who?'

'Our oldest sisters,' Euryale answered, her black eyes shining. 'They share our blood, and so we have a deep connection, although not as deep as with each other, and you, of course.'

The knot in Medusa's stomach eased a little at that, and a twinge of shame tugged at her as the source of her discomfort became clear. Jealousy. She had gotten so used to being the centre of her sisters' attention and devotion, the mention of other siblings had rankled.

'We have not heard from them in many years,' Stheno continued, 'and so them calling out to us is alarming.'

'What did they say?' Ismene asked, the worry evident in her voice. 'Are they in danger?'

'We cannot be certain,' Stheno replied, 'their messages are more feelings than words. But one thing was very clear – they are in distress, and are calling us to them.'

'Then you must go.' The other women turned to Medusa again. 'You have done so much for me.' She squeezed Ismene's hand. 'For us. You cannot abandon your other sisters. Go, quickly, and make sure they are all right.'

Relief flashed across Stheno's face, but some concern remained. 'Are you sure you will be all right on your own?'

'You have left us alone before.' Medusa shrugged, refusing to let her own fears bubble to the surface. In truth, she always felt safer knowing Euryale and Stheno were nearby, but she could not expect them to babysit her forever.

'For several hours at most.' Euryale sighed and moved closer to Medusa, placing a hand on her shoulder. 'This is not a short journey, and once we reach our sisters we do not know how long it will take to aid them. I hate to leave you unprotected, but...'

'But nothing.' Medusa planted her hands on her hips, looking from Euryale to Stheno. 'I value your company immensely, but your other siblings need you right now. This island is secluded, and unknown to most. We will survive until you return.'

'You are right,' Stheno murmured, 'but there is one thing we can do to ease our concerns while we are gone. Euryale, give Medusa your Sense.'

Euryale nodded. She grasped Medusa by both shoulders and turned the smaller woman towards her. 'Now,' she said quietly, staring into Medusa's eyes with an unnerving intensity. 'This might feel unpleasant, even painful, but I need you to stay perfectly still.'

'What are you going to do?' A nervous flutter rippled through Medusa's chest. She trusted Euryale with her life, but she only understood a fraction of her abilities, and truly did not know the extent of the power her sisters could wield.

'I have an ability,' Euryale murmured, closing her eyes and moving her fingers up to Medusa's temples. 'One that enables me to sense and locate any trespasser on the island. While we are gone...' She pressed into Medusa's head, her clawed fingers digging into the flesh. 'I pass this ability to you.'

A flash of white erupted in Medusa's vision. Pressure built behind her eyes, pulsing harder and harder until it felt her head might burst. Medusa squeezed her eyes shut and tried to breathe through the discomfort, reminding herself that Euryale would not hurt her. She was safe.

'Stay still...' Euryale's voice seemed distant, clouded by the thick throbbing in Medusa's head. 'Remain calm.'

Pain bloomed in Medusa's skull, a searing heat spreading from Euryale's fingertips. She clenched her teeth, and breathed. Euryale would not harm her. Euryale would not harm her.

A burst of stars, and then it was over. All at once, the pain vanished, and Medusa blinked her eyes open. Euryale's gentle face greeted her, a small smile on her lips.

'You did well,' Euryale cooed, dropping her hands and stepping back. 'It is done. How do you feel?'

'I... I feel fine.' In fact, Medusa felt more than fine. She felt... wonderful. Euryale's magic thrummed through her veins, filling her with a rejuvenating warmth. Euryale nodded, a glint of understanding in her black eyes.

'Good. Until we return, if anyone other than us steps foot on this island, you will know. We are well-hidden, so I hope you never need it, but it will soothe us to know you are protected.'

'Understood. Thank you.' Medusa wrapped her arms around her sister and held her tight. 'Don't worry, we will be fine.'

'We should go.' There was reluctance in Stheno's voice, but Euryale pulled back from Medusa all the same.

'Go,' Medusa murmured, releasing her sister and standing by Ismene's side. 'Let's not waste time with lengthy goodbyes. Go, help your sisters.'

'Do not stray far from the temple,' Stheno called as she and Euryale made their way to the doorway. 'There is still plenty of food in the storage room. Ismene, make sure Medusa rests often.'

'Stop fussing,' Medusa replied, though she couldn't help but smile. Her sisters cared so much, and it filled her heart with a joy she never knew she could experience. 'The sooner you go, the sooner you can return. Take care of yourselves, and your sisters.'

Stheno nodded.

'We will be back as soon as we are able,' Euryale said, her voice wavering even as she walked further from where Medusa and Ismene stood. 'Stay safe. We love you both.'

'We love you too,' Medusa called, waving.

Euryale looked as though she wanted to say more, but thought better of it. She waved a hand limply, took one last look at Medusa, and allowed Stheno to steer her through the door.

Within seconds, the beating of great wings could be heard through the temple walls, and Medusa and Ismene were left alone.

The morning sun streamed into the room, bathing the bed in golden light. Medusa curled up against Ismene's back, burying her face in the comfort of her chestnut ringlets. Winter was approaching, and there was a bite in the air which made her reluctant to leave the bed any earlier than she needed to. There was no Euryale brewing a morning tea for them all to share, no Stheno preparing breakfast. The entire temple was cold and quiet, and a little unnerving.

Ismene murmured, still half asleep, and shuffled back so their bodies were pressed together. Medusa relished the warmth, and laid an arm over Ismene, her heart fluttering as she felt the curves of her body under her clothing.

'Mmmm...' Ismene sighed, rolling over and resting her head on Medusa's chest. Medusa's heart jumped again, and she laid a soft kiss on Ismene's forehead.

Her smooth skin tasted like the finest olive oil, and her scent was reminiscent of ripe figs and herbal honey. Medusa could quite easily spend all day drinking it in, holding Ismene in her arms and revelling in the feeling of her body pressed against her own. There was nowhere else she would rather be.

'Good morning,' Ismene murmured, curling herself around Medusa and entwining their legs together, sending a fresh ripple of warmth through Medusa's body. This woman's touch still thrilled her every time.

'Good mor—*Ah!*'

A wave of pain tore through Medusa, beginning in her feet and crashing over her abdomen. She sat up, grimacing, and rubbed her protruding belly. It felt harder than usual, as if tightening from the pain.

Ismene sat up next to her, brow furrowed with concern. 'What's wrong?'

'It hurts...' Medusa said through gritted teeth. And then, as quickly as it came on, the pain subsided.

'Are you all right?'

'I... I think so? The pain has gone now.'

'Is it the baby?' Ismene's voice was barely a whisper. 'Is it time?'

Medusa's pulse quickened. 'I don't know, but I hope not. It seems early still... and I wanted my sisters to be here when the time came – they know what to do.'

'Don't fret.' Ismene said more cheerfully than Medusa felt, gently caressing Medusa's stomach. 'I'll start a fire and get some tea brewing, and you can relax. If the pain passes, that's good, and if it progresses, I will look after you. Everything will be fine, don't you worry.'

Medusa nodded, but her chest remained tight. She was not ready for the baby to arrive, not yet. Not without her sisters.

Ismene climbed out of bed and helped Medusa to her feet. The chill in the air did nothing to ease Medusa's nerves, but she followed Ismene to the living chambers nonetheless, with a blanket hung around her shoulders to stave off the cold.

It took a short while for Ismene to get a fire burning in the hearth, but soon the heat of the flames reached Medusa, and she welcomed their comforting embrace. As Ismene busied herself preparing one of Euryale's simpler tea recipes, Medusa rubbed her stomach, gasping as another wave of pain washed over her. It was brief, but intense, a fleeting crescendo warning her that more was to come. When it passed, she took in a steadying breath and considered her situation.

The child was fathered by a god – would that ensure the birth happened safely? That it would grow up hardy and strong? Medusa prayed that would be true; there had to be some benefits of the babe's parentage.

'The baby is blessed, you know,' Ismene said as she hung a pot over the fire and began filling it with herbs.

'What do you mean?'

'Stheno told me.' Ismene disappeared to the next room, leaving Medusa waiting anxiously for the rest of her story. When she returned with a small water jar, Medusa stared at her until she tipped the water into the pot and finally continued. 'She asked for their father's blessing,' she said as she emptied the jar fully and placed it carefully on the tiled floor. 'According to your sister, Phorcys has promised a safe birth, and a healthy child.'

Medusa's breath caught. 'Truly? You mean that?'

Ismene dropped the prepared herbs into the bubbling water and sat down beside Medusa, placing a gentle hand on her knee. 'I do. Stheno assured me that her father agreed to her request. You can relax, my love – your child will be fine. I promise.'

A swell of relief flooded Medusa's body. She took Ismene's hand and kissed it. 'Oh, thank you. Thank you for telling me.'

The pain returned, but now she knew the child was blessed by a powerful god, it was no longer accompanied by the sting of fear. It flared briefly and then disappeared as quickly as it came. Perhaps the baby was on its way, but knowing it was not in any danger, Medusa allowed herself a touch of excitement.

Soon, she would be a mother, and she would give her child all the love and affection she had dreamed about growing up.

As the morning drifted into the afternoon, Medusa's cramps became more frequent, and Ismene's anticipation rose.

She kept a relaxed demeanour for Medusa's sake, but under her calm exterior, a million butterflies tore through her insides. The blessing Phorcys had promised soothed her nerves to an extent, but being the only one at Medusa's side at such a critical time sent Ismene's heart pounding. She tried to keep busy, keeping Medusa well-fed while preparing linens, oil and water for when the birth began in earnest.

'How long do you think it will be?' Medusa asked as Ismene handed her a fresh cup of the only herbal tea Euryale had taught her to brew. It was supposed to be calming, and providing Medusa with a constant supply helped Ismene to feel useful.

'I don't know.' Ismene wracked her brain, trying to remember when she was a very young girl, and her mother had helped a few local women through their labour. She poured herself a cup of steaming tea, and sighed. 'I might be wrong – my memory has faded, but I seem to think Mother said it could be anywhere from a few hours to several days.'

Medusa let out a low whistle as Ismene sat across from her. 'Several days... Gods. Although, that means my sisters may return in time, then.'

*That's true!*

Perhaps Ismene wouldn't have to help Medusa through the ordeal alone. Standing by the side of her semi-divine lover trying to figure out how to prepare for the birth of the child of an Olympian god, Ismene felt completely impotent. She had spent her life being told how useless she was, but never had she felt it so keenly than in this moment. She hoped with all her might that Stheno and Euryale would return soon.

'I'm sure they're already on their way,' Ismene replied, forcing a reassuring smile across her face. 'They know you so well, they've probably sensed the child is coming and are racing to be by your side in time for its delivery.'

Medusa nodded, but it was clear she didn't believe those words any more than Ismene did. 'Stheno will be furious if she is late.' Medusa forced her own smile, but it quickly disappeared as a fresh wave of pain took her. Ismene could only watch, helpless, as Medusa breathed through it, clutching her stomach with her free hand, her eyes clenched shut.

'You're doing amazingly,' she breathed, and those words she truly meant. People often called childbirth a miracle, but that did a disservice to the incredible women who made it happen. It took strength no man could ever understand to bring life into the world.

Medusa's eyes fluttered open as the pain subsided once more, and she huffed a small laugh. 'I'm not sure you will still be saying that when I'm screaming and crying at the end.'

Ismene opened her mouth to respond, but froze when a strange look fell over Medusa's face. Her features slackened and her eyes glazed over for a moment. The cup of tea she had been cradling crashed to the ground, the clay shattering against the hard tiles.

'Medusa?' Ismene asked, a cold sense of dread creeping down her spine. 'Medusa, can you hear me? Are you all right?'

Medusa blinked, and the terror that contorted her features turned Ismene's insides to water.

'What? What is it?'

Medusa paled, as if she might vomit at any moment. 'There... There is someone here. A man just stepped foot onto the island.'

Ismene's stomach soured.

*No, not now. Any time but now.*

'What? Who?'

'I don't know.' Medusa fidgeted with the fabric of her dress. 'What could he want?' Her eyes widened; she was already starting to panic. 'What if Poseidon sent him to reclaim me, or your father sent him to fetch you?'

Steeling herself, Ismene rose to her feet. She had to keep her composure and ensure Medusa remained calm.

'He might be lost, or seeking shelter on his way to another destination.' Ismene worked to keep her voice as mild and passive as possible, but it was clear Medusa didn't believe her, and if she was truly honest with herself, she didn't believe her words either. But she had to try, for both their sakes, and most importantly, for the baby. 'Try not to panic – he might not come anywhere near here. But, if it soothes you, we can take precautions in any case.'

Ismene fetched another water jar and tossed the contents into the hearth. The fire disappeared with a hiss, sending a burst of smoke billowing through the vent in the ceiling. She waved her arms, clearing the air as quickly as possible.

'With any luck,' she said, continuing to waft the remaining wisps of smoke away, 'he won't know there is anything here.'

Medusa nodded, but the fear still shone in her large, dark eyes. Ismene handed her a blanket, which she took silently with unsteady hands.

'Wrap up warm, now we don't have the fire, and I'll get you something to eat. You still need to keep up your strength.'

Ismene walked into the small room adjacent to the living quarters where Stheno and Euryale usually prepared food for them all. She prepared a simple meal of bread and honey and returned to find Medusa still clutching the blanket with trembling fingers.

'Here,' Ismene murmured softly, handing Medusa a piece of honey-dipped bread. 'I know you're afraid, but try to eat. You need energy to get through the birth.'

Medusa nodded, and took a tentative bite, but from the distaste on her face Ismene knew she would struggle to swallow. She had to try something else.

'If he does happen upon us,' she said slowly, straining to bring some levity to her voice, 'it is him I worry for. Does he not know he would be coming face to face with the mighty Medusa, who could turn him to stone in the blink of an eye?'

A small laugh fell from Medusa's lips. It didn't sound wholly genuine, but it was a start. 'I hope not. I would rather him think we're entirely uninteresting. Besides,' she continued, a worrisome look creasing her features, 'I have never used my gaze on another person deliberately. I'm not sure that I could.'

'Well,' Ismene replied, bending to kiss Medusa on the top of her head, 'let's hope for his sake we don't have to find out. I would hate to have a statue of some big, ugly man to deal with.'

A true chuckle burst from Medusa then, and it warmed Ismene's heart. If she could find a way to bring that rich, melodic sound out every single day, she would. She opened her mouth to speak again, but was cut short when Medusa let out a great gasp and her eyes glazed over once again.

'He is coming closer,' she murmured, 'heading straight for the temple, and quickly. He knows where we are.'

'We don't know that,' Ismene replied, but the quiver in her voice betrayed her own fear. How did this man know to come in this direction? As far as the outside world was aware, this island was uninhabited, abandoned many decades ago after it was sacked during a particularly brutal war. 'But just in case,' she continued, pulling Medusa to her feet. 'Let's go somewhere more secure until he leaves. Follow me, and try not to worry. It's just a precaution.'

Ismene scooped up the linens she had collected and led Medusa out of the central chamber and down a dilapidated corridor to the storeroom. Rows and rows of huge storage vases crowded the dusty, old room, most of which Ismene knew were empty. This was no longer a busy working temple, and with only four women to support, the volume of storage available was beyond anything they would ever need.

Choosing a path between two rows of vases at random, Ismene spread the linens on the ground and fashioned a makeshift bed for Medusa.

'Here,' she said with more confidence than she felt. 'You make yourself comfortable and I'll bar the door. And remember.' She wrapped an arm around Medusa's waist and kissed her forehead. 'This is just a precaution.'

'He is getting close.' Medusa said quietly, closing her eyes and bringing her fingers to her temple. 'He is in the woods now, coming here.'

Ismene rushed to the doorway and pushed at the open old wooden door. It was thick and heavy, and had obviously not been moved in some time. It took considerable effort to slowly inch it closed. The hinges screamed as Ismene finally shoved it into place, breathing heavily, sweat beading on her brow. A cracked leather strap hung from the wooden bolt on the back of the door. Ismene wrapped it around her wrist, braced herself and pulled.

The bolt didn't move. She heaved with all her strength, but it remained firmly stuck in place.

'Damn it!' she hissed, letting go of the strap. Ismene might be a woman, but she had grown up lugging equipment and pots around for her father, and so had built up a reasonable level of strength. She heaved and heaved, but it wasn't enough. She shook out her hands and flexed her fingers, and readied herself to try again.

Ismene grasped the leather strap and threw herself back, straining against the ancient bolt. She groaned and gritted her teeth, and closed her eyes as she prepared for one final pull.

The wood held for a moment before finally releasing, and Ismene almost barreled backwards to the ground. She opened her eyes to see Medusa hanging off the other end of the bolt where she had been dragged forward by its sudden movement.

'What are you doing?' Ismene cried, a little more forcefully than she intended.

'You looked like you needed help,' Medusa replied, straightening and brushing the dust from her dress.

'I told you to rest.' Ismene planted her hands on her hips and glanced down at Medusa's swollen stomach, which the other woman clutched subconsciously, no doubt still battling with the recurring cramps that were only getting worse.

'I prefer to stand.' Medusa held her head high, defiant, some of the authority she used to command as the priestess of Athena returning. 'Just in case.'

Ismene raised her eyebrows, but she knew from the way Medusa held her chin high that there was no convincing her to stand down. The woman before her, dark eyes blazing with purpose, a halo of pale serpents writhing and hissing atop her head, would be coddled no longer.

'This could get dangerous, Medusa,' Ismene said with more than a hint of warning.

'Then I will protect us.' Medusa's voice was quiet but powerful. Hard. 'If this man wants to harm my beloved and my child, he will have to get through me.'

Ismene's chest tightened, pride and fear at war in her heart. 'But Medusa, you're—'

'I know.' Medusa inhaled and let out a long breath. 'But I have been through too much to back down now. I have been violated and cursed by the gods, driven out of my sanctuary and my home, thrust into a strange, new life I never could have expected... but finally I am happy. I have love, I have a caring family, I have the promise of a joy I have always thought was out of reach... and I will be damned if I let this man reduce it all to nothing without putting up a fight.'

Ismene chewed her lip. Every instinct in her body told her to defend Medusa, to put anything and everything between the woman she loved and the danger drawing ever closer. It was true Medusa possessed powers Ismene could not, but she was in labour, and vulnerable, and precious beyond anything else in Ismene's world.

'I need you to promise,' Medusa continued, grasping Ismene's hands and pulling her close. 'Promise that if something happens to me—'

'No.' Ismene shook her head. 'No, I will die before—'

'*Promise me*,' Medusa cut in, squeezing Ismene's hands tight. 'That if the worst happens to me, you will take care of the child, by any means necessary. They must survive, no matter what.'

Ismene stared into Medusa's wide eyes, which darkened to almost black as they searched Ismene's face. She swallowed, her mouth dry. Medusa was everything to Ismene. She loved her with every fibre of her heart and soul, and just the thought of losing her was more than she could bear.

'Please don't make me do this,' Ismene whispered, her heart in her throat. 'The danger may pass; this might all be a false alarm. I will not, I *can* not speak of a life without you. It will break my heart just thinking of it.'

'He's almost here, Ismene.' Medusa's hands trembled in Ismene's fingers, but there was more than just terror in her eyes. There was a fierce determination that sent Ismene's pulse racing. 'It is me that he seeks. I can feel it now. I need you to promise me. I need you to promise that you will take care of our child, no matter what.'

'Medusa,' Ismene breathed, 'I can't—'

'Please,' Medusa whispered, cupping Ismene's face with her hands. 'I need to know my child will live, or I cannot face this.'

Tears trickled down Ismene's cheeks. She knew what she had to do. She knew, and it broke her heart. 'Of course.' She heard the pain in her own voice, but forced herself to continue. 'I promise, Medusa. As long as there is air in my lungs and blood in my veins, your child will live.'

Desperate lips crashed into hers, and Ismene returned the urgency as she fell into Medusa's deep kiss. Time stood still, and there was nothing but the two of them, drinking each other in as if it was their final breath.

When they broke apart, they pressed their foreheads together, chests heaving.

'I love you,' Medusa whispered, her sweet breath caressing Ismene's cheek. 'I will always love you, Ismene.'

'And I you,' Ismene breathed. 'Nothing in this world could take away my love for you.'

Medusa smiled, and the two women held each other for one brief, perfect moment before a distant crash tore their world apart.

'He is here,' Medusa whispered, her eyes wide. 'He is inside the temple. Quick, get behind me.'

'Medusa, no, I can—'

'Do it!' Medusa ordered, pulling Ismene behind her and backing them both up away from the door. 'I cannot be sure you won't be affected also.'

Ismene opened her mouth to question her, but snapped it shut as she saw Medusa spread her arms wide, the serpents atop her head darkening as they thrashed and hissed. As they writhed and spat, their scales rippled, turning first a bloody red and then the black of night.

'Stay back.' Medusa's voice was low, an otherworldly power thrumming through her words. 'I will try to stop him.'

Ismene stood still, her heart pounding, a nervous energy vibrating through her entire body. They listened, the only sounds their own rapid breathing and the vicious hissing of Medusa's ink-black serpents. Ismene's stomach tightened as another crash sounded: a door breaking somewhere deeper into the old temple. She couldn't think, could hardly breathe.

There was silence for what felt like eternity, and then footsteps, somewhere on the other side of the door.

Ismene looked over Medusa's shoulder, terror gripping her insides. She scanned the floor around her, searching for anything she might use as a weapon, anything she could put between this threat and the woman she loved, but there was nothing. Whoever this man was, Ismene would be useless against him.

Something struck the old wooden door to the storeroom, and Ismene started, her heart slamming against her ribs. She reached a trembling hand forward and entwined Medusa's fingers in hers, squeezing tight.

'I will protect you,' Medusa whispered, squeezing back.

The door banged again, as if a bull rammed it from the other side. Ismene held her breath.

*Maybe he will give up. Maybe he'll realise there's nothing here for him and leave.*

Another bang, rattling the very hinges of the door. Medusa backed up further, pushing Ismene back with her. Another bang, and the door splintered, the bolt bending back almost to the point of breaking. Ismene's insides turned to water as a curved blade broke through a crack in the wood and sliced through the remains of the bolt like butter. The splinters fell away, dropping uselessly to the ground and leaving the entryway open for their intruder.

Ismene's fingers trembled in Medusa's hand, but Medusa stood strong, ready and waiting for whoever had broken into their home.

Another bang and the door swung inward, revealing a tall, broad-shouldered young man. He bore a gleaming shield in his left hand, and a curved blade in the other, with its twin hanging from the belt around his waist. Strangely, he did not look straight ahead, instead peering into the shield, which shone like a perfect mirror.

He angled the shield until Medusa's face appeared, her eyes black and blazing with fury, and cold terror shot through Ismene as a wicked grin spread across his face.

'Finally,' the man said darkly, turning the handle of his blade deftly in his long fingers. 'I have found you, *monster*.'

He raised his blade, and Ismene's heart jolted as a terrible realisation struck her. Medusa's gaze would not protect her. This man could attack her freely, using his shield as his eyes.

'Stop!' she screamed, letting go of Medusa's hand and throwing herself at the intruder. She grabbed the arm that wielded the blade as he stumbled back, scrabbling with desperate fingers to loosen it from his grasp.

'Ismene!'

She heard Medusa cry out as she tried to twist the man's muscular arm to force the blade out of his hand. His other arm was strapped to the great mirrored shield, which limited his movement, but he was strong, stronger than any man she had dealt with before.

The man grunted and shoved Ismene backwards, but she leapt at him again, this time clamping her teeth down on his hand and biting as hard as she possibly could.

The man shouted in pain and released the blade, sending it clattering away from them, but before Ismene could react, he swung his muscular arm and threw her to the ground. Ismene's head collided with the hard tile, and stars burst in front of her eyes. A heavy foot collided with her ribs with tremendous force, sending a searing pain shooting up her side, and Ismene screamed.

'Stop!' she heard Medusa shout through the haze of pain, and the sounds of a scuffle began.

'Medusa,' Ismene groaned, pushing herself up onto her elbow. Fresh agony jolted through her and her vision rocked and swayed. She blinked rapidly, forcing her eyes to focus, and fresh terror shook her.

The man stood over a fallen Medusa as he drew the second curved blade from his belt and held it high.

'NO!' Ismene scrambled to her feet, ignoring the pain that flared through her body, and launched herself at him. He lifted his gaze from his mirror for a brief moment, just enough to lock eyes with Ismene and ram the shield into her, sending her tumbling back.

Blinding agony rocked Ismene as she crumpled to the ground. She pushed herself up to kneeling and managed to blink her vision clear, but it was too late. The man swung his blade down into Medusa's neck, severing her head from her body in one impossible strike.

An inhuman scream erupted from Ismene, tearing at her throat as her heart shattered in her chest.

*No.*

*NO!*

Medusa's still, decapitated body lay a short distance ahead of Ismene, a pool of dark, glistening blood spreading across the tiles as her very life ebbed out of her. Great, heaving sobs wracked Ismene's body and she screamed again, the sound almost bestial in its savagery and echoing all around until there was a cacophony of shrieks screaming back at her.

She knelt, chest heaving, the walls closing in around her. She couldn't breathe, couldn't believe her eyes. This couldn't be happening. It wasn't real, it couldn't be.

*Medusa...*

Ismene looked up at the intruder, the beast who in one effortless motion had destroyed her entire world. Her eyes darted to his hands, and an acrid, sickening breath caught in her throat. There, facing away from her, her serpents grasped by the man's thick, bloodied fingers, hung Medusa's head.

'NO!' Ismene screamed once more, her ruined throat so raw the word was completely intelligible. She threw herself at the man, but he was ready for her, blocking her frenzied attack easily with one hand.

'Stand back!' he shouted, grabbing Ismene by the arm and pulling her farther away from his grotesque prize. 'I would rather not kill you also. Stand down.'

Ismene did not listen. She lunged forward, reaching for Medusa's serpents, desperation overwhelming her senses. She just had to free Medusa from his grasp, and then she could save her. There had to be a way. This couldn't be it. It just couldn't.

The man pulled her back once again, but there was no violence in his action. It was slow, and almost gentle. 'Stop this,' he said, a trace of something akin to sympathy in his deep voice. 'It is over. She is dead.'

'No, she can't be dead!' Ismene beat at the man's breastplate, hot tears streaming down her face as she brought down her fist over and over until the skin broke and her knuckles bled. 'She can't be dead! She can't be!'

The man pushed her back a few steps, and for the first time, Ismene looked into his eyes. The eyes of a murderer. Yet, where she expected to see evil, she saw something different entirely. Confusion and pity mingled in his dark gaze, and where there should have been a smirk of victory on his lips, there was only a thin, grim line.

'Go,' he said with no trace of cruelty in his voice, gesturing at Medusa's lifeless body. 'Mourn. There is nothing else you can do for her now.'

Ismene's heart leapt into her throat. There *was* something she could do. The only thing that mattered now.

'Get out.' Ismene spat at the intruder, her pulse racing. She didn't know how much time she had, but the man could not be here for this; it wasn't right. When he didn't move, she stepped forward, pointed at the open doorway and screamed, 'GET OUT!'

The man looked at Ismene for a moment longer with a strange sort of sadness shining in his eyes, and silently turned to leave. Without hesitation, Ismene rushed to Medusa and knelt by her side, warm blood soaking up the skirt of her chiton, sending bile crawling up her ruined throat. Her entire body shook as she placed her hands on Medusa's abdomen, hot tears streaming down her face.

'I-I promised...' Ismene managed to stammer between gasping sobs. 'I p-promised...'

Medusa's child still lived, but for how long? She needed to do something, and quickly.

A terrible thought occurred to her, and Ismene scrabbled around on the dusty floor, heart hammering in her chest, until her trembling fingers found the man's first blade, abandoned and forgotten in the fray. She held it over Medusa, the blade glinting in the dim light, but terror held her shaking hands in place.

'I... I can't...' she breathed, sobs choking her between each word. 'I... I...'

Medusa's words drifted through Ismene's mind, strong and firm. The words of a mother who valued her child's life above all else.

*Promise me.*

*I need to know my child will live.*

Ismene took a deep breath and brought the blade down, slicing through Medusa's flesh. Blood poured out of the wound, and panic threatened to overwhelm Ismene, but she repeated Medusa's words over and over until her hands steadied enough to continue.

'I promised,' she whispered, cutting deeper and pulling away the layers of flesh protecting the child from the outside world with trembling fingers. Cold horror curdled in her gut, but she forced herself onwards. 'As long as there is air in my lungs...' She plunged her hands into Medusa's abdomen, her stomach twisting and her mouth filling with bile that she struggled to swallow down. Finally, her heart fluttering with relief, her fingers closed around a small body. 'As long as there is blood in my veins.'

Ismene pulled out a small, blood-soaked baby, and held it to her chest, breathing heavily as she cradled its tiny body against her own.

She had done it. Deep, burning pain scorched her soul in a way she had never felt before, but she had done it. She had saved the baby.

But before Ismene could process the situation further, she glanced down and her heart leapt back into her throat. Medusa's stomach was moving.

There was another child.

Clinging to the first baby with one hand, Ismene held her breath and plunged her other hand back into Medusa's abdomen. Warm blood spilled over her flesh once more as desperate fingers searched through the gore of Medusa's ruined body, but Ismene forced herself to fight through the horror. When she felt the soft skin of the second child beneath her fingertips, she could not hold back the sob of relief that burst free from her throat. With one hand, she managed with some difficulty to lift the unexpected twin out of its trappings, her eyes widening as she noticed a small pair of wings folded on the babe's back.

Breathing heavily, Ismene cradled the child on her chest next to its sibling, unable to care that all three of them were now drenched in blood.

'I promised...' Ismene whispered, holding the babies tight against her, tears flowing down her cheeks like scalding rivers. 'I promised.'

The first child coughed and spluttered, letting out a soft cry. Relief washed over Ismene in waves, almost overwhelming her as the second child joined its sibling, returning its call and announcing its presence to the world.

'I promised, Medusa,' Ismene breathed, fresh sobs shaking her chest. 'They're alive, just like I promised.'

The warm summer sun shone down on the lapping waves, the clear blue water glittering like it was made of sparkling diamonds. Two small boys frolicked in the surf, chasing the tide as it pulled away, and running away giggling as it came after them.

Chrysaor was the bolder of the two children, with skin that gleamed as if it was spun from pure gold, and the attitude to match. He barked orders at his sibling, instructing him when to run and jump from the encroaching waves, and always chose the next game. Pegasus, on the other hand, was meek and mild. Taller than his twin, he stood pale and lithe, a pair of delicate white-feathered wings protruding from his angular shoulder blades. He followed his brother's orders with grace and gratitude, never arguing or growing upset. They were as different as they were beautiful; two perfect little boys.

Ismene took a deep breath, enjoying the tang of salt that pricked her tongue. The beach had become her favourite place in recent years, a place where the boys could play with unbridled freedom, away from their temple home and the memories that haunted Ismene still.

She watched the children play, a pleasant breeze blowing off the waves and bringing with it the wonderful freshness of the sea and world beyond. Ismene had not left the island since the day she arrived years ago, and she wasn't sure she ever would. There was nothing beyond the horizon for her anymore.

Chrysaor, apparently tired of the chasing game, began picking up stones from the wet sand and tossing them into the sea, cheering every time he managed to throw a farther distance. He turned to Ismene after each new victory, beaming with pride, and her heart swelled to see such joy on his face.

*If only your mother could have seen you*, she thought, a twinge of sorrow tugging at her.

'She would have been so happy to see them like this.' Stheno's voice startled her, and Ismene turned to see the woman standing behind her, a sad smile on her face. She longed for the day her hearing would be sharp enough to hear the winged woman's approach. Even after all these years, she still surprised her.

'I know,' Ismene finally replied, not bothering to question how the demi-god knew what she was thinking. She and Stheno had grown close since Medusa's death, openly sharing their grief where Euryale preferred not to address it, instead channeling all of her energy into raising the children. Consequently, Stheno now knew Ismene inside and out, and whether through divine powers or the intuition of one who has grown to know everything about the other, she seemed to always know what was on her mind.

Ismene looked back out over the sea, and beckoned for Stheno to sit down beside her on the soft sand. 'It breaks my heart every day that she will never meet them.'

Stheno lowered herself to a seated position. 'She will,' she said quietly, looking straight ahead at the two boys, now engaged in a competition of who could throw the farthest. 'Their souls will be reunited, when the time comes.'

Ismene nodded, Stheno's words offering little comfort. 'That will not be for some time, gods willing.'

A low chuckle tumbled from Stheno's lips. 'It will not. But in the meantime, we will love them, and we will cherish them, and they will want for nothing.'

'I do love them, Stheno,' Ismene said softly, her throat tightening as a great swell of emotion rose from her chest. 'I love them as if they were my own.'

'They *are* your own.' Stheno wrapped an arm around Ismene's shoulders, and drew her closer. 'Medusa loved you more than anything, little sister. Her love flows from you, and into them. They will grow up feeling their mother's presence through you.'

'I hope you're right.'

Ismene rested her head against Stheno's arm, relishing her closeness, the warmth of her body a comfort, even under the heat of the sun.

The pain of Medusa's death would never leave her, Ismene knew that. It would be with her until the end of her days, a bone-deep sorrow she would carry for all time. They would meet again one day, in the meadows of Asphodel, and her heart would be whole once more.

Until then, between the unconditional love of her sisters, and the endless love she bore for her two sons, Ismene would survive, and she would learn to be happy again.

She had to; it's what Medusa would have wanted.

# Acknowledgements

I can't believe we're here. I've been a fan of Greek mythology ever since I was a little girl in primary school, when I learned about Theseus and the Minotaur and began dreaming of an ancient world full of powerful gods and fantastical creatures. Since that day, I have been obsessed with each and every story, but what always stuck with me were the parts that we never got to hear more about. We are always told about the heroes of the story, the men who achieved greatness and glory through their adventures, but what about the rest? What about the women, the side characters, the "monsters"? Eventually, I swore to myself I would tell Medusa's story, and show she was more than just a dangerous creature the hero needed to overcome to achieve his goal. Well, I finally did it, and I really hope you enjoyed getting to know my favourite snake-haired girl.

Every novel is a team effort, and I'd like to thank my wonderful beta team, Audrey, Astrid and Merlina, for your invaluable feedback. You helped me to see what I needed to do to make this story as good as it could be. A huge thank you also to my fantastic editor, Adie Hart, for your encouragement and support, and for making this manuscript shine. I apologise for all of my errant commas!

None of this would be possible without the online writing community. I feel very lucky to have found my people – you know who you are, and I am forever grateful for your support, friendship and encouragement. You keep me going when times are tough, and I couldn't do any of this without you.

A special extra thank you goes to my fellow Greek mythology geeks, Em and Audrey. Thank you for always thinking of me when you see anything Medusa-related, and for always being there to geek out about all things mythological with me.

A final thank you goes to my husband, Ryan. We differ in many ways, but a love of the ancient world is something we both share. Thank you for exploring ancient ruins with me, for climbing a mountain in 32°C heat with me to see the birthplace of Zeus (just for it to be blocked by snow), and for waiting patiently while I stood and stared at a giant sculpture of Medusa in Corfu. You get it.

**If you enjoyed *OF SERPENTS AND SORROW*, please consider leaving a review on Goodreads, StoryGraph and / or Amazon. Every review helps get this book into the hands of more readers.**

# About the Author

Katherine Shaw is a Yorkshire-born multi-genre writer of both long and short-form fiction, based in a little fisherman's cottage on the bank of the Humber Estuary.

Despite being a chemist by training, she has been a writer ever since she could pick up a pencil, and feels she was born with an innate need to write stories. Her parents still ask her about the fantasy series she was dreaming up as a child on the beach during a family holiday at Bournemouth.

When she isn't working or daydreaming about new characters, Katherine is an avid Dungeons and Dragons player (and fledgling DM), a reader of all genres, a mediocre choir singer, a lover of daily yoga practice, and a player of vintage video games. Some may say that she's a geek...

OF SERPENTS AND SORROW is Katherine's second published novel. Connect with her online to keep up to date with the launch of her next release.

Instagram and Threads @katherineshawwrites

facebook.com/katherineshawwrites

BlueSky @katheroony.bsky.social

www.katherineshawwrites.com

www.ingramcontent.com/pod-product-compliance
Lightning Source LLC
Chambersburg PA
CBHW030028200726
48283CB00013B/2097